LAST
DANCE
IN
REDONDO
BEACH

Also by Michael J. Katz

Murder off the Glass

LAST DANCE
IN
REDONDO BEACH

Michael J. Katz

[signature: Michael J Katz]

G. P. PUTNAM'S SONS/NEW YORK

G. P. Putnam's Sons
Publishers Since 1838
200 Madison Avenue
New York, NY 10016

Library of Congress Cataloging-in-Publication Data

Katz, Michael J., date.
Last dance in Redondo Beach / Michael J. Katz.
p. cm.
Sequel to: Murder off the glass.
I. Title.
PS3561.A772L3   1989   88-22828 CIP
813'.54—dc19
ISBN 0-399-13445-X

Printed in the United States of America
1   2   3   4   5   6   7   8   9   10

For my Mom and Dad, this time in lights.

Special thanks to Dick and Rosemary
for spiritual guidance.

1

The sweet, surly sounds of a blues harmonica floated over the harbor at Redondo Beach, filtering through the rows of empty sailboats and cruisers, wafting past the roped-off docks which were empty except for a quorum of uniformly dressed television technicians sporting khaki shorts, red pullover shirts, and bright yellow windbreakers bearing the insignia of their network on the back.

Andy Sussman always brought his harmonica with him on road trips. Back in the old days, when he'd been working his way up the sportscasting pyramid, serving stints in places like Bozeman, Montana, and Green Bay, Wisconsin, the harmonica had been a reminder of where he was from and where he wanted to return. Chicago—the Loop and the lakeshore, the great sports traditions, Lincoln Avenue with its vintage blues scene—Orphans, the Wise Fools Pub, Kingston Mines. So what if he had been born and raised in Highland Park, on Chicago's affluent North Shore, and had about as much in common with Muddy Waters and Willie Dixon as he did with the Queen of England? When you're sitting in a Montana blizzard in the middle of February, waiting to do a live remote of a Big Sky Conference basketball game that's being watched by the few thousand people who aren't skiing or hibernating or smart enough to be on their way somewhere else, you have a right to wail away on your Hohner harmonica, complete with chord book and the Marine Corps hymn—even Muddy or Woody Guthrie or Sonny Terry would have admitted that.

The thing was, Andy Sussman was not spending February in Bozeman, or even in Chicago, where he had most recently been employed as the voice of the Chicago Flames, an allegedly professional basketball team. He was in Redondo Beach, California, where it was a breezy eighty-two degrees, and he was now a handsomely paid employee of CBS Sports. The appropriateness of invoking the spirit of Muddy Waters to express these circumstances was, Sussman had to admit, dubious. Nonetheless, he struggled through a few more chords of "Walkin' My Blues Away" before settling into the bunk on the docked cabin cruiser where he was hiding from his producer.

The reason that Sussman was lying low could be witnessed through the windows of the yacht or schooner or whatever it was—Andy had chosen the boat for its view of the marina, not for any great love of the sea. Out on the dock, two extremely large and muscular men, dressed only in tank suits, although one of them wore a mask, were standing toe-to-toe, pointing fingers in each other's faces, and exchanging taunts which Sussman could not hear, but assumed had something to do with eye-gouging chokeholds and flying scissors and body slams and hammerlocks and possible complete physical incapacitation and moral humiliation for one or the other—or both. The two were being assisted by their seconds, one of whom was a manager of some sort and had no business being anywhere near the production, a blatant breach of security for a network as self-aggrandizingly efficient as his. The other was a female rock star who, try as he might, Sussman had been unable to avoid noticing on TV talk shows and music videos as he flicked through the thirty-two available channels in various hotel rooms on various assignments. She was here legitimately, at least—she was part of the production which Sussman was doing his best to ignore, except for the hour or so that he was actually required to announce it. The production was called *Celebrity Network Superteams* and it was being taped for showing during the ratings sweeps in May. It was not exactly what Andy Sussman had had in mind when the network offered him permanent work after the basketball playoffs a year ago.

"Andy?" said a meek voice. Cliff Trager, his producer, had been chasing the harmonica riffs through the boat slips and had finally located Andy, supine on the bunk bed. Trager poked his bespectacled head through the cabin door and placed his clipboard down on a coffee table. "Andy, we're having a little, uh, tiff down on the dock and the cameras are getting it and everything, and we were wondering if it might not be too much to ask if you might, uh, go over there and sort of, uh . . . cover it?"

Sussman stirred from his bunk and walked across the cabin, opened the Refrigerator of the Unknown Sailor, and pulled out a can of some type of apricot-strawberry nectar. "Cliff, old pal, have a seat. Join me for a salute to bizarre fruit concoctions."

"Well, actually, Andy, we have this little situation and I think we're missing out on it and—"

Sussman popped open the can of nectar and split it into two highball glasses. He really did not want to be too hard on Cliff, who was not really the producer, he was an assistant producer who was taking over for Merle Summers, a man whom Sussman actually did have to answer to occasionally. Summers produced what the network euphemistically referred to as "Non-Traditional Sports Events," which could be anything from Ice Skate Barrel Jumping to the Strongmen Refrigerator Pull, and which the print media less charitably called "TrashSports." Despite the content of these shows, which Sussman considered uniformly moronic, Merle Summers was not a bad guy. He actually had a master's degree in history from Princeton and had worked in news for several years before shifting over to sports, for reasons Sussman had never quite understood. He had always assumed that Summers was just another closet sports junkie who really wanted to produce basketball and football games, until several months ago, when the network had granted Merle a new series called *Adven-*

ture! Summers had pounced on it with the passion of the two snow leopards that devoured a wild sheep at the beginning of each program.

Adventure! was a ninety-minute show to be seen on Saturday afternoons, a sort of eighties version of *The American Sportsman.* A celebrity would be flown into some remote place, teamed up with the *Adventure!* host, and sent to climb a Himalayan peak that had last been ascended by Tibetan monks in 1374, or raft down some river in South America filled with piranhas, headshrinking natives, and Communist guerrillas. This, apparently, was what Merle Summers had been waiting for all this time, and he was so busy organizing the new productions (and so mindful of how much hosting *Celebrity Network Superteams* would piss Sussman off) that he had barely had time to outline Andy's assignment before catching the next plane to South America, where he would be stalking rare Peruvian yaks in some remote foothills of the Andes.

So Cliff Trager, a civil, if overorganized trooper who had mostly been assigned to events like figure skating and bobsled racing for *Sports Spectacular,* had been designated to produce *Celebrity Superteams.* Sussman really *was* trying to be cooperative with him in such matters as timeliness, preparation, and even, when the red light was on, something that was darn near close to enthusiasm. Unfortunately, the format and personnel of *Superteams* had put Andy in conflict with one of the two strict Holy Taboos which he had ordained for himself at the beginning of his sportscasting career.

During the long years from Bozeman to Reno to Green Bay to Chicago, Sussman had been willing to go anywhere, do almost anything to get a story, to get on the air or on tape. He had done girls' basketball in Iowa, rodeos in Montana, high-school hockey in Wisconsin, he had stood knee-deep in a Sierra trout stream at five in the morning to report on opening day of the fishing season at Tahoe. There were only two rules that Andy Sussman had stuck to, and stuck to resolutely: No wrestling. No roller derby.

Now, it was not his fault, Sussman reasoned, that professional wrestling had undergone a revival in the mid-1980s. These things happened once or twice in a generation. Wrestling seemed to come and go on the same tide with Republican presidents and evangelical ministers. It was not, on the whole, any more or less stupid than hula hoops or yo-yos or music videos. Commercially speaking, Sussman could not deny that pro wrestling had acquired a great deal of legitimacy the last several years, sprouting all over the cable and late-night network shows and into major arenas like Madison Square Garden and the Rosemont Horizon. He had been, he considered, extremely polite to Dr. Double-X and The Thing during the entire week of shooting—on a professional level they were easy to work with, never missing a cue, always knowing where the camera was. But there *was* a future to look after, there were standards of dignity to be maintained. When Andy Sussman looked in the mirror every morning, he saw the future lead sportscaster of the NBA championships, the anchor for the '92 Olympics, the Walter Cronkite of Sports. And he was goddamned if he was going to stand between two preening, steroid-pumped muscleheads, waving and bleating like a used-car salesman and trying to avoid being strangled to death by the microphone cord or suffocated by two hairy sternums.

Cliff Trager, in the meantime, had not exactly made himself at home in the cabin cruiser. He was standing by the table, looking nervously at the apricot-strawberry nectar, which had the consistency of transmission fluid, and sneaking a look back at the pier, where Dr. Double-X, his face hidden by a black mask with X's above both eyes, appeared to be strangling his own manager, a short, burly, bald-headed man with immense forearms who was known as Wireless. "Now, Andy," Cliff said, peering through the window, "I know this isn't exactly your kind of thing, but, you know, it's all in fun, and after all, Ted Dirking let himself get in a chokehold, and he's one of ABC's most serious dramatic actors—"

Sussman sighed and took a look at the twelve-jewel captain's clock that was clanging in the kitchen, signaling the arrival of 2:30. Time, he knew, was his ally. The technicians and camera crew, as well as all of the participants, held union cards, they were all paid generously and by the hour. The paddleboat race, the final event in the five-event competition, was supposed to start in twenty minutes and there was every reason to believe it would be on time, just like the tug-of-war and the obstacle course and the wheelbarrow/beanbag/boiled-egg-in-the-spoon race—the network had been surprisingly good about that sort of thing of late, ever since the Great Purge. All this meant that in a few minutes the contestants would have to start warming up and testing the boats and he would have to conduct formal interviews with the captains, which left only another few minutes for The Thing and Double-X and Wireless and Leona Z, the rock star, to engage in mutual assured verbal destruction. So Sussman gulped down his fruit nectar, patted Cliff on the back, and finally acquiesced to leaving the cabin cruiser.

"I really didn't mean to be so tight-assed about the whole thing, Cliff," Sussman said, feeling much freer to confide in Trager, now that the final event was almost at hand. "But you know, this is a visual medium, and certain images stick in people's minds. Ted Dirking can clown around with those guys and still go back to the set and turn into Conrad Hale, but I play Andy Sussman all the time, and I'd just like to keep a little distance from some of the more outrageous stunts, if you don't mind."

Trager shrugged and looked at his clipboard; Sussman wondered if there was a little item on his checklist that said "2:31 P.M.—Massage Ego of Sportscaster." "Well," Trager muttered, "you've made a noble effort. And they seem to be about finished—maybe we can do

a voice-over later. Do you have the lineups for the paddleboat race?"

Sussman followed Trager from the boat slip back to
the main section of the pier, which had been closed off
by the Redondo Beach police but was still ringed with
onlookers. Most of them were tourists from the nearby
hotels, although the number of local residents milling
around had increased throughout the week, as news of
the production had spread down the beach. Redondo,
part of a cluster of South Beach communities which
included Hermosa, Manhattan, and Palos Verdes, was
slightly different in character from the beaches a few
miles north, like Santa Monica and Malibu. It was not
as heavily frequented by Hollywood types or muscle
builders or the general flotsam and jetsam that seemed
to wash up around Venice. And it was not a stranger to
competitions such as this: the beach volleyball championships were held here each summer, as well as the
contests for Miss Budweiser and Miss Nissan Hardbody,
which did not turn out to be pageants for boat racers
or female weight lifters, Sussman was not disappointed
to learn. It was a polite crowd. Most of them had not
seen Andy in his limited network exposure and didn't
know him from Adam; after the first few days the security had let more and more of them get closer to the
competition, which was held either on the beach or in
the marina.

"Now, we've got a nice little finish coming up," Trager
was saying to his clipboard. "ABC and NBC are tied
with thirty-two and a half points, and we've got thirty,
so that means whoever wins the paddleboat race wins
the whole schmear." Trager pulled a sheet off the clipboard. "Here, Andy. The boats are color-coded, otherwise you'll never tell them apart once they're in the
water."

Sussman stopped about ten yards from the long section of pier where the boats would start; he studied the
rosters while Cliff Trager went ahead and started organizing the teams and double-checking the camera

placements. The *Celebrity* teams were a collection of actors, entertainers, and bona fide athletes whose shows or sports were affiliated with the networks they were competing for. As he glanced back up at the marina, Sussman could see three rubber dinghies, red, yellow, and blue, bobbing against the dock. The boats, more like rafts, were low to the water and looked awfully small for four people. Sussman guessed they had been chosen specifically for their total inability to steer and their high probability of capsizing. There were little plastic oarlocks on each side, but this was to be an oarless race—the contestants would be paddling the boats with their hands.

Sussman studied the roster one final time and then approached the dock, where the teams, dressed in swimsuits the same color as their boats, were milling around the starting point. Like all the events, there had been several practice runs, and in this case, some preliminary heats; each network had started with two boats, and presumably the best teams were in the finals. But the contestants seemed a little wary; they poked the boats' plastic sides and touched their toes gingerly to the bottom without getting inside—the race would start with them sitting on the dock and then leaping into the boats. There had been several spills in the prelims.

"Two minutes, Andy," Cliff Trager said to Sussman. "You do forty-second interviews with the captains of all three teams. Then we stop tape for a commercial break, then we start the race."

Sussman let a makeup girl do a final check on his face. He straightened out his yellow blazer, which looked faintly ridiculous with the Bermuda shorts, but he hadn't had any choice on the attire and didn't want to press his luck with Cliff. Fortunately, none of the wrestlers had been chosen captain, so he wouldn't have to interview them. Ted Dirking was leading the ABC crew and he neatly stage-managed a forty-second scene in which Kristie Halimon, a Wimbledon semifinalist last year, demonstrated her forearm paddle and Tony Price, a leftfielder on the Giants, used a bat for a rudder, and Monica Cummings, a soap-opera heroine whose character only yesterday had been abandoned at three in the morning in a wine-barrel factory in Santa Barbara, explained that she wore those rubber tabs on her nails to keep from puncturing their vessel.

Leona Z, who had hosted NBC's *Friday Night Videos*, was captaining their boat. She gave Dr. Double-X a stiff elbow in the gut and then kissed The Thing on the cheek. "Thingie's *so* excited," Leona told Andy, who was silently counting off the forty seconds, "and we're going to put him right in the front and let him paddle both sides, and I'm going to rudder in the back, and the skinny little broad over there"—Leona pointed at Barbara Simms, a figure-skating silver medalist in the last Olympics, who now skated for the Ice Capades—"oh, really, isn't she just *cute* as a dimple! Oh, the judges'll just *love* her."

"Sorry, Leona," Sussman said, playing along. "No judges—"

"*What!* No judges! But . . . but . . ."

"No, Leona, there's nothing subjective about a race," Andy said, using this opportunity to describe the course to the audience. The dinghies would leave the pier and zigzag through a maze of boat slips, then head out toward open water, where a number of bright red buoys would mark their course. Then they would make a ninety-degree turn and head for a small manmade lagoon that had been built especially for the event, concluding with a mad stretch run for the beach.

"Well, I don't know what little Barbie's gonna *do*," whined Leona. "No *style* points, even? We'll have to have someone swim beside us and throw roses or something."

"Sorry," said Sussman, looking for a graceful exit. "Any predictions on the outcome, Leona?"

"Andy," said the rock singer, wrapping a lithe but muscular right arm around Sussman's waist and pinching him on the rear end, "we are going to kick tush." Leona pecked Sussman on the cheek and Andy slid to his left, where the team representing his own network had gathered around their co-captains, Hal Barron and Carol Vivian, the latest co-hosts of the struggling morning news show.

Barron was a skinny avocado-and-bean-sprout type who was alleged to have competed in several ten-K's, according to his bio sheet, but his hands looked frail and his arms scrawny—he didn't appear as if he would be of much help in an inflatable dinghy. Carol, by contrast, looked like an exercise video waiting to be produced. Her well-defined arms and thighs, tanned and coconut-oiled, glistened against her standard network one-piece yellow swimsuit. It was none of Sussman's business, but having the two of them standing next to each other half-naked was not, in his view, doing much for Hal's sex appeal. Sussman guessed that their presence on *Superteams* during ratings-sweeps week was not entirely due to their athletic prowess, although their boat *had* somehow won one of the preliminary heats. This was due mainly to Dr. Double-X, who had attacked the water with a maniacal fervor, double-windmilling with his arms until the boat had actually risen out of the water for an instant, like the Hovercrafts at Le Havre.

Double-X, thankfully, was several feet out of the picture while all this was going on, getting a last-minute rubdown from Wireless and chomping on a wad of chewing tobacco. A nauseating drool slid down his cheek. Hal and Carol bubbled on for a few seconds about his brute force, taking the interview away from Sussman, who was quite happy to let them have it. "Cindi!" shouted Carol, waving to Cindi Beamon, who was jogging in place a few feet away. "Our secret weapon, Andy—you have no idea how strong these volleyball players are! I mean, they play two people on a whole *court*, on the *sand*—do you have any idea what kind of shape that girl is *in?*"

Cindi's shape, as it happened, had not completely escaped Sussman's attention. She was a slim blond, with light sandy hair pulled back in a ponytail. Her red zippered sweatshirt hung loosely from her shoulders; she stared straight ahead as she warmed up, occasionally licking her lips in a way that Sussman would have found sensually attractive if he were looking for that type of thing, which he was fairly sure he wasn't.

"Well, it's sort of Beauty and the Beast, then," laughed Hal Barron. Sussman looked back to Cliff Trager, who was nodding his head and tapping his wristwatch. "We might have to be a little scientific here, to keep up with the Peacock," Barron concluded, "but it's all on the line, Andy, and we are *ready*, right, Carol?"

"You got it, captain!"

"Well, there you have it," said Andy Sussman, "it's all come down to this: two and a half points separate these three teams as they go for the championship, and we'll have the race for all the marbles, when we come back!"

Cliff Trager waved his arm and the cameras dropped back. The technicians moved back off the dock so that the contestants would have plenty of room to get their start organized. In the several minutes that followed, the twelve entertainers stretched, hyperventilated, and put on their life vests. They patted each other on the back and joked lightly amongst themselves, except for the two wrestlers, who were sworn enemies and could not be seen fraternizing in public, even though the cameras were off.

The crowd buzzed, mostly in amusement. The docks lining the pierside restaurants were filled with people now, and there was another crowd lined up near the lagoon, at the finish line. Finito, Sussman thought, projecting twenty minutes ahead. The race would be about five minutes of frenetic dog-paddling, then the wrap-up interviews, then this whole idiotic thing would be over.

"Coming up on ten," said Cliff Trager, his hand in the air, and ten seconds later Andy Sussman, standing on the dock about twenty feet in front of the three teams of celebrities, took the cue and started the final segment. He briefed the audience on the water temperature and the wind conditions, reset the personnel on the boats, and described, in what he considered an informed and polished manner, the different strategies each boat would be using. Then, to his great relief, someone shot off a starter's gun and the race began.

"They're off!" Sussman reported. "Here we go, folks, the deciding race! It looks like they're all off cleanly— hang on there, Barbie—" Barbara Simms, the figure skater, had fallen a little short on her jump from the dock, but Leona Z had grabbed her by the arm and flung her to the front of the dinghy like a Frisbee; she bounced off the bow and was caught by The Thing, who gently placed her in the back. "Boy, you've gotta admire that team for its raw strength," Sussman said. "Now, there's ABC and CBS going neck and neck, trying to catch up . . ."

Sussman, in truth, could not see a thing. All three boats were dog-paddling furiously, frothing around and bumping into each other. A few shrieks came from the water. Sussman thought he heard a "Move it, fat ass," from Leona, but he couldn't tell because the boats were zigzagging through the marina and his view was blocked by the boat slips. There were cameras stationed at two of the turn points, of course, and Sussman assumed he could dub in some more commentary later, in post-editing.

"So all three boats are just about clear of the harbor now," Andy said as the three dinghies broke into open water. The NBC boat was ahead by about a length and a half, he guessed, with ABC second and CBS third. He had expected his crew to be closer, but now it appeared that Dr. Double-X, paddling almost single-handedly, couldn't quite pull it off by himself. "They're approaching the last buoy," Sussman reported, "then they'll turn back and head for the lagoon . . . let's see who can cut it sharpest, every inch could be crucial!" The NBC boat still maintained a slight lead, but the blue ABC dinghy actually did cut the buoy sharper and Sussman thought he deserved some credit for inventing expert analysis for all this. "Boy, the home team's really dragging now . . . there's Dr. Double-X, reaching for something extra and . . . Wait, they're in trouble, I think they've swamped!"

Sussman held his hands over his forehead to block out the glare. "It looks like Dr. Double-X lurched forward to try to give the boat an extra surge—I think he must have upset the balance there, and the boat just turned over. There they all are, swimming around . . . Meanwhile, NBC continues to lead, but here comes the ABC boat!"

Sussman kept his eyes on the two competing boats as they approached the last hundred yards of straightaway leading toward the lagoon and the beach. Ted Dirking was a little stronger than Andy had given him credit for; he actually seemed to be outpulling Price, the Giants' outfielder—the boat kept spinning to port—but the NBC entry, with The Thing, Leona Z, Barbara Simms, and Barry Hansen, another soap-opera actor, had pulled away to a lead of several lengths. "They're headed toward the finish and it looks like . . . yes . . . it's NBC!" shouted Sussman as the boat hit the beach with a squish and the triumphant dog-paddlers bounded ashore. "NBC has *won* the Network Celebrity Team championship with an unbelievable dash to the finish, fighting off a plucky bunch of ABCers and, we're sorry to report, the CBS boat is *way* behind—" Sussman looked back toward the buoy. "As you can see, they seem to be having a little trouble there . . ."

Back at the edge of the harbor, the four paddlers were swimming around several yards from the capsized dinghy, which was beginning to float away. Sussman saw a few hands waving, frantically, he thought. He looked quickly in back of him, where Cliff Trager was waving his finger in front of his throat, signaling him to cut to commercial. "Well, we seem to have a little bit of a mishap out there, we'll get the Coast Guard out right away. NBC has *won* the race, though, and we'll be back in a minute to talk to the champions."

Sussman turned back to Cliff, who gave him the okay

sign and leapt up on the dock. "What the hell happened, Andy?"

"I have no idea, Cliff. They swamped."

"I can see that . . ."

A couple of motorboats sped out to the four swimmers—or actually, Sussman noted, three swimmers. All three were struggling with the body of the fourth, and Sussman thought he saw the black hood of Dr. Double-X at the top of it. It took all three of them, plus two lifeguards in the motorboat, to haul the wrestler out of the water. One of the swimmers, either Carol or Cindi, Sussman wasn't sure, got in the boat with him, and the other two were pulled into the second boat. The two boats sped through the marina back to the long stretch of dock that Sussman and Trager were standing on. The lifeguards, meanwhile, had cleared a path from the dockside to the nearest road outlet, and an ambulance had been called.

All this seemed to happen in an instant. By the time the motorboats pulled up to the dock, the men with Dr. Double-X were already working furiously, trying to give him mouth-to-mouth resuscitation. They didn't miss a beat, even as several policemen, coming from the dock, rushed out and helped to remove the wrestler from the boat and lay him down on the dock.

"Move it, lookout," shouted a raspy voice working its way through the crowd. Sussman looked up and saw Wireless, wearing pink-and-purple Tahitian swim trunks, the sunlight bouncing off his bald dome, leap onto the scene like Quasimodo. "Hands off the mask! The mask stays on!"

Several policemen, apparently unsure as to what species Wireless belonged to, let him move all the way up to the fallen wrestler, but he did not accost anyone and didn't seem to know what to do besides flail his arms around and scowl at the television cameras. The policemen had made no effort to remove the mask; there hadn't been time—they were breathing right through the mouth hole, trying to revive the wrestler.

Andy Sussman, standing a few feet away, tried to sneak in a glance, and noticed a CBS camera bumping against his shoulder. He didn't think they could pick up much, except that Double-X's face seemed awfully blue, and so did his fingernails. A few seconds later, the ambulance roared up to the dock. The trauma unit hustled out with a stretcher, and in a matter of seconds Dr. Double-X, his lips and eyes appeared lifeless through his mask, was whisked into the ambulance.

Sussman looked over at Cliff Trager, who was staring at his clipboard, shaking his head mournfully. "The son-of-a-bitch better not check out on us," Trager said, clicking off his stopwatch. "Or the whole program's right in the dumper."

"I hear you," said Andy, but they had both seen the wrestler's right arm slide lifelessly from the stretcher as they carried him into the ambulance. The emergency vehicle gunned its motor, and the last thing Andy Sussman saw was Wireless bounding into the back, his equipment bag slung over his shoulder, just ahead of the slamming doors. The ambulance pulled away, lights flashing, sirens blaring, heading toward the nearest hospital.

2

Andy Sussman was lying on the king-size bed in his suite at the Sheraton Redondo Beach Hotel, trying to garner bits of truth from the six-o'clock news while he carried on a conversation with his agent, who also happened to be his girlfriend.

"Well, at least they won't be able to pin this one on you," said Susie Ettenger, who was lying next to Andy on the bed, her otherwise naked body wrapped in a bath towel. "And I gather if the entire program never sees the light of day, it won't exactly be a calamity. Dignity preserved, shall we say?"

"Well, I didn't need the guy to drown for it," muttered Sussman, fumbling with the TV remote control. He switched around the local news shows, but it was all pretty much the same. CBS hadn't released the actual show footage, but once the ambulance call had been intercepted, camera crews had come right out. All the stations had it. Sussman saw himself standing on the dock as Dr. Double-X was carried away; then he saw the coroner standing outside the emergency entrance at Harbor Hospital, announcing that Dr. Double-X, who didn't seem to have any other identity, was dead of an apparent heart attack and drowning. In the background, Wireless, still dressed in his Tahitian swimsuit, clutched his fists and bawled like a baby.

"Did you hear anything about a police report?" asked Susie, wrapping her soft brown hair in another towel, which she tied around her forehead like a turban.

"I suppose there'll be a more sophisticated coroner's report, and I guess they'll check for drugs; they almost have to in a case like this, just to stifle the rumors. Let's assume they don't find anything, though, just for convenience's sake." Sussman pulled himself out of bed and headed for the little refrigerator by the television set. "I don't think they'll need anything more out of me."

"Well, we've got the hotel suite till the end of the week," Susie purred. "And my tan is *not* complete yet."

"Better get to work, sweetheart. They certainly aren't going to air the show now, and they'll probably want to cut costs—"

"As your agent, Mr. Sussman, let me point out that the untimely demise of Mr. Double-X—"

"*Dr.* Double-X."

"Whatever. It ain't your fault, the perks are in your contract, and we're staying till I get rid of this little white spot where my wristwatch was. And that includes all meal expenses, and you deserve every penny of it for acting extremely professional in a situation that was far afield from your contractual area of expertise," recited Susie, as Sussman poured himself a Michelob. "Fix me a gin and tonic, will you, sweets?"

Sussman twisted the top off a bottle of tonic water, poured some into a glass, and added two healthy slugs of gin. A little drunkenness seemed appropriate for the occasion, and probably wouldn't do their relationship any harm either. When he'd originally retained Susie as his attorney, after his first season broadcasting basketball games on WCGO radio in Chicago three years ago, Andy had entertained some faint hopes of getting a date with her. That goal had quickly become secondary when his career was threatened by the murder of his broadcasting "color man" Lester Beldon, almost a year ago exactly. Andy had been suspected, for no logical reason except spite, by WCGO's management, to whom he had not exactly endeared himself during three years of telling the truth, as he saw it, about the performance of the perennially last-place Flames. Somewhere in the fight to clear his name and grab the network offer that he knew was waiting, Andy had managed to win the affections of Susie—he supposed it never would have happened if he had consciously plotted things out.

Susie had negotiated the contract with CBS and even moved to New York with him for a few months, but circumstances just hadn't allowed a permanent live-in arrangement. Having invested the previous three years ascending the cobwebs of Chavous and Birnbaum, a prestigious Chicago law firm, Susie found that she was not sufficiently compensated by her one-man broadcasting clientele to give it all up. She understood Andy's desire to be located in New York for the time being. That was where network management was; it helped to be visible. They'd both adjusted to the new terms of their relationship, which, if not exactly thriving, had at least survived, feeding on weekends and road trips.

"I just think we'd better watch the expenses," Sussman said, handing Susie the double gin and tonic. "If the Great Purge ever hits the sports department—"

"Andy, you have an ironclad contract, please cut it out. It's forty degrees and raining in Chicago, this is my first real vacation in six months, I've been listening to you piss and moan about your image all week. Now that the whole thing's over one way or the other, can't we just go out dining and dancing and have a great time?"

"I wasn't pissing and moaning. You want me to end up as the network point man for *Wide World of Geeks?*"

"Andy, you're not the only sportscaster on the damn network and I'm trying to keep you on the air! The only other thing happening between now and April is golf and Merle Summers' cockamamie thing. He wanted you to do an *Adventure!* segment, 'Roughing It in the Rain Forests of Java'—is that what you wanted?"

Sussman sipped his beer and admitted that he did not want to go roughing it in Java. His idea of "roughing it" was a motel room without cable television. He kissed Susie on the cheek, climbed back on the bed, and began discussing which overpriced Beverly Hills restaurant they would dine at and charge to the network, when the phone rang. Sussman considered letting the hotel switchboard take a message, but no one down there seemed to be paying attention. He answered it and heard Cliff Trager's stammering voice trying to find its way across the line.

"Well, you see, Andy," Cliff ventured, "this whole thing with Dr. Double-X has been causing quite a commotion here and we really don't have any choice but to cover it."

"That's what we have a news department for, isn't it, Cliff?"

"Uh, well, that's true, Andy, but it *was* a CBS Sports presentation and you were the anchorperson for it, and it seemed kind of logical for you to continue with it—"

"What about Hal and Carol? They're hosting the *Morning News*, this would be a great chance for them to do some firsthand reporting—"

"Well, the thing is, Andy, they've got to go to New York," Trager mumbled, stopping several times to clear his throat. "And we just don't think it's advisable to tie them up for who knows how long with this wrestling thing."

"Oh, I get it," said Sussman, tapping Susie on the shoulder and pointing to the bathroom. She scurried inside and grabbed the suite's other telephone. "But it's okay to stick *me* with this wrestling thing?"

"Andy, covering a news event isn't necessarily a bad break for you. Remember how Jim McKay handled the Olympic thing at Munich—"

"Cliff, the two are hardly comparable—"

"Andy, listen. I think we're only talking a few days here. The coroner's report could be the end of it, if it turns out the guy's heart just gave out. In the meantime, there's just three little things and I'd sure appreciate it if you'd handle them. I'm sure Merle would too, and everybody else . . ."

Sussman looked toward the bathroom, where Susie held the phone with one hand over the speaking part of it. She shrugged and said, "Hear him out."

"Shoot," Sussman said.

"Thank you. First, get a reaction from some of the wrestlers. They've got a big match at the Sports Arena tomorrow night, I've got the ad in front of me . . . The Thing and El Destructo and a couple of tag-team matches and a cage match at the end, whatever that is—"

"Cliff, you're not really expecting me to cover that. I'll interview a couple of them if I have to, but I will not—"

"We've already called the promoter, Andy. Some guy named Ben Garrison, he's all over the cable. Just get there about an hour early and do some interviews, you can go home before the whole thing even starts."

Sussman looked at Susie, who had put the phone down and was plucking her eyebrows. "Fine, Cliff, I'll handle it. Get a crew ready, I'll be at the Sports Arena by six—"

"Make it five-thirty, for the local news show." Trager cleared his throat. "Two: attend the coroner's report, which should be Saturday morning at the hospital. If everything's on the up-and-up, we'll probably call it a wrap right there."

"Let's hope so—"

"And third, Andy, can you, uh . . . do you think you could find out who the guy was?"

"Dr. Double-X?"

"Uh-huh. Sorry to trouble you with that, but we have no idea about the guy's real name, and we're all feeling a little silly."

"Well, didn't the hospital say—"

"They didn't have a clue. Nobody showed up except that cretin Wireless—can you believe he wouldn't even let 'em take off the goddamn mask when they got to the emergency room. They finally had to call six cops, and even then he wouldn't leave. He claimed there was a will, for Chrissakes, says he's supposed to be buried in the thing."

"Well, honestly, Cliff, I think that's just a lot of hype. The guy gets checks made out to him, he had a home somewhere, it shouldn't be too hard to find out—"

"Good, then I can count on you to handle it—"

"Cliff!"

"Well, I've got to go, Andy, the missus made reservations somewhere. Go out and have a good meal somewhere, you deserve it."

Sussman slammed down the phone and guzzled the rest of his beer, while Susie, who had heard the end of the conversation, replaced the bathroom receiver and started to dry her hair. "I think he's right," she said over the hum of her hair dryer.

"Whattaya mean, Suse? Look at my contract, it says nothing about news reporting—"

"I mean about dinner. I think it's our night for Spago."

"Forget it."

"Andy!"

"I'm not hungry."

"Andy, will you please stop this sulking!" Susie stalked over to the bed, waving her hair dryer at him. "This is a challenge, you can show everyone at Black Rock how you can take a potentially farcical situation and turn it into serious, insightful, dignified reporting—"

Sussman pushed the hair dryer away with his pillow, he grabbed his harmonica from the bed table and started wailing out a few bars of "Freight Train," or maybe it was "Lost and All Alone," he wasn't sure and he didn't think his audience would know the difference. Susie, who was not exactly a Lincoln Avenue regular to begin with, responded with a truly pained expression and started crooning into her hair dryer, remarkably on key: "Oh, I've really got the blu-u-u-es, I'm getting paid to spend a week in Redondo Beach and I make two hundred grand a year and I've got to go interview-w-w-w, some stupid wrestlers, oh yeah, oh yeah."

Sussman blushed and plunked the harmonica down on his pillow. "Oh, all right," he said, "here's the deal.

I can't handle Spago tonight, there'll be too many biz people there."

"Tomorrow'll be better?"

"Well, at least I'll be done with the dirty work. Let's go to P and W's tonight. We'll have margaritas and enchiladas and dance the night away, and then tomorrow we'll splurge."

"P and W's again, I can't tell you how thrilled I am." Susie banged her hair dryer down on her dresser and returned to the closet, where she yanked out a pair of designer blue jeans. "Andy, what are we going to do with you?"

"Feed me some margaritas and guacamole and cheeps," Sussman said, "I'll probably be okay."

And that is exactly what they were doing about an hour later, at Pancho and Wong's, a Chinese-Mexican restaurant and bar that was conveniently located right across the street from the Sheraton, a few yards from the ocean. They were nestled into a booth, polishing off their fifth bowl of corn chips and salsa, trying to tune out a bad rock-and-roll band that was playing old songs by the Turtles and Elvis and the Animals, songs that Sussman had played himself when he was in high school, hacking away at an electric guitar. He was on his third or fourth margarita by now, and he vaguely suspected that Susie was making an attempt to get him plastered. She wanted him to take her out to some glitzy Hollywood nightclub, or at least to the Blue Moon Saloon, a slightly more upscale place down the street. The main course came and they wolfed down some enchiladas and chile relleno—after several days experimenting, he had learned that Pancho cooked considerably better than Wong. Sussman, by now, had just about washed tomorrow's assignment out of his mind when his eyes focused, more or less, on something either revolting or familiar, or possibly revoltingly familiar, that was flashing on the twelve television screens bolted to the walls and tuned into ESPN.

"Lookit!" said Andy, pointing to the screen above his

head, which was filled by a couple of professional wrestlers plugging their next match.

"Andy, forget about it, worry about it tomorrow. Finish the enchilada, we're going dancing—"

"No, no, lookit, Suse! Christ, it's . . . it's Lennie Weintraub."

"Right, Lennie Weintraub. Oh, miss!" Susie shouted
as a waitress headed past them.

"Two more margaritas?"

"How about some coffee and a check."

"I'm serious," Sussman said, staring at the TV screen.
"I swear to God, that is Lennie Weintraub, pal of my
youth."

On the screen, a huge man with thick greasy hair and
muttonchop sideburns was screaming, "I'll tear his heart
out, I'll slaughter him like a dumb animal! I will destroy
him! I will mutilate him! No one gets out of the ring
against El Destructo—"

"Lennie Weintraub," said Susie, opening her purse.
"I'll cover this one."

"No, no, not him . . ."

The camera panned to the left and a sharp retort came
from El Destructo's adversary in a steady, cocksure,
British-sounding voice:

"Who knows himself a braggart, let him fear this;
   For it shall come to pass,
   That every braggart shall be found an ass!"

"Uh . . . him?" said Susie, but before she could go any
further, El Destructo seized the spotlight again.

"He's been ducking me for years," bellowed the wrestler. "He's a yellow-bellied, lily-livered coward, but he
can't hide from me tomorrow night! I will crush him! I
will mutilate that limey twit—"

The camera panned over to the object of all this scorn,
a slightly smaller but nevertheless well-built man dressed
in a pair of black tights and a black satin cape. He had
short black hair and a neatly trimmed Vandyke beard.

Beneath his cape he wore a white jersey, which bore his name in black Old English lettering: "The Renaissance Man."

"Him," said Andy Sussman, slurping the remains of a margarita and leaving a residual arc of salt on his forehead. "Leonard Weintraub, the Bard of Braeside Junior High."

The Renaissance Man, having heard El Destructo's taunts to the end, cried out:

> "Am I a coward?
> Who calls me villain? Breaks my pate across?
> Tweaks me by the nose? Gives me the lie i'
>   the throat
> as deep as to the lungs? Who does me this, ha?
> 'Swounds, I should take it! For it cannot be
> but I am pigeon-livered and lack gall
> to make oppression bitter, or ere this
> I should have fatted all the region kites
> with this slave's offal. Bloody, bawdy villain!
> Remorseless, treacherous, lecherous, kindless
>   villain!
> O, Vengeance!"

El Destructo stared into the camera, scratching his head, then grabbed the microphone back from the hapless announcer. "This man is an embarrassment to wrestling," he announced, pointing his finger in his opponent's face. "You're a pansy! You're a weak-kneed limey. I'm gonna destroy you tomorrow night in the ring, just like I destroyed the Mauler. They'll be picking up your bones one at a time and sending 'em back to England—"

The Renaissance Man whipped off his cape and snapped it at El Destructo. "S'blood!" he exclaimed.

> "You starveling, you eel skin, you dried
> neat's tongue, you bull's pizzle, you stockfish—
> O for breath to utter what is like thee! You tailor's

yard, you sheath, you bowcase, you vile standing tuck!"

"Vile standing tuck?" mumbled Sussman, but at this point the announcer broke in between the two wrestlers and tried to establish some decorum. He was a chunky man with a round face, he wore large black glasses, had a fat mustache, and wore a plaid sport coat. Now there, Sussman thought, is a man who is not destined to become the Walter Cronkite of Sports. "I have no idea what any of that means," the announcer shouted, "but it sounds like the Renaissance Man means business—and he'll have to if he wants to have a chance against El Destructo. Yes, sir, fans, it's all part of the great WFA wrestling card tomorrow night at the Los Angeles Sports Arena. You'll see The Blob against Super Enforcer Three, The Thing against the Mexican Mauler—and there's more, sports fans! A special cage match! Eighteen wrestlers, locked in—that's right, *locked in a cage* until there's only one left standing. Call *now* in Los Angeles, 213-555-8393 . . ."

"Lennie Weintraub?" said Susie Ettenger, leaving a generous tip for the waitress and leading Andy back into the parking lot. "Pal of your youth?" They were standing outside Pancho and Wong's now. The ocean breeze had stiffened and she was shivering slightly; the margaritas were not having much of a warming effect.

"I swear to God," said Sussman. "I went to high school with the guy. He had the lead in every production we ever did from seventh grade through junior year, then he went off to New York in some special program for talented kids."

"Andy, I don't suppose you'd consider the possibility that you've overimbibed."

"Nah," said Sussman, carefully putting one foot in front of the other and tracing the lines on the parking spaces. The familiar sight of Lennie Weintraub, along with the damp ocean chill, seemed to sober him up. Susie grabbed him by the arm anyway and they strolled across the parking lot toward the Blue Moon Saloon. "I'd recognize him anywhere, Suse. We all followed his career, the neighborhood kind of kept up with him. My parents used to send me his clippings. I remember he was doing summer stock for a while—he spent a year at the Guthrie in Minneapolis, it was when I was doing sports up in Green Bay. I was up there for a Packer-Viking game and I caught a Saturday matinee. I think it was *The Tempest*."

"He played Prospero?"

"Naw, he was understudy to Caliban, but it was still a big deal at the time. I thought he was on his way." Sussman stopped at the entrance to the Blue Moon Saloon—the restaurant section had been closed for several hours, but the bar was full and a band was playing, he thought he could make out some old Beatles songs. He didn't feel like going inside quite yet. He'd had enough noise and booze and cigarette smoke. The dead wrestler was beginning to kick in, too, and now there was good old Lennie, it was all a little on the overtly strange side of things.

"But you weren't exactly good buddies or anything," Susie said. "I never heard you talk about him."

"No," Sussman admitted. "The fact is, we used to pick on him a little. You know how it is, high-school jocks and all that. But he didn't seem to care, he took it all, and by the time he left, we all sort of assumed he'd make it. I thought I heard he was in New York. I wonder what happened . . ."

Susie stopped and kissed Sussman on the cheek, then kissed him again on the lips. They held each other and leaned against the wall of the Blue Moon Saloon. Sussman wondered how it was that she always knew when he was feeling really, legitimately bedeviled by life and not just pissing and moaning, as she put it, and how she knew just what to do about it. "Andy," she said, "tomorrow, babe. Everything falls into place." She kissed him again, and said, "How about one dance, for old times' sake, and then we'll call it a night."

Inside the Blue Moon Saloon, the band was playing the Beatles' "Yesterday"; they could hear it faintly, but they both knew the words and could hum it themselves. They held each other tightly and danced through the ocean mist. It was not exactly Hollywood, it was just the parking lot at Redondo Beach, but it was all they needed.

"Tomorrow and tomorrow and tomorrow," whispered Sussman. He was just drunk enough to remember his old high-school Shakespeare, and just sober enough to make it back to the Sheraton before collapsing in bed.

3

Andy Sussman leaned against the ropes of the wrestling ring that was set up in the middle of the Los Angeles Sports Arena, grasping the increasingly obvious fact that he was being set up. The clock on the scoreboard above his head read 5:30. By this time he had expected to be nearly through his interviews—his sober, dignified reports on the day-after reactions to the death of an athlete. But the arena was empty, except for Sussman and the cameraman and a lighting technician provided by the local CBS affiliate. Cliff Trager had not made it, he had flown back to New York to go over the videotapes of *Celebrity Superteams* with the network pooh-bahs. The only reminder of Cliff was the bright yellow blazer with the CBS insignia on it which he had instructed Sussman to wear, despite Andy's protests that this *was* a news event, after all, and that Dan Rather and Diane Sawyer were not required to wear CBS blazers when they interviewed the President.

Mainly, though, Sussman knew he was being set up by the wrestlers. They were going to make an Entrance. The promoter was going to parade out whomever he wanted to be seen, and expect Sussman to stand there like the buffoon announcers on his TV shows while they put on their act. Well, he wasn't going to stand for that, no, sir!

Still, Sussman couldn't help but suppress a smile when Ben Garrison marched somberly into the arena, dressed in a black suit with a black tie, followed by Wireless in a tuxedo and a black veil, and The Thing in black wrestling trunks and a black robe. All three of them wore dark glasses and carried bouquets of roses, which they held silently at their chests until they saw the red light on the camera go on, then placed them in the center of the ring.

Ben Garrison, a tall man in his mid-thirties with slick black hair and a perfectly postured gait, was a familiar sight even to Sussman, who rarely watched wrestling on television. Several years ago Garrison had bought out the Wrestling Federation of America, at the time a local tour headquartered in Long Beach and seen mostly on the West Coast and Nevada; scarcely a year later he had turned it into a national phenomenon, thanks mainly to cable television. Garrison had been the first promoter to really exploit that medium; he had bought huge blocks of time on several of the cable networks and developed a national audience. Riding the crest of pro wrestling's new popularity, Garrison's WFA soon became the dominant wrestling league in the country. Wrestlers from all over began dropping their affiliations with local circuits and joining up with him, much to the chagrin of the regional associations, who were suddenly struggling to survive. That, of course, was several years ago; now, with the proliferation of cable channels, several wrestling associations had gotten their share of the airtime and were rivaling the WFA. But Garrison's head start had paid off handsomely; he still had the best cable outlets and the most exposure. It was WFA wrestlers who were most likely to show up in music videos or network late-night shows, it was WFA cards which attracted the overflow audiences at Madison Square Garden. It had all, no doubt, made Ben Garrison a very wealthy man.

Money, however, was not on Ben Garrison's mind tonight. This he confessed as he stood in the pool of television lights and poured his heart out to Andy Sussman. "The Doctor was a beautiful human being, Andy; it's hard for me . . . it's just so hard to conceive of this tragedy. Here we see a great champion, and a man I considered to be a close personal friend even as I was just getting to know him, cut down in the prime of his great career—" Garrison tried to keep from crying, while Sussman tried to keep from throwing up. "The potential that this man had. This was a man destined to be a world champion . . ."

"Ben," Sussman said, "I wonder if we could focus on the personal aspect for just a minute—perhaps you could just spend a moment and tell me about the man behind the mask."

"Andy, I'm truly glad you asked me that. Because this champion, Dr. Double-X, whose memory we'll be honoring tonight right here in this ring at the Sports Arena at seven-thirty on cable stations all across America—"

Sussman looked up at the clock—he had a limited amount of time, the local affiliate wanted the tape for the evening news and the network wanted a copy for their morning news show; he knew he had better get control of the interview. "Ben, I'm sure the Doctor's friends and family were shocked by this sudden and inexplicable death. I've heard you say many times that your wrestlers are the most superbly trained athletes in the world, and a lot of people are wondering how someone in that physical condition . . ."

Sussman's attempt at investigative reporting never reached the end of the sentence. Wireless, standing behind him, had broken out sobbing. He began pounding the turnbuckle so hard that the whole ring was shaking. "Andy," Garrison said as The Thing walked over to Wireless and embraced him, "as you can see, the man is heartbroken, the man is devastated, I can't tell you how much courage it took just for him to come out here and face these cameras—"

Sussman sighed, jerked the microphone away from Garrison, and stepped back toward the ropes. "Okay, fellas, cut it right there."

The cameraman did as he instructed. Wireless stopped blubbering and The Thing stopped consoling him. Ben

Garrison, evidently accustomed to being his own writer, director, and stage manager, stood with his hands on his hips, gaping at Sussman.

"Gentlemen," Andy said, "I am here to do a news interview on the death of one of your colleagues. I am not here to do a five-minute free promotion for the WFA."

Garrison stooped down in the center of the ring, picked up a bouquet of roses, and held them to his heart. "Mr. Sussman, feel these, they are real flowers. And this, in our own way, even if it isn't your way, is our very real way of expressing grief."

"I'm sure the Doctor would be touched, Ben. Now, gentlemen, look—I only have a few questions for you, there's no sense in us wasting each other's time. How about giving me about two minutes of yours and then I'll leave you alone."

Garrison nodded solemnly and tossed his roses back into the ring. "Okay, Andy, it's all yours," he said with a thin-lipped smile, and Wireless and The Thing retreated to neutral corners.

Sussman signaled his cameraman and the red light went on again. "Ben, there's been a lot of confusion regarding the actual identity of Dr. Double-X. I wonder if you could fill us in on that."

"Andy," said Garrison, staring forthrightly into the camera, "I'm afraid I never learned the man's real name."

"I see. This man who was destined to be a world's champion—"

"It was part of his mystique, Andy. It was part of what *made* him a champion, and who am I to tamper with that?"

"But, Ben, certainly there must have been contracts, you did pay him, after all—"

"I only dealt with his manager, Andy. Perhaps this gentleman can shed some light on the matter."

Andy walked over to Wireless's corner. Slumped against the turnbuckle, the manager was red-faced and his eyes still tearful. His tuxedo was wrinkled. It hadn't exactly fit him to begin with; he was not the type of person that could get formal wear on short notice. "We're talking to the man known as Wireless," Sussman said to the camera. "He was Dr. Double-X's manager and closest associate. Wireless, I know this is a moment of great loss for you, but I wonder if you could tell us a few words about your friend?"

Wireless snuffled back some tears and wiped a stubby hairless right arm against his nose. "He was an enigma, Andy. The man was truly an enigma, and now, to all our great dismay, there are questions we're destined never to know the answer to."

"Well. One question I do think we can answer is, 'Who was he?' "

Wireless choked back some more tears. He snatched the microphone from Andy's hand and walked toward the camera. "Andy, it was a dark January night, nearly a year ago—I was sitting at my good friend Harvey Pulaski's bar in Kansas City, and out of the shadows, out of the cold, snowy night, comes a man in a mask. And he says, 'Mr. Wireless, I am going to be the next wrasslin' champeen of the world.' And I'm telling you, Andy, I'd had *nothing* to drink, and I looked at those cold blue eyes, which were the only thing I could see through that mask of his except his lips, of course, and his nostrils, and the two little holes for his ears, but you can't really tell from looking at a man's ears, Andy, I know, I've been around this sport for a long time—"

"I understand. Wireless, you were his manager—I take it you saw to it that he got paid?"

"Absolutely, Andy, every penny of it, and let me tell you, no one worked as hard as that man—"

"Well, who did you write the checks out to?"

"Checks?"

"Paychecks."

Wireless coughed and Ben Garrison, walking over, slapped him hard on the back. "Dr. Double-X did not take paychecks," Garrison said. "He took only cash. One of his little quirks."

"Thousands of dollars in cash? After every match?"

"Andy, he was not the type of man who had to worry about carrying around large quantities of money."

"Well, what did he do with it?"

"That I do not know."

"Did he have any family?"

"I'm sure he was a wonderful family man, as befits a great champion with his legions of admirers—"

Sussman turned back to the manager. "Wireless, do you know where his family lives?"

Wireless wiped a tear from his eye. "He never mentioned it to me, Andy. He was a very private man about those things."

"Where was his hometown?"

"I have no idea."

"Did he have brothers and sisters?"

Wireless shrugged. "The man was an enigma."

"Well, what did he do on his birthday?"

Wireless growled and turned around to Garrison. "I baked him a cake! Look, the man's not even in his grave, all of us are trying to do him a little reverence . . ."

Sussman backed away; he decided he was willing to invest about thirty more seconds in this interview and then he would let Cliff Trager worry about it. "Let's get a final word from The Thing," he said, turning to the wrestler, who opened his black robe to show a chest that was built along the lines of the Berlin Wall. "It must shock you that a superbly conditioned athlete, just like yourself, could be so vulnerable, so suddenly mortal."

"Andy," said The Thing, resting two huge paws on Sussman's shoulders, "I put my faith entirely in the Lord. And when the Lord calls me, as He called for Dr. Double-X, I'll be ready, for I am but His humble servant."

Time to go, thought Sussman, reasoning that whatever minuscule chance he had to retain his dignity would be overwhelmed by the combination of wrestling and religion. "So you think," he asked The Thing, "that the Lord called Dr. Double-X Himself?"

"He lived as the Lord wished, and died according to His plan."

"Paddling a rubber raft in the Redondo Beach marina for the Battle of the Celebrity Superteams?"

"We all saw it with our own eyes, Andy."

Now, it happened that, as aggravated as Andy Sussman was, he was not incapable of seeing this whole situation from the wrestlers' point of view; he could rise to such heights of understanding, especially when he had no other choice. He had known their profession was a font of outrageous hype all along, and he supposed that he couldn't expect them to appear on network television and treat Dr. Double-X in death any differently from the way they had in life—they had professional standards to maintain, too. Besides, he thought, as a taciturn Ben Garrison threw a white handkerchief onto the pile of roses and led his charges back into the locker room, there had to be ways of identifying Dr. Double-X—tax records came to mind—and the hospital would probably have some more information by tomorrow. Really, this whole thing would be cleared up in a couple of days.

And finally, there was Lennie Weintraub, whom Sussman was eager to see anyway; he was actually going to attend the match tonight just to see Lennie wrestle, or soliloquize, or whatever it was that Lennie did. So Andy Sussman, relieved that the interview had run its course, unhooked his microphone and handed it to the soundman. He picked up several stems of red and yellow roses—he hoped they would look nice with whatever Susie was wearing tonight. He was meeting her for dinner at a Thai restaurant near the USC campus at six o'clock. They would be only a couple of minutes from the Sports Arena and, with a little luck, they could have a nice meal and not miss a single minute of exciting WFA action.

4

The good news, according to Susie, was that Sussman was going to be making a network appearance on the basketball game that Sunday between the Los Angeles Lakers and the Boston Celtics. "Cliff Trager called from New York," Susie explained over a cup of sweetly delicious wonton soup at the Thai place on Jefferson Street. "They're getting deluged with phone calls over the Dr. Double-X thing, and they're actually going to be airing a whole segment from *Celebrity Superteams* before the game. It'll be on at ten in the morning here."

Sussman wasn't sure whether he could bring himself to get out of bed at ten o'clock on a Sunday morning to watch himself hosting taped highlights of *Celebrity Superteams*, especially when he knew that one of the local independent stations showed his favorite Rocky and Bullwinkle cartoons at the same time. Sussman had taken a lot of grief from Susie about *that* last Sunday. She was convinced every intelligent person over the age of ten was watching *Meet the Press*, until a set of commercials interrupted Moose and Squirrel with messages from the Waterbed Store and Ralph Williams Ford. There was obviously a large semiliterate audience out there keeping Sussman company.

The lead-in to the Lakers-Celtics game was another matter. "Let me understand this," Andy had said, making a token effort to use his chopsticks on the combination of chicken pa-nang and kung prik-pao shrimp that he and Susie were splitting. He made several futile spears at a shrimp before flagging down a busboy, who churlishly presented him with a fork. "Let me understand this," he repeated. "Directly preceding the greatest rivalry in professional sports, which I, one of the outstanding young basketball broadcasters in the nation, would give my eyeteeth to announce—"

"You know, it really wouldn't hurt to learn to use the chopsticks," Susie said, neatly swooping up some rice, shrimp, and water chestnuts and showing it to Andy for an instant before gobbling it down. "We've got some depositions at work concerning some clients in Taiwan and there's a chance they might send me over there for a week. I thought maybe you could come along."

"I may *have* to go there," Sussman said, impaling a piece of chicken with his fork. "It's the only place in the free world where they won't remember me as the guy who interviews professional wrestlers before basketball games."

"Look, Andy, you're the one who's dragging me to a wrestling match on our last Friday night in LA. I've got a couple of *très magnifique* outfits that've been sitting in the closet all week waiting for the big Spago-and-dance-till-dawn-on-Sunset-Strip celebration and I just didn't have the heart to put on all those sequins for El Destructo and your friend Lennie."

Sussman didn't have much response to that; actually attending the matches had been his idea. He tried again to use his chopsticks and wondered why this wrestling thing always seemed to work out with him on the wrong side of the argument.

As it turned out, Susie probably could have worn her sequins to the wrestling match. The dress codes seemed to have changed dramatically since the old days in Green Bay, Montana, and even Chicago, when the dressiest outfit he ever saw was the plaid sport coat worn by the beleaguered TV announcer. It was probably the rock-star connection, Sussman guessed. When they arrived at the Sports Arena, Leona Z was already there, prancing around at ringside, her red spiked hair in something that resembled an open bear trap, a scarlet-and-black cape flouncing over her tight silver body suit. The entire first three rows seemed to be taken up by Leona's entourage. There was champagne flowing and a lot of hugging and dancing going on to some music, evidently Leona's. She was lip-synching the lyrics that thundered over the loud-speaker. A few rows back, the crowd melted into a combination of curiosity seekers and wrasslin' regulars—they were the ones with the programs rolled up, the stogies and the three sixteen-ounce cups of beer stashed underneath their seats.

There also seemed to be a lot of journalists present. Sussman could see the TV cameras from the local news shows; the press table seemed awfully crowded—no surprise really, given yesterday's drowning. But he hadn't used his press pass to get in. He'd bought two tickets in the first tier above the ringside seats, and instructed Susie to bring a change of clothes to the restaurant. He was now dressed in jeans and a Grateful Dead T-shirt, with an old White Sox cap in case he needed complete anonymity. Susie had opted for her designer jeans and a loose-fitting sweatshirt that said "Chicago" in faded blue script on the front. It looked nice on her. She had enough class for the two of them, Sussman thought.

During the first several matches Andy tried to explain the fundamentals of professional wrestling to Susie. Basically there was a good guy and a bad guy, and the bad guy usually was alleged to come from someplace like Turkey or Iran or South America and tended to hit the good guy in the few places on his body that were covered by clothing. Generally any combative maneuver, including kicking, slapping, and biting, was acceptable as long as it did not involve firearms or nuclear devices. The wrestlers were supposed to stick with the natural strength the Lord had provided them, although the bad guy was generally armed with the dreaded "foreign object" concealed in his boot or his trunks or his corner and used to gouge the good guy's vital organs out.

The only other figure of importance was the referee, whose job it was to ignore the bad guy completely, penalize the good guy occasionally, wave his arms at the moon every once in a while, and pound the mat twice when it looked like somebody might get pinned, or three times when someone actually did get pinned, or was supposed to.

By the end of the third match, when the Mexican Mauler threw Rough Reggie Randolph through the ropes, dragged him back into the ring, tied both his arms to his right kneecap, and plunged on top of him with a swan dive from the turnbuckle, Sussman could see that his girlfriend was catching on. Susie was screaming epithets at the Mauler, things she couldn't have possibly learned in law school, insulting the referee with gibes she might have learned in law school, and generally adapting to her surroundings much better than he was.

"I am determined to have fun my last weekend in Los Angeles, before returning to the cold, the slush, and three cases on tax evasion in the soybean pits," was her explanation, as the Mexican Mauler sneered at his fallen opponent, hurled some warm tortillas into the crowd, and stalked back to the dressing room. "Is your friend Lennie up next?"

Lennie was up next, but he did not come out right away. The crowd needed a few minutes to settle down from the previous match and get three or four more sixteen-ounce cups of beer, or whatever Leona and her friends were using to maintain their state of frenzy. Then, as a swelling of boos rose from the stands, a single grappler made his way out from the locker room.

"Ladeez and gentlemen," rasped the ring announcer through the crackling PA system, "introducing the Western States Champion, from Buenos Aires, Argentina, weighing in at two hundred and sixty-five pounds, El-l-l-l Destructo!"

The crowd greeted El Destructo with a standing boo and Susie whispered into Sussman's ear, "He really doesn't look Argentinian, does he? Last night he sounded like he was from Brooklyn."

"I'm sure he's just assimilated into the melting pot," Sussman said. But Argentinian or not, El Destructo was one of the larger accumulations of flesh and bones Sussman had ever seen. His legs were about the girth of a side of beef, his shoulders looked like cement mixers as he whirled his arms around to loosen up; whatever they were paying Lennie Weintraub for this, it was not enough.

"And in this corner," blared the referee, continuing with the introductions, "the challenger-r-r, from Stratford-upon-Avon . . . the Renaissance Man-n-n-n!"

From out of the runway emerged, not Lennie, but two young boys with Prince Valiant haircuts, each carrying a standard and a yard-long bugle. They stepped into the ring and blew a royal herald. Then, into the ring swaggered Lennie Weintraub, the Renaissance Man himself. He wore the same black tights and cape they had seen on television, and on his head was an outrageous black hat adorned with several white plumes. The cape had his name spelled out on one side; on the other was a sequined reproduction of the *Mona Lisa*.

The crowd, in the meantime, had started to hoot and even boo a little. "I thought El Destructo was the bad guy," Susie said.

"Uh, one of those little things about Lennie, babe," Sussman said as the boos started to swell. "There always was something about him that seemed to attract derision. But geez, he really built himself up—lookit him!"

The Renaissance Man stood in his corner, flexing his biceps to Leona Z and her friends, who were standing behind his corner throwing peanut shells at him. He was only about five-feet-ten but his muscles were sinewy and taut; unlike El Destructo, whose gut rolled over his trunks, the Renaissance Man's stomach was flat and rigid. Behind the Vandyke beard was a look of arrogance and determination.

The referee brought the two grapplers together and explained the rules: the match would be one fall or forty-five minutes, whichever came first, that was about it. The bell rang, the two of them parried around the ring for a few moments, feeling each other out. Suddenly El Destructo grabbed the Renaissance Man by the arm, twisted him with a vicious jerk, and flung him into the turnbuckle.

"I don't think I want to see this," said Susie, and for good reason: as his opponent slid down to the mat, El Destructo turned toward the crowd and pulled a foreign object from his boot, completely in view of all ten thousand people in the arena except the referee, who was sweeping some peanut shells out of the ring, and the Renaissance Man, who nonetheless must have sensed that something was wrong, for he shouted out, "Something is rotten in the state of Denmark!"

To Sussman's astonishment, the Renaissance Man had a small remote microphone wired to him; his words could be heard all through the arena: "I prithee, take thy fingers from my throat," he proclaimed as El Destructo leapt on him and put him in a hammerlock.

> "For though I am not splenitive and rash,
> Yet I have in me something dangerous,
> which let thy wisdom fear. Hold off thy hand!"

El Destructo, hesitating only for a moment, slugged his opponent in the face with the foreign object, which appeared to be a nail of some sort. The Renaissance Man began to bleed profusely. The referee jumped in and wagged his finger at El Destructo, who feigned innocence, looked insulted and, as soon as the referee turned his head, kicked the Renaissance Man in the face and laughed so loudly that he could be heard all through the arena without benefit of electronics.

"O villain, villain, smiling damned villain!" the Renaissance Man cried out, rising slowly to his feet, his face streaked with blood.

"My tables, my tables, meet it as I set it down
that one may smile and smile, and be a villain!"

The crowd let out a rancorous boo and El Destructo
kicked the Renaissance Man again, leaving him writhing
on the ground and pounding the mat. The Argentinian
raised his arms and waved his fist at the crowd, then
turned and spat at Leona Z, who had gotten out of her
seat and was spitting back. She had changed her alle-
giance, she seemed to have found some type of artistic
bond with the Renaissance Man and was the only one
coming to his defense.

The Renaissance Man, taking note of this distraction,
rose to his feet. With one swift and vicious move he
kneed El Destructo in the small of the back, sending him
to the mat in a heap. He stomped on El Destructo in a
fit of rage, he punched him hard in the eye, unleashing
a torrent of blood. The crowd was booing with a ven-
geance now, except for Leona, who had climbed onto
the ropes and was swearing a blue streak at the fallen
wrestler.

The Renaissance Man flexed his biceps, he leaned over
his fallen opponent, ready to go for the pin. But as the
crowd roared, he backed off; he recoiled in horror and
held his blood-soaked right hand to the klieg lights and
cried out:

"Will all great Neptune's ocean wash this blood
clean from my hands? No, this hand will
rather the multitudinous seas incarnadine . . ."

El Destructo slowly began to pull himself off the mat.
The crowd built up to a din, but the Renaissance Man,
still facing the seats and clutching his blood-soaked hand
in remorse, did not see the danger.

"Out, damned spot! Out, I say . . ."

Now El Destructo was back on his feet and the crowd
was in a frenzy. He threw the Renaissance Man with a

vicious flying mirror, pounced on him, grabbed his beard and pummeled his head against the mat again and again and again. The crowd shrieked its appreciation. As the referee flopped down on the mat for a better view, El Destructo put all his weight on the Renaissance Man's shoulder and went for the pin.

"One!" pounded the ref, but the Renaissance Man sprang up, sat on one knee, and cried out:

> "I am dead, Horatio, wretched queen, adieu!
> You that look pale and tremble at this chance,
> that are but mutes or audience to the act,
> had I but time (as this fell sergeant, Death,
> is strict in his arrest) O, I could tell you—"

The crowd, which had fallen deadly silent, applauded politely, but El Destructo was unmoved. He grabbed the Renaissance Man by the throat and smashed him to the canvas again, harder than before. He stomped on his opponent's face until the mat was soaked red with blood; then, as the crowd went delirious, he went into his pin once more. The referee pounded the mat twice this time, but before he could hit it a third time the Renaissance Man bounced determinedly back up and shouted:

> "O, Horatio, what a wounded name
> (things standing thus unknown) shall live behind
>   me.
> If thou didst ever hold me in thy heart,
> absent thee from felicity awhile,
> and in this harsh world draw thy breath in pain
> to tell my story."

A few of the spectators applauded again this time, but the crowd was growing restless. "Die already!" someone shouted, and the familiar chorus of boos began to cascade down as El Destructo tried once more to apply the coup de grace. He picked up the Renaissance Man in a fireman's carry and spun him around, threw him onto

the mat, then leapt as high as he could, which fortunately for the Renaissance Man was only a few inches;
El Destructo did not have a great vertical leap. He came
down on his chest with a bone-crushing thud. The Renaissance Man appeared done for, but as the referee scurried down and pounded the mat, "One! Two! Thr—",
the bearded grappler sprang up one last time and cried:

> "Oh, I die, Horatio!
> The potent poison quite o'ercrows my spirit.
> I cannot live to hear the news from England
> but I do prophesy the election lights
> on Fortinbras. He has my dying voice.
> So tell him, with the occurrents, more or less,
> which have solicited—the rest is silence."

And with that the Renaissance Man flopped over on
his back and the referee counted him out as El Destructo
harmlessly looked on.

By this time the arena had fallen completely silent.
The participants remained still until the referee, in an
uncharacteristic flash of alertness, raised El Destructo's
hand in victory. The crowd broke into tumultuous applause as El Destructo put on his championship belt and
stalked out of the ring, except for Leona Z and her friends,
who showered him with beer and peanuts and champagne.

The Renaissance Man, meanwhile, was still flat on his
back. When the din subsided he rose slowly, wiped the
blood off his face, and bowed toward the audience.

The crowd booed.

He bowed toward all four corners of the arena, and
the booing became a deafening din.

Finally, he took his cape and placed it on his back
with a dramatic swirl. The haughty arrogance returned
to his face and the Renaissance Man, to a chorus of
catcalls, made his exit from the ring.

"Ahem," Susie said to Sussman as she cupped her
hands and made a futile attempt to give the defeated

wrestler a small measure of support as he made his way to the locker room. "Well, sweetheart, do you have an athletic or artistic appraisal that you could offer to the fans back home?"

"Marvelous," said Sussman, standing up and applauding as the Renaissance Man disappeared into the tunnel toward the locker room. "It was vintage Lennie."

5

Sussman wanted to get a few words in with Lennie Weintraub after the match, confidentially if possible. He pulled his baseball cap over his forehead and walked through the stands and past the ring, where The Thing was warming up for his match with Sir Alec Peckerwood, Champion of the British Isles. The Thing had managed to delay proceedings by insisting that his girlfriend, Leona Z, sing the national anthem of his native Transylvania before the match started, giving Sussman the chance to slip almost unnoticed into the tunnel to the locker rooms—there was only one security guard and he was easily waved off by Andy's network ID.

Sussman wandered through a small hallway, past the "authorized personnel only" sign. He entered the locker room, tiptoeing through the rows of small lockers and past the showers, until he reached a small lounge at the end of the dressing area. He sat quietly on a bench behind a row of lockers and surveyed the situation: most of the wrestlers were still in their costumes, clustered around the lounge. Sitting at a table at the back were four of the largest men he had ever seen, and Andy Sussman had spent the better part of his adult life around professional athletes. They were playing bridge.

"Two hearts," said one of them, whom Sussman recognized as the Mexican Mauler. He repeated, more firmly, "Two . . . hearts."

"I heard you," said the next player. It was El Destructo, a towel draped over his shoulder. The blood had been mostly wiped from his face and arms. "Three spades."

"Herman," said another wrestler, who was standing behind Destructo, "you can't jump to three spades with that hand."

El Destructo turned around with a hideous scowl. "I think I can do this without your help."

"Sorry."

"Pass," said the Mauler's partner.

"Pass," said Destructo's partner.

"Pass," said the Mauler. "They're your spades, Herman."

"Thank you."

El Destructo's partner, whom Sussman identified from an earlier match as the Vulture, laid his cards down and walked around the table to see his hand. "He's right, Herman. We have no business being in spades. When I bid one no-trump, I was asking for another suit. You've got to start paying more attention to the bidding—"

"Jesus H. Christ!" shouted El Destructo, his face turning a deep red. "Would you mind if I just played my own hand? Can't we discuss my attention span some other time?"

"Gentlemen, gentlemen!" trumpeted Lennie Weintraub, trooping over from the shower in his birthday suit. "Problems? Can't we discuss this rationally?"

"No problems," said El Destructo. "Just cut out all the damn table talk. Everybody thinks they're goddamn Charles Goren around here." He threw down the ace of diamonds. "Everybody shut up and play their own hands and there won't be any problems. Pass the beer nuts."

Lennie shrugged, grabbed a towel from a nearby pile and wrapped it around his waist, then walked away toward a row of lockers only a few feet from Sussman.

"Lennie?" Sussman whispered, edging over, making sure he was shielded from the bridge game by the lockers.

Weintraub turned around and feigned a look of surprise at the sight of Andy. He rolled his eyes and twitched his beard and said, "My goodness, as I live and breathe!" Then, in a near-whisper, added, "Andrew, how the hell are you!"

"Well, I'm hanging in there, Lennie."

"Keep your voice down. I don't think your presence is particularly welcome here, old chum."

"I gathered that," Sussman said, looking anxiously around him. "I just happened to be in the audience and, uh, I thought I'd drop by and say hello."

Lennie toweled himself off—he seemed in a hurry. He continued to talk as he pulled on his socks and underwear and dried his hair. "I knew you were in town, of course. I'd been talking to Leroy just the other day, I was on the road till the last day of your little tournament—"

"Leroy?"

"The Thing. Reports you were polite but a little terse. And not a big wrestling fan, which didn't surprise me, so I'd also calculated that you didn't know what I was about these days."

"Well, you should have called, Lennie, if you knew I was here—"

"I did call your network, actually—it was after the unfortunate demise of the Doctor, I'd just gotten back from Sacramento. Your people are a little secretive about giving out hotel rooms."

"Thankfully."

"Listen, Andrew, why don't we—"

At that point another wrestler entered the locker room, he was bleeding profusely from his head and Sussman guessed he had just lost his match, it didn't seem to have taken long. He walked toward the bridge game, mumbled a few words to the card players, then stopped over by Weintraub.

"Hello, Bernie," Lennie said. "Getting a bit thick out there, is it?"

"I hate following your act," said Bernie, wiping the blood capsules off his forehead. "You get the crowd up to such a pitch. Leroy's still trying to get through the mob. I could do without that cage match, I'll tell ya . . ." Bernie wandered away, completely oblivious of Sussman.

"Sir Alec Peckerwood?"

"The very same. He's had an inner-ear infection, he could really use some time off." Lennie poked his head around the lockers and looked briefly at the bridge game. "Listen, Andrew, I'm sorry to say the boys were a bit sensitive about your line of questioning this afternoon—"

"I'm just trying to get the facts, Lennie. Believe me, I didn't volunteer for the assignment."

"Oh, I'm sure you didn't. Although," Lennie said, barely concealing a smirk, "as a lifelong acquaintance, forgive me if I gleaned a sliver of humor from the situation."

"Yuk yuk. And vice versa, for that matter."

"Oh, so true. But don't despair, old chum, they tell me Brent Musberger used to do the Strongman Refrigerator Pull. Now, tell me, what palace of splendor has CBS quartered you in?"

"The Redondo Beach Sheraton."

"Capital, Andrew! My wife and I live only a few blocks away."

"Wife?"

Lennie grinned. "Unlikely as it may seem, I've found a compatible mate."

A security man poked his head into the locker room and informed the wrestlers that the cage would be constructed for the final free-for-all in ten minutes.

"One more hand," grunted the Mexican Mauler. "Your deal, Herman."

"You're passing up the cage match?" Sussman said to his friend, who was the only wrestler getting back into his civvies.

"I'm afraid so—my performances tend to get lost in eighteen-man free-for-alls. A little contractual thing I managed to work out with Ben Garrison—who incidentally should be dropping in here any minute, and you and I need much more time, Andrew. Do you know where Pancho and Wong's is, down by the pier?"

"All too well."

Lennie emitted a Rasputin-like cackle. "Stick with Pancho. And there's nothing wrong with their margaritas, I could use one or two to unwind myself. Meet you there at eleven-thirty?"

Sussman looked at his friend, surprised. Margarita drinking was not an activity he had remembered sharing with Lennie Weintraub; then again, he could understand: doing the death scene from *Hamlet* at the theater was not quite the same as doing it from underneath three hundred pounds of El Destructo. "Fine," he said, and started to head back out of the locker room, when the security man poked his head in again.

"Five minutes, boys, the crowd's gettin' surly out there."

"Curtain's going up," Lennie shouted to the bridge players. "Shake a leg."

"Let's bid this one out," said the Mauler, who had just picked up his hand. "We can finish it later."

"I pass," said the Mauler's partner, taking a perfunctory look at his hand.

"I pass," said the Vulture.

"Pass," said the Mexican Mauler. "It's to you, Herman."

El Destructo stared at his hand; his stubby fingers poked at the edges of the cards as he totaled up the points. "Oh, damn," he said softly to himself, then slowly recounted his cards. He gazed at them for a second, then flung them disgustedly into the center of the table and pounded his fist with a report so strong that the lockers shuddered halfway through the cavernous dressing room. *"Damn!"* he shouted, backing away from the table and knocking his chair backward onto the floor. "I just never get any cards."

So Andy was back at Pancho and Wong's, without Susie this time. She'd had enough excitement for the evening and had decided to rest up for a day of intense tanning and roller-skating. Besides, she explained, she didn't want to get in the way of a tearful childhood reunion, which would inevitably be full of grade-school stories and high-school references that she had absolutely no interest in.

"My apologies for not having you back to the homestead," Lennie said, licking the salt off the rim of his margarita glass. They were sitting at one of the booths in the restaurant section, which was still crowded. It was a Friday night; they had waited several minutes just to be seated. "My wife's got her cousins in from St. Louis and their kids are asleep, and we had Bernie in for a few days too, he's from Minneapolis—"

"Sir Alec?"

"We try to put some of the guys up when they're traveling through, it makes the whole grind a little easier. I think my wife could use a little privacy, about this time."

Sussman nodded, he stared through the cigarette smoke at his thespian friend. Lennie was wearing a pair of baggy white slacks and a pink shirt, he blended in with all the tanned Californians with their pastel-colored shirts and sun-bleached hair. Andy, by contrast, was pale. He was still wearing his Levi's and Grateful Dead T-shirt, he was aware that a few girls were staring at them from the bar, or more accurately, staring at Lennie—this was not how he remembered things from their youth.

The next several minutes were spent discussing the turns their lives had taken. Weintraub had not had much difficulty following Sussman's career, it had proceeded more or less according to plan since the last time they had spoken, after Lennie's Guthrie performance in Minneapolis. "I've seen you on the network a few times, of course," Lennie said. "I tune in the basketball games every once in a while to see if you're on. I figured we'd eventually be in the same town at the same time, although I never guessed you'd be covering my profession, as it were."

Lennie's profession, as it turned out, was a result of a much more labyrinthine path. He'd spent nearly five years in New York, scratching for any stage role he could get. In the summers, he traveled the country, appearing in everything from the Guthrie, which had turned out to be his high point, to the traveling Renaissance Faires which popped up all over the country, in which he played farcical roles in the Royal Court and got "considerably pudged out" on the myriad of Elizabethan foods and candies.

He had migrated west almost two years ago, found an agent and scored with a few commercials and some small theater roles. Eventually he got a bit part in a TV hour-adventure show, for which he'd found it necessary to shed some of the excess weight he had gained on the Renaissance Faire circuit. "That's when I really started working out," he explained. "You'd be surprised how many of these TV actors have their own personal trainers; I guess with all that money they can afford just about anything. I started working with one of them, a fellow named Paul St. Clair, and it turned out he worked with several of the WFA people, including Leroy Wedbush—"

"The Thing?"

"We do try to avoid those nicknames when we're not performing. Anyway, Leroy has this uncle in Tarzana who teaches theater at UCLA, and we sort of got into this conceptual thing with the Renaissance Man. I was working out fairly regularly by then, so I started scrimmaging with Leroy, you might say, and I found I could hold my own quite well."

"And you didn't have any second thoughts about abandoning your acting career?" Andy asked, signaling the waitress for some more chips and salsa. "After all that time you put in? I know people sometimes have to wait a long time for their big break, but I always figured you had the talent—"

"Well, I suppose I could give you the party line, which is all about bringing culture to the masses. Shakespeare *was* a popular writer, you know. He wrote violent, raucous plays for the Elizabethans—that was what the public wanted to see. If he was alive today, I suppose he'd be writing sitcoms or car chases."

"Uh, Lennie, you're stretching the old credibility there, even for a basketball junkie."

"I know, I know." Lennie grinned, he took his margarita and lifted it in front of his eyes, like Yorick's skull. "Alas, poor Lennie. But there's family considerations, I'm forced to admit. Mortgage to keep up, and we've got a child on the way. The truth is, Ben Garrison pays terribly well, even to someone like me who's still on the undercards. And believe it or not, if my act ever *does* catch on, and I think it's beginning to, Andy, it'll attract so much attention, I'm sure to get some acting opportunities."

In back of them, on the stage, the same bad rock-and-roll band that had been playing the night before was doing a poor impersonation of the Rolling Stones. Sussman would have almost preferred to sit through an hour of MTV than have to listen to someone bungle the chords of "Satisfaction." He could begin to feel a whole pitcherful of margaritas calling his name, but there were a few curiosities to be sorted out, specifically the questions about Dr. Double-X.

"Now, this isn't the kind of thing we could discuss in the locker room," Lennie said, expounding on the subject without much prompting. "And I'll expect you not to repeat it."

"You have a reporter's word."

"But it is rather interesting, actually . . ." Lennie Weintraub sipped on his margarita. "It turns out that the late, lamented Dr. Double-X won a match he was not supposed to win."

Sussman arched his eyebrows. "He un-threw a match?"

"Allegedly. It was a few months ago, back in the IWA."

"What's that?"

"The International Wrestling Association. One of Ben's

rivals. Dr. Double-X wrestled with that circuit for a year and a half, culminating four months ago when he won the IWA heavyweight crown in a shocking upset of the legendary Harvey 'Crash' Kopeck.''

"Ah hah," said Sussman, munching on a corn chip. "And this, I take it, was a particular shock to Harvey 'Crash' Kopeck?"

"Let's put it this way. Harvey 'Crash' Kopeck owns fifty-five percent of the International Wrestling Association. So I have some difficulty believing that he would have arranged to lose his own championship to Dr. Double-X, who was not, incidentally, even considered one of the top challengers."

"And I don't suppose Harvey 'Crash' Kopeck would publicly admit that the loss was 'unscheduled,' let us say?"

"Naturally, no such admission could be made. And, to make things curiouser, two weeks after Dr. Double-X won the IWA crown, he defected to the WFA."

Sussman drained the last few drops from his margarita. "So. Poor Harvey not only lost his championship, he lost his champion."

"Not to mention his chance for a rematch. His career, personally, never recovered. He's in his late forties. The only reason he'd held on to the belt at all was that he owned the league. And now the league's lost stature; I'd say Harvey's going through some decidedly rough times."

Sussman crushed a corn chip on the table. He was not exactly thrilled to be discovering all this. If someone had the motive to deal out Dr. Double-X, then this assignment had the potential of dragging on much longer than he wished. But that much was out of his control, he'd wait for the autopsy report; his only real commitment was to find out Double-X's identity.

"I'm afraid I can't be much help with that one," Lennie said, stifling a yawn. "We're talking about an odd bird here, as you've no doubt gathered."

"I thought they were all a little odd."

"Tut, tut."

"C'mon, Lennie, you're telling me the guy never took off that mask, not even in the locker room?"

"Sorry, Andrew. He didn't hang around there much. The nights we were on the same card, he came in right before his match, left right after. That's all I saw of him, except for the promos and the shows he did on the cable."

"Well, what about the other league? He wrestled there for however long, someone must have known him."

"A bit of intrigue there too," Lennie said. "Of course, there *is* a certain amount of that in this profession, isn't there? A lot of it's pure hyperbole, I'll admit, carefully managed and choreographed. But we do attract our share of legitimate weirdos. We can't really help that, can we?"

"I'm not holding you personally responsible. I'd just like to finish this assignment, Len, and get on with my life."

"Well, I can only tell you a few sketchy things I heard." Lennie settled back in the booth. "There was always a certain amount of speculation about who he really was, of course. A good many of the fellows have athletic backgrounds—college football or wrestling, especially—but no one seemed to be able to place him. There *was* a rumor that he wrestled in the MWA for a while, before it folded—"

"MWA?"

"Midwest Wrestling Alliance. Detroit, Toledo, Milwaukee, Chicago. It was a casualty of the Cable Wars."

"But he didn't wrestle as Dr. Double-X, I take it?"

"No. All this was just a rumor, of course. I think he was the 'Silent Assassin,' something like that. There was supposedly some problem with the name, might have been a copyright infringement of some sort. I think it was some type of contractual thing, not exactly my neck of the woods."

"Mine either. What about Wireless? Was he working for him then?"

"No, no, Wireless works strictly for Ben. You really don't follow us much, do you?"

"I'm afraid not, Lennie."

"You're missing all the fun," Lennie said, but Sussman was quite obviously not in his Mr. Fun mode, and Lennie continued. "Wireless was a minor character as a wrestler, a good second man on tag teams, but not quite big enough or nasty enough to contend. As a manager, though, he's great theater. He's handled Rough Reggie Randolph and the Vulture and the Mad Elk. When Ben has a talent who he thinks needs that extra boost to get an audience, he teams him up with Wireless. Sometimes they do tag teams, usually they stay together for six months, a year—"

"But Dr. Double-X hardly needed the hype, Len. He'd just won the IWA crown and jumped leagues, presumably he was getting plenty of attention."

"Point well taken, Andrew. Maybe Ben just wanted to capitalize on all the notoriety." Weintraub tugged on his beard as he stifled another yawn.

"Or maybe he just wanted to keep close tabs on someone who had a record of not always doing what he was supposed to do."

"Hmm . . . it's possible. Of course, those *are* the things one thinks about when a person turns out unexpectedly dead." Lennie glanced at his watch; it was nearly one and the bumps and bruises of battle, muffled somewhat by the tequila, were nevertheless beginning to manifest themselves. "Andrew, old chum, I'm afraid it's time I moved along. Ten-o'clock flight tomorrow morning, sad to say."

"Where to?"

"Denver. On the road for ten days: McNichols, then Albuquerque, Santa Fe. Tucson, then home."

"Sounds brutal."

"Oh, we get used to it," Lennie said, not very convincingly. "I'll slow down come August, when the baby's due. If the concept continues to go over, maybe I can stick to the larger cities."

"Well, it was a remarkable performance, Lennie. Best Hamlet I've ever seen."

"Sprinkled with Macbeth. I'm working on a few new ideas too. In the meantime, Andrew . . ." Weintraub pulled a business card from his wallet and gave it to Sussman. "I don't suppose you'll be around when I get back. But call if you're ever in town. And if you need any more help with this Double-X thing, give Leroy a call." He scribbled The Thing's number next to his own. "Leroy's a good egg. But stay away from Ben, that's my suggestion. He's very nice to family, but a bad man to cross."

"Point taken, Len."

Sussman took out his MasterCard and charged the margaritas to CBS. Lennie was parked near the restaurant and offered him a ride home, but Sussman had only a short walk to the Sheraton, and he was not nearly as plastered as the night before. He stood at the edge of the pier for a moment, watching Lennie drive away, then jogged across the parking lot and back to the hotel.

It may have been the margaritas, or it may have been the fog or the hour, but Sussman had the impression that someone was following him slowly in a small sports car—the two beams seemed to be tracking him as he jogged up to the lobby, then they swerved away and disappeared into the night.

6

The Murray Question was bound to come up sooner or later; Sussman had felt it in the back of his mind ever since Dr. Double-X's body had been hauled off in the ambulance. He had put off discussing it with Susie; in the first place, there was no reason to believe that a murder had been committed, hence no need for a detective, private or otherwise. Second, Susie could not stand the living sight of Murray; she regarded him as a leering, repulsive sleaze, she could not tolerate him anywhere within a radius of, say, two or three states.

The fact that Murray Glick had effectively solved the Lester Beldon murder, paving the way for Andy's CBS job and Susie's new status as quasi–Power Agent, had barely softened her opinion. It was not merely that Murray unashamedly made a pass at every attractive woman he had ever met between the ages of fifteen and forty, including Susie herself several times, and had a disgustingly high success ratio (Susie's rejections being more in the line of the exception that proved the rule). It was also the general nature of Murray's work—he had gotten out of the hard-core detective market several years ago and opened up an office of Glick Investigations in the Northbrook Court shopping mall, sandwiched in between Fanny Mae Candies and the Footlocker athletic-shoe store. He spent most of his waking hours tracking down who was wearing what to the next country club Ball, and finding out which cheerleaders had which social diseases, or figuring out who was stealing someone's mother-in-law's chocolate-chip-cookie recipe. He no longer did murders; he'd taken on Andy's predicament only as a personal favor, and only on the condition that Andy do all of the footwork.

This, of course, had not prevented Murray from taking all the credit once the case was solved. He couldn't help it that he was at Charlie Hathaway's restaurant when the killer was flushed out, it was not his fault that flocks of newspapermen had descended upon him afterward, or that TV news shows had featured him on everything from *PM Magazine* to the Chicago Celebrity Bar-B-Q'd Rib Cook-offs. He was a professional; what was he supposed to do? Turn the business away?

But Susie had this little blind spot; she was otherwise a completely fair and understanding person. Sussman could, on balance, understand how it was possible for Murray to rub some members of the female persuasion the wrong way. So he'd decided to avoid the Murray Question for as long as possible, but the events of the last several days, to his great regret, were not proceeding in the direction of MQ avoidance.

Saturday had seen the results of the autopsy, or more accurately, the nonresults. There had been no traces of any drugs in Dr. Double-X's system. The death had been ascribed to heart failure; it was unusual but not unheard-of in a well-conditioned athlete. He had been stricken, apparently as the boat went over, and his lungs had filled with water; the combination of the drowning and the heart attack had killed him.

There were bound to be questions, of course. Given the training procedures and the impressive musculature of professional wrestlers, and the current controversies over steroids and other muscle bulkers, there would no doubt be all sorts of speculation over what had contributed to the heart attack, but there was no suggestion that the death had been anything other than accidental. That was fine with Sussman.

CBS would not drop the story, though; the autopsy had not cleared up the identity thing; if anything, it had muddled it up even more hopelessly. The coroner, in his press conference, referred to the deceased, without any apparent embarrassment, as "Deceased Dr. Double-X." According to the hospital, not a single relative had called; there had been no one at all inquiring at the hospital since Thursday except Wireless, and Wireless had not shown up at the coroner's inquest; no one from the Wrestling Community, as Sussman had so eloquently described it in his taped pregame report, was in attendance. When Sussman had returned to the Redondo Beach Sheraton following the inquest, he had found Cliff Trager waiting for him in the lobby, slightly bleary from his bi-coastal shuttling, but carrying joyful tidings of high ratings.

"The interest has been phenomenal," Trager reported, juggling several folders and pulling out some papers, which he spread over the small cocktail table in the hotel lounge as he described yesterday's network powwow to Sussman. "We haven't seen so much switchboard traffic since we preempted the soap operas for the Iran-Contra hearings. We think the story has legs, Andy."

"We?"

"Those who give us our marching orders. I think we're going to have to follow this one all the way."

"All the way where, Cliff? You heard the coroner's report, I take it?"

"Well, Andy, we did discuss all the probabilities, and uh . . . of course there's that whole identity thing."

"It's a little complicated, but I'm working on it—"

"Which is exactly why it has such appeal! 'Who Was Dr. Double-X?' What was his secret?"

"I give up."

"Well, there had to be some reason why no one can figure out who the hell he was." Cliff gathered his papers back into his folders and sat up straight. "Andy, we've decided that we'd like you to cover the funeral."

"What funeral?"

"The funeral of Dr. Double-X."

"There isn't going to be any funeral, Cliff, they haven't

identified the body yet! They'll keep it in the deep freeze until someone puts in a claim."

"I understand, Andy. But there *is* going to be a memorial service."

"For *who!*"

"For Dr. Double-X," Cliff said, reading from a press release. "At the Sports Arena Wednesday evening, Ben Garrison's organizing it—"

"Cliff! You want me to cover a memorial service for an unidentified professional wrestler? Thrown by the very people who are probably hiding his identity?"

"Well, Andy," Cliff said weakly, "if that's the case, maybe you can find out something."

"Cliff, that service is going to be nothing but a farce for the benefit of Ben Garrison's cable TV network. If he even lets us in, I'm sure it'll only be for the express purpose of making buffoons out of us."

"Honestly, Andy, I've seen all the tapes, and we all think you're doing a solid job, dead solid. Oh, and incidentally . . ." Cliff looked up at the clock on the wall; it was almost two'clock. "We need you over at the studio at three, just for half an hour. We want to tag on interviews with Hal and Carol and Cindi Beamon to your pregame show, and Cindi's got this volleyball match tomorrow, so we thought we'd do it this afternoon."

Sussman took a deep breath, counted to ten, and let it out slowly.

"Well, they were in the boat and everything, Andy, and we've got an isolated tape."

"I assume the police saw it?"

"Oh, of course, but our viewers haven't. Look, Andy, if you've got any other suggestions, we'd all sure like to hear them. In the meantime, I think we're moving in the right direction."

The suggestion that came to mind was the Murray Question, and Andy had done his best to push it off at least one more day. He had promised Susie a last glorious weekend in LA and didn't want to upset her. So, as a second-to-last resort, he had called the Redondo

Beach Police Department. He was not used to this type
of investigative reporting, but the CBS identification had
helped. He'd been transferred directly to a Captain Stevens, who explained that there was a limit to what his
department could contribute to the case, in terms of
time and resources. There wasn't any evidence of a crime,
after all. They had looked at all the tapes and hadn't
seen anything suspicious. Dr. Double-X was a celebrity;
if he had any friends or relatives out there, they certainly
would have been heard from by now. In the absence of
any such interest, about all the police could do was run
some dental charts into the computers and see if anyone
saluted. Otherwise, that was it—at least until the tax
people started nosing around, and that wasn't likely to
be nearly soon enough to get Sussman out of Wednesday's Dr. Double-X Memorial Service and Beer Blast.

So Sussman went out Saturday night and treated Susie
to the best Beverly Hills could offer, compliments of the
network that was putting him through all this idiocy.
They had aperitifs at the Beverly Wilshire, dinner at
Spago, after-dinner drinks and dessert at some French
place he was too looped to remember by that time. These
were followed by dancing until two in the morning at
the Coconut Teaszer on the Strip, where the rock and
roll was slightly more polished than at Pancho and
Wong's, although getting back to the Redondo Beach
Sheraton was slightly more of a challenge.

It was Sunday morning now. It occurred to him, as
he sat half-awake in his bed watching Rocky and Bullwinkle cartoons and trying to decide if Ralph Williams'
Used Fords really were a bargain that he couldn't turn
down, that his alcohol intake for the last several days
was far greater than normal, and that there was a limit
to the things that could be charged off to CBS or blamed
on CBS and cirrhosis of the liver was not one of them.
So, hung-over and staring at Boris and Natasha, who
were about to blast Moose and Squirrel back to Frosbite
Falls, and satisfied that Susie would stay soundly asleep
for several more hours, Sussman went into the bath-

room, picked up the telephone, and dialed the phone number of Murray Glick.

"This is Glick Investigations," said a voice that sounded like Murray's receptionist, Peggy, who did not usually answer calls from Murray's living room. "How may I help you?"

"Uh, Peggy?"

"Yes, this is Miss Terrell."

"Peggy, this is Andy Sussman. I could have sworn I called Murray's apartment."

"Oh, hello, Mr. Sussman. I'm sorry, all of Mr. Glick's phone calls are being referred to his office while he's on his cruise."

"Cruise?"

"The Murray Glick Mystery Singles' Cruise to Martinique."

"Are you kidding," mumbled Sussman, who had lost track of Murray's entrepreneurial undertakings.

"Would you like me to read you the brochure, Mr. Sussman?"

"Uh, sure . . ."

" 'Murder in Paradise! Who killed Lance Balmoral? Was it the beautiful movie star, or the scorned heiress? Or the ship's steward, or the captain himself? YOU SOLVE THE MYSTERY, aboard the USS *Whodunit*, in the glorious Caribbean, February 5–15. Visit the sparkling beaches of Martinique, dine at the West Indies' most famous cafés, and solve a spine-tingling mystery with MURRAY GLICK, world-famous Detective. $1475, all travel included. Singles only. AIDS test results required twenty-four hours before boarding.' "

"I don't believe it," muttered Sussman, then quickly corrected himself. "Yes I do. When's he going to be back, Peggy?"

"He'll be back on the mainland Tuesday."

"I don't suppose there's a ship-to-shore telephone or anything like that?"

"I'm afraid not, Mr. Sussman. Murray doesn't want

any calls to interfere with the sense of realism generated by his mystery."

"Well, what if it's an emergency?"

"He'll be checking in with me tomorrow. I'll tell him you called, okay?"

"Thank you, Peggy."

"Oh, by the way, who do you think killed that wrestler?"

"Excuse me?"

"I've been watching your show! I think it was that weasel news guy, Hal. I think he was jealous of Dr. X, he looked so *masculine* in that boat next to Carol—boy, he was a real dreamboat, except for that mask, of course."

"Peggy . . ."

"Yes, Mr. Sussman?"

"Good-bye, Peggy."

"Good-bye, Mr. Sussman. I'll tell Murray you called."

Sussman looked back at Susie, who was still asleep and didn't show any signs of waking up anytime soon. She did not stir until an hour later, when Andy was so engrossed in the first quarter of the Celtics-Lakers basketball game, he'd almost forgotten his aggravation over not being there to cover it himself. When Susie had showered, Sussman ordered up some room-service breakfast. The two of them sat on the bed and munched on croissants, scrambled eggs, and bacon. The second quarter had just ended and Andy was mortified to find that highlights of his pregame report on the Double-X murder had been spliced into the halftime show. "Aargh!" he moaned.

"Shush," said Susie, grabbing Andy's arm just as he was about to change channels. She edged forward and watched a close-up shot focusing on the CBS boat just as it capsized. "I hadn't seen that before."

Andy fell back onto his pillow; he would have crawled under the covers, but he figured Cliff Trager would find a way to preempt his dreams. "That was our remote," he muttered. "We had two cameras covering the race—

we'd have dubbed over the commentary later." On the screen, he could see a slow-motion replay—Dr. Double-X was windmilling furiously with his arms in the bow of the little dinghy; Hal and Carol were in the center of the craft dog-paddling away, while Cindi Beamon was in the stern, ruddering.

"I really couldn't tell what was happening at the time," Hal Barron was explaining on the tape. "But it looks like, maybe . . . I think Dr. Double-X jerked right there . . . freeze that . . . yeah, I wonder if maybe that's where he had his seizure . . ."

"I think it was," chimed in Carol, "because we really lost our balance there. Look, you can almost see the boat fold a little, there, and then it went right over."

The boat had turtled, flipping into the air and landing on top of Hal and Carol and Dr. Double-X. Cindi, who had been in the stern, had been tossed a few feet backward, and she had immediately swum toward the boat and tried to push it away.

"Well, I was mainly worried about them being forced underwater," said Cindi, her face showing on a little inset in the upper-right-hand corner of the screen. "I thought, you know, they might be trapped. Fortunately I'm tall and I was able to push it up . . ."

"She's a pretty girl, isn't she?" commented Susie. She was definitely awake now; she rubbed Sussman's back as he gobbled down the last of the scrambled eggs.

"I hadn't noticed."

"Oh, please. I get worried when you lie so blatantly."

"Well, all right. I do kind of like the way she purses her lips when she's concentrating, like when she was first warming up."

"Uh-huh."

"Or when she serves in volleyball. I saw her in the NCAA championships last year in San Diego—"

"That's enough," Susie said, poking Sussman in the ribs.

On the television, Cindi had managed to lift the boat slightly out of the water, and Hal and Carol had slithered out. At that point the camera had left the raft and panned down the beach, to catch the end of the race. By the time it returned, Hal, Carol, and Cindi were struggling with Dr. Double-X, trying to keep his head out of the water.

"You could tell he'd swallowed a lot of water," Cindi said, talking in a small, whispery voice. "I used to be a lifeguard, I was trying to get his throat clear. But he was so big!"

"She's a pretty tall girl, herself," Susie commented.

"A big family. Her brother was a basketball player, freshman of the year in the MVC. Illinois State, I think. Had some sort of a swimming accident, I don't think he played at all this year."

"What was he doing at ISU?" Susie asked. "I thought she was from California."

"Family's from Indiana. She went to Ball State two years, then transferred to Santa Barbara."

Susie sipped on some orange juice and pulled closer to Sussman. "Aw, Andy. I gotta go back tomorrow. It's no fair, you get to stay out here all week."

"It's no treat, believe me. I wish I could get this thing wrapped up and go home."

"Back to that lonely apartment in Manhattan?"

"It's not that lonely if they've got me working," Sussman said, realizing as he spoke that it wouldn't hurt to admit to a little loneliness. He took the breakfast tray and put it on the desk. "Anyway, I certainly can't afford to move away from there now, being stuck on this wrestling thing and everything." He sat back on the bed and ran a finger along Susie's leg. "Can't you stay here a couple more days?"

"No way, chief. I was pushing it, taking the whole week. I'm dreading to see my desk when I get back. And there's that Taiwan thing—at the very least I'm going to get the grunt work on that one."

Sussman sat quietly on the bed for a moment, his arm around his girlfriend. The interview with Cindi and Hal and Carol had ended; he and Susie watched silently as several NBA players did a shoe commercial and a league promo. This life-style problem of theirs was going to have to be addressed sooner or later—with a little luck, he could delay it till their next weekend. Not that there wasn't at least one obvious solution he had considered; but it involved one of them making a career sacrifice, and he didn't think it was going to be him. And besides, he wasn't sure if he was ready for the whole permanent-relationship thing. He could handle the separations, he thought. The gnawing regret when Susie's plane taxied away would linger for a while, then subside, it always did when he was busy with an assignment.

Still, he knew the topic was dancing around in the air between them, he could feel it in the silence. He was almost happy when the commercial ended and his interview with Ben Garrison and Wireless and The Thing flashed on. It created an atmosphere that was too ludicrous to allow discussion of permanent relationships—he was relieved, but he wasn't sure why. He got up and turned off the television, then took Susie's hand and pulled her off the bed. "Well, if this thing drags on, you can come back out here for the weekend."

"If I can get away."

"Bring the work out with you. If I'm still here through Wednesday, I'm sure they'll give me the whole week."

"Sounds like you're beginning to like it," Susie said, reaching for the pair of blue-framed sunglasses she had bought on the boardwalk at Hermosa Beach.

"Beats freezing my ass off."

"It's a dirty job, but someone's got to do it."

Sussman admitted that he had played the sympathy angle about as far as it could go, especially in the presence of someone who was about to be buried in snowbanks and paperwork. He gulped down the rest of his coffee and donned his swimsuit; a few minutes later he was escorting Susie out to the beach. It was a gorgeous Southern California winter's afternoon, and they still had most of the day left before he would have to drop her off at the airport.

7

There is a certain serenity that comes from being in a helpless situation, and Andy Sussman really couldn't have felt more serene as he cruised in his rented Chrysler out into the California desert. With Susie back in Chicago and Murray in the middle of the Caribbean, he was completely on his own. He had forty-eight hours to find out the real identity of Dr. Double-X, or at least present his bosses in New York with a reasonable programming alternative to Ben Garrison's Wednesday-night wake at the Sports Arena.

Left with no other options, he'd taken Lennie Weintraub's suggestion and put in a phone call to The Thing. It was not the way Sussman usually spent his Monday mornings, but he kept saying to himself, "Leroy Wedbush, Leroy Wedbush," and it didn't sound quite so bad. The last time they had spoken, in the center of the ring at the Sports Arena, The Thing had found God and given Him responsibility for calling Dr. Double-X home. Leroy Wedbush, thankfully, was not so religiously inclined. He didn't know where to find the Lord, but he did know where to find Harvey "Crash" Kopeck, which was why Sussman had phoned him.

Andy had planned on running up a significant phone bill from the Jacuzzi at the Redondo Beach Sheraton, tracing Dr. Double-X's career in the IWA and the MWA. He was sure this would reveal his identity; it just couldn't be such an impenetrable secret. But as it turned out, Harvey "Crash" Kopeck was relatively nearby, by California driving standards, anyway. According to Leroy, who had defected from Harvey's circuit in less suspicious circumstances, Kopeck had retreated to Palm Springs for a few months, more specifically to La Quinta, a sleepy little desert town a few miles away, where he was licking his wounds and trying to plot the resurgence of the International Wrestling Association.

A phone call might have been sufficient, Sussman thought, as he drove past the Joshua trees and the tumbleweeds, through the miles of arid nothingness that separate Los Angeles from the rest of the universe, but there was nothing like the personal touch. The truth was, it was a relief to get away from the hotel; the beach just didn't have as much appeal without Susie around, and it was especially nice to be unreachable by phone, at least for a few hours—whatever ridiculous new suggestions Cliff Trager had could wait until evening.

Sussman had made contact with Harvey Kopeck that morning. He had kept up with the Double-X story, of course, but they didn't discuss it at length over the telephone. Harvey was happy to extend an invitation to La Quinta; he could surely use a little network publicity and he couldn't resist the opportunity to rub it in Ben Garrison's face a little. Kopeck was thus surprised when Sussman pulled up to his small rented house alone, in a rented car, with no camera crew and no cameras, period. "You're it?" he said, plainly disappointed.

"Well, I'm sure we could get a crew in from Palm Springs if there's any need for it," Sussman said as he stood outside the front door of the small wooden frame house, waiting to be invited in. He had never had any intention of calling in a camera crew; there was no way that Harvey was going to talk about the things he wanted to discuss in front of television cameras; it would all be a monumental waste of time and money. "I thought maybe it would be fun to talk a little about the wrestling business, then we could lay the groundwork for a longer feature."

Harvey shrugged. He was a swarthy man, about six feet tall, with a squashed nose that was worthy of the name "Crash." He was mostly bald and what hair remained was cropped short. He was deeply tanned, he had evidently been out in the desert for a while. He wore a pair of wrestling shorts and a white T-shirt that said "International Wrestling Association" in large red letters, he had dressed for the occasion. "Oh, come on in," he said with an open, friendly smile that didn't seem a bit forced. Whatever Harvey's problems with the IWA were, he didn't have that hangdog look about him. "Sorry the place is such a mess; my wife went back to Milwaukee last week to visit her mother. Have a brewski?"

Sussman accepted the offer, which turned out to be a Leinenkugel's Beer, brewed in Chippewa Falls, Wisconsin. Harvey had five cases stacked against the kitchen wall, two of them filled with empties, all returnable. "The old ticker's still in Wisconsin," laughed Harvey, opening the beers with a church key. "Ah, yes, a Leinie's and a smoked brat, what more can a man ask for?"

"Women?" suggested Sussman, taking a long swill. "Money?"

"Too fickle," chortled Harvey. "And I know, I've had 'em both. Come on into the den, Andy."

The den was only a few steps from the kitchen; the whole house, in fact, seemed only slightly larger than Sussman's suite at the Sheraton. There were files and folders spread all around. Posters and fliers for upcoming wrestling cards lay haphazardly on the couch and were piled on a stained wooden coffee table. A few photographs were tacked to the wall, mostly of a younger Crash Kopeck; some of them were with his wife. There were a few wrestling pictures, but there were also several football pictures from Kopeck's days at the University of Wisconsin. Sussman recognized some of the other players in the pictures. Dale Sorrell had been a defensive end on several championship teams with the Packers and was now an executive with the Eagles; Sussman had interviewed him during his six-month stint at Green Bay. Harry Breland had coached the Browns to several playoff appearances.

"What a collection of lowlifes, eh?" said Kopeck, straightening one of the pictures. "I'm the only one who found honest work." He cleared away a pile of posters and motioned for Sussman to sit down on the couch. "I've got one of those computers back in Milwaukee, it works fine with the secretaries. Myself, I like to have the work in front of me."

"You know, I'd completely forgotten you'd played at Madison," Sussman said, still staring at the pictures. "I graduated from there—"

"No kidding! I bet you were there during the crazy times! I swear, my boys were in grade school then, I vowed I'd never send 'em there, all those bombs and tear gas, it was terrible! And the football team went to hell, that's for sure!" Kopeck guzzled the beer. He seemed much more familiar now to Sussman, especially with those Madison memories recalled. Kopeck had probably wrestled there dozens of times, he'd been on the TV wrestling shows every Sunday morning; Sussman had never paid any attention to them, of course, but the memories were there. It was like all those rock songs that were around; even if you never liked them or bought any of the albums, you still remembered them.

"Well, things have calmed down since then," Sussman said. "Even the football team wins a few games now." He picked up one of the posters and looked at the card that was advertised; it was for next month at the MECCA in Milwaukee. He didn't recognize any of the names. "Looks like you're keeping busy, Harvey. Introducing some new talent to the Midwest?"

Harvey took a swig of beer. "Oh, a few new ones. But we're very environmentally conscious," he said, this time with a laugh that wasn't quite as carefree. "We believe in recycling."

"Uh, huh." Sussman looked over at the desk. Included among the papers were several contracts; he couldn't tell if they were for arenas or television companies, or maybe individual wrestlers. "Speaking of recycling, I heard that Dr. Double-X had been recycled when he wrestled with you—at least once that I know of."

"Could have been, it's not unusual. Sometimes a persona doesn't work, the fans just don't respond. Get a tattoo, wear a mask, change your image. Be a bad guy, that's where the money is. That's how I got started."

"But you reformed," Sussman said, grinning; he was beginning to like Harvey.

"I repented. I found Truth and Justice. I owned the goddamn league," laughed Harvey. "That's one way to make truth and justice work." He guzzled down the rest of his Leinie's. "Most of the time, anyway. Such is life, fellow Badger."

Sussman sank into the couch a few inches and sipped on his beer. Harvey seemed a little too blasé about Dr. Double-X's background, he thought, considering that the guy had taken his belt and bolted the league and left him to pick up the pieces. "So it must have come as quite a shock, I take it, when this unheralded mystery man took away your title?"

"Anything can happen in the ring, Andy; that's why wrasslin's the great sport that it is."

"Even when it goes against the script?"

"Script?" Kopeck winked. He looked out the window for a second, at the small cactus garden that had been started in the front yard. "I hardly think you can claim that a match is scripted, my friend, when a lowly ranked grappler defies the odds and upsets the champion of the world."

"And owner of the league."

"It showed great courage, didn't it?" Harvey "Crash" Kopeck smirked, thumping the Leinie's onto the coffee table.

"Harvey," Sussman said, choosing his words carefully, "Harvey, fellow Badger, I have a dilemma."

"How can I help you, buckaroo?"

"Well, my network, in its honor and wisdom and search

for high ratings, wants me to find out the identity of Dr. Double-X. Now, I'm figuring, Harvey, that since he worked for you, and seems to have played a pivotal role in your recent career, you might have been overcome with curiosity to find out who he was."

Kopeck belched. " 'Nother Leinie's?" he said, pulling himself off the couch.

"Maybe one more."

"Always room for one more!" Kopeck said, stepping into the kitchen. He put the two empties back in the case with the others and returned with two more cold ones. "Now, the truth is, I was curious, but knowing his real name doesn't do me much good. I knew where he was, after all—what difference did it make whether his name was Bill Smith or Joe Jones?"

"Maybe he had something to hide. Wouldn't you like to know, Harvey? Especially after he jumped ship?"

Kopeck lopped the caps off the two beers and silently gave one to Sussman.

"Harvey, the issue never came up? You always paid him cash, just like Ben Garrison?"

"Naw, naw, nobody pays cash. Garrison's blowing smoke, a big operation like that?" Kopeck settled back into the couch and started digging through some old posters. "He came in with that mask on one day, I must've had a million things to do. Said he had experience in Canada, asked for a tryout." Kopeck found what he was looking for, a frayed poster that had one of Dr. Double-X's matches on it, a single-fall bout with Gaucho Gil Gilberto in Minneapolis. "I had him wrassle with a few of the guys—he was good, he was experienced, that much was obvious."

"And you didn't ask any questions?"

"Oh, sure. But he was so clammed-up about the whole thing, I figured, hell, it's a great put-on. He had a company set up: Dr. Double-X, Inc. All paychecks went to the corporation, so I didn't have to put his name on any tax forms. We had a clause in the contract, of course: no member of the corporation was in violation of any statutes, was wanted for anything, that kind of thing."

"And that was it?"

Kopeck wiped a ring of water from underneath the beer bottle. "Look, Andy, I got sixty, seventy wrestlers working for me at the time. Sure, all this looks important now, 'cause he beats me and he jumps leagues and then he dies. But at the time, I got seven cards over fifteen days, including my own matches. I'm not in Milwaukee enough to kiss my wife hello. I got schedules to work out months in advance in all these different arenas. So I got one more stiff, he wants to wear a mask and be a big mystery, you think I ain't seen weirder things in thirty years in the sport, Andy? I was in Alaska with the Creeper and Kenny Bossone, the Mad Elk—not his kid, who wrestles now, the original. We're in a goddamn bush plane between Fairbanks and Juneau, this was in the fifties, it was all prop planes, and Kenny all of a sudden decides he's afraid to fly! He wants to get out! He's six-three and two hundred eighty pounds, and he grabs a goddamn parachute and starts pounding on the door at thirty thousand feet—"

"Harvey, look—I appreciate that it might have been hectic, but if this guy was such a good wrestler, someone must have seen him before. I heard something about him being the 'Silent Assassin,' or something like that, back in the MWA, whatever that is."

"Was," said Harvey. "It was a rumor. Coupla guys'd wrestled there—tank-town circuit, places like Toledo and Fort Wayne. It's possible, I checked it out later."

"After the big upset?"

"I was curious. Turned out there were three or four different Assassins. Hell, one of 'em was a midget. And we're talkin' six, seven years ago. And they'd all been gone a couple years before Double-X showed up, outta sight completely. The league had folded by then, they didn't have much in the way of records."

"Well, why would he want to change his name? And go to so much trouble, with this corporation and everything?"

"Beats the hell outta me, Andy. It could be there was licensing problems, maybe somebody held a right to the name. Hell, it could have been anything. Girlfriend, agent, taxes. Or maybe he was just a paranoid schmuck son-of-a-bitch, which is my personal opinion."

"Ever see any relatives?"

"Nope."

"Friends? Girlfriends?"

"He was a loner. What he did away from the ring, I have no idea."

Sussman glanced around the living room; at first the place had seemed too small for Crash Kopeck. It wasn't much larger than a wrestling ring, even the furniture seemed scaled down, the couch barely held the two of them. But Kopeck didn't seem cramped, maybe he was used to making the most out of small places. "Harvey," Sussman said, "did it ever occur to you to look at the checks you paid him? After they came back, I mean. He had to endorse them."

"Tried it," Kopeck said. "Endorsed with a company stamp. Had my accountant call the bank to find out who the principals were; the bank said it was privileged information."

"I don't suppose you remember where the bank was?"

"Sorry, like I said, my accountant checked. He's off skiing somewhere now, but I could have him look it up, or send you a copy of one of the old checks."

"Could you, Harvey? Front and back?"

"No problem, Andy. Maybe the bigshot networks can figure it out." Kopeck took a cursory look at a contract that was lying on the coffee table, then folded it and tossed it back on the pile. Sussman couldn't read much of it, but he thought there was some reference to an arena in Cedar Rapids. "Naturally, Andy, I'd be curious to find out."

Sussman glanced at his watch. It was three o'clock, he had wanted to get on the road back to LA before the traffic accumulated, he didn't want to spend an hour stuck in the Ontario smog. Perhaps he'd just drive into

Palm Springs and take a tennis lesson or something; it wouldn't hurt him to have some expertise in one of the country-club sports, he could even get in a game with some of the vice-presidents. "Harvey," he said as Kopeck showed him out the door, "do you mind if I ask you a hypothetical question?"

"Not my favorite kind of question," said Kopeck. "I prefer stark realism. But take your best shot."

"Well, let's suppose," said Sussman, "that a wrestler gave an account of himself in the ring that did not coincide with, uh, what was expected of him as a professional."

"Hypothetically," said Harvey. "It's an unpredictable sport."

"Of course. Now, would that person be in any jeopardy from those who were dissatisfied with said lack of professionalism?"

"Jeopardy?"

"Of a physical nature."

Kopeck cleared his throat. "I don't think he'd be getting many golf dates, if that's what you mean."

"And would it be normal for another wrestling association, even if it was a competing one, to open up its arms to this athlete?"

Harvey Kopeck leaned against the door of his bungalow and took a deep breath of dry desert air. "Andy," he said, "times have changed; values, they've changed. In the old days, there was respect and camaraderie, we all had our territories . . ." Harvey finished his Leinenkugel's and set it on top of a parched metal mailbox. "Guys like Garrison, they don't know no boundaries. It's a new ballgame, they do whatever they goddamn please. Maybe they have to answer for it later, I don't know."

"Answer to who?"

"I don't know, Andy. The Man Upstairs?"

Sussman smiled and headed toward his car. When wrestlers started referring to the Man Upstairs, he'd learned, it was time to hit the road. He said good-bye to Harvey, reminded him to send him the copies of Dr.

Double-X's paycheck, and drove out into the desert. It was 3:15, too late to set up a tennis lesson, and too early to have dinner. Sussman took his chances on the traffic and managed to do passably well until he got to the downtown intersections. Fortunately the car had a tape deck, and what was the big hurry, anyway?

It was 6:30 when Sussman got back to Redondo Beach. When he got there the desk clerk had three messages for him. Susie Ettenger had called, Cliff Trager had called, neither of them had left a message. And there was a note for him, typewritten, in an envelope with no postmark on it. It was not signed. It read:

> Roses are red,
> Violets are blue,
> Mind your own business,
> Or I'll break your fucking neck.

8

"Merle Summers broke his kneecap," said Cliff Trager, sprinkling some salt and pepper over a plate of scrambled eggs and bacon. He and Sussman were cramped into a small booth at Polly's, a greasy spoon at the foot of the pier at Redondo Beach, about fifty yards from Pancho and Wong's.

"He broke his kneecap?"

"He was charged by one of those South Peruvian yaks, or gnus, or whatever it was. They'd tracked it down and stunned it, or thought they had, and Merle took the hand-cam and tried to get a close-up, but it turned out the yak was only grazed and it charged him." Trager sipped on a glass of watery orange juice. "Merle tried to make it to the Land Rover but he couldn't quite get inside, so he leapt onto the hood and smacked his knee right on the winch. They say it's broken in two places."

"Well, at least he didn't have his life threatened."

"You want to go face-to-face with a grazed yak? One that's never seen an American in a Land Rover before?"

"An avoidable risk, Cliff. Look, I'm wondering if I should call the police."

"Now the word we're getting from Peru," said Trager, dunking his toast into his eggs-over-runny, "is that Merle is hors de combat for the next few weeks—and of course we've got a whole crew down there, and the meter's running."

"I'm sure the network has some type of injury insurance for a show like that, Cliff. Besides, Merle's not irreplaceable."

"No kidding. I actually heard they were thinking of sending *me* down there to finish up the show, Andy. Merle's first choice, I'm flattered to say. Except, of course, that I'm deeply involved with this Dr. Double-X affair, and I couldn't possibly leave the country until it's cleared up."

Sussman choked on some scrambled eggs. "Let me get this straight, Cliff," he said, trying to wash the greasy eggs down with some scalding-hot coffee. "I'm supposed to risk my life and jeopardize my career trying to track down the identity of a dead wrestler, just to keep you from being shipped to Yakland?"

"Andy," said Cliff, referring to his omnipresent clipboard, which was resting on his lap, "let me answer that in several ways. One: if your life actually *has* been threatened, then clearly we have a story which we can't possibly ignore. CBS does *not* stand idly by while its employees are threatened, Andy."

"I wasn't suggesting we stand idly by. I was kind of hoping we'd run like hell."

"One-A: This whole secret-identity thing has to be leading to something big, if someone's willing to send you these threatening letters in blank verse."

"I don't really think they went to all that much trouble—"

"And two, considering our viewer interest, we can hardly just drop the story—even if we do find out who Double-X was, we need to know what he was hiding. And I really think you're overreacting to this threat business, Andy. Remember, these wrestling characters threaten each other with that kind of stuff all the time, nobody takes it seriously."

"Sure, Cliff. You think he just meant to attack me with blood capsules? And who says it was a wrestler?"

"I think you're perfectly safe behind the cameras, Andy. And incidentally, I wish you'd let me know when you're going off to do your investigative reporting. We should've had a camera crew at Crash Kopeck's home. We don't have a thing on tape from that."

Sussman tried to douse his coffee burns with some cold water but it was too late, his taste buds were already on the disabled list. "Cliff," he said, ignoring Trager's reprimand—it was impossible to explain to production people why or how a story could be done without cameras—"I really think we should go to the police about this. I think someone was following me the other night, too."

"No objections, Andy, go ahead if it makes you feel better. But I don't think you want to go around with a police escort, it might scare people away."

"I certainly hope so."

"And then there's the wake tomorrow night—"

"Cliff—"

"Andy, I have to hand it to you, you were absolutely right. The whole thing's part of Garrison's *Wednesday Night Grapplers* thing on the cable. We can't exactly cover it like a news show."

"Good. I'll work on the checking-account angle from Harvey, then—"

"But Garrison's agreed to have you on the wake as a guest, Andy, and we're free to use any segments that you appear in for our own coverage. And I understand that rock singer's going to be there singing a hymn or something, and I think that a ten-minute segment from their show, combined with a studio analysis thing that we tag on Saturday, could give us a nice twenty-minute segment on *Sports Spectacular* and keep the story in front of our audience."

"Right. And keep you out of the Andes."

Cliff Trager took his glasses off and tapped them on the table. He spoke to his clipboard, his eyes almost rising to meet Sussman's. "Andy, do you know what kind of shots you have to get to go to that place? Malaria. Dysentery. Cholera. I don't like shots, Andy, my arm swells up for a week."

"I'm awash in sympathy for you, Cliff."

"As much as I could expect." Cliff got up and pulled a yellow CBS windbreaker off the back of the chair. "Oh, and would you mind picking up the tab? We're going slightly over budget, and I'm low on cash."

Sussman paid the check; it was only ten bucks for the two of them. He hoped the assignment ended before Cliff saw the Spago bill. He also hoped that Harvey Kopeck might get him the copy of Double-X's paycheck post-haste, but one day was obviously too soon, and that was assuming that Kopeck was not the joker who'd sent him the threat.

Who had? he wondered.

He didn't think it was Leroy, aka The Thing. Leroy was a friend of Lennie's, and Sussman trusted them both implicitly. Ben Garrison and/or Wireless seemed more likely, although why would Garrison allow him on his "Memorial Service" show if he didn't want him around?

And why would someone threaten him in the first place? There were two possibilities, the first of them obvious: Dr. Double-X had been hiding something, and Someone didn't want it to come out, now that he was dead. The second possibility was a little farther in the back of Sussman's mind, but it was beginning to gnaw its way out: Someone had killed him.

9

Leona Z was really a small woman when you talked to her close up, which Sussman had several times during the *Celebrity Superteams* competition. Take away all the splashy clothes, the spike heels, the jewelry, and the punk hairdo that seemed to make her a foot taller, and she was not all that imposing, except for her breasts, which stuck right out at you rather defiantly, Sussman thought. He'd gotten a good look at them during the first day of shooting, when Leona had shown up in a tissue-thin bikini, which the networks had made her replace with the standard one-piece NBC red swimsuit.

Sussman wondered to what degree Leona's pyrotechnics were just part of the act, whether deep down she was a lover of Shakespeare or Bach or Tony Bennett. Somehow he doubted it. Leona worked too hard at her public persona, she made so little effort to separate it from her private life. She didn't seem to have a locker room to retreat to after performances like the wrestlers did—according to what Sussman had heard on the set, the scenes inside her dressing room after concerts were as wild as the concerts themselves.

But that was unfair, he thought, you couldn't believe everything you heard from technicians and cameramen and assistant producers. And this whole wrestling relationship with Leroy Wedbush, The Thing, which was splashed all over the tabloids, the cable, and *People* magazine, seemed completely contrived. Leroy, after all, was Lennie Weintraub's mentor, he had helped conceptualize the Renaissance Man, he did not seem the type to become involved with a rock star. So Sussman was surprised when he found the two of them standing together behind the counter of an empty concession stand in the upper-deck lobby of the Sports Arena. He had been roaming around by himself prior to the start of the "Memorial Service," trying to plot strategy for avoiding complete embarrassment at the hands of Ben Garrison.

"Yo, Andy, babe!" shouted Leona. "You gotta stand up straight and walk with *authority*, love—that'll keep those goons away from you."

The news of the threat had apparently leaked out, as Sussman was sure it would. He had called Captain Stevens at the Redondo Beach Police Department, who had promised to keep an eye out for him; Stevens had alerted security at the Sports Arena and there obviously wasn't any way to keep that news from Ben Garrison.

"Popcorn's hot, help yourself!" said Leona, who had connected one of the machines and was popping up a batch. "Whoever heard of a funeral without popcorn!"

"Or a nice cool gin and tonic," said Leroy, pulling a bucket of ice from the ice-cream cooler and fixing himself a drink.

"I do say, weah getting highly civahlahzed heah," Leona replied in an accent that was sort of Southern-British.

"I'm sure Dr. Double-X would be pleased," Sussman said, helping himself to the drink.

"I'm sure he wouldn't give a horse's petunia, the lying faggot son-of-a-bitch. It's just like him to not even show up at his own funeral."

"I take it you had more than a passing acquaintance with the gentleman?"

"I'm not sure anyone had more than a passing acquaintance with him," cut in Leroy, his arm around Leona.

"I went out with him once," Leona said, as Leroy winced in obvious disgust. "Well, come *on*, Lee-Roy, don't be a whine-o. It wasn't like I thought he was better-looking or more intelligent or anything—God *knows* I didn't go out with El Scumbucket twice."

"I'm sure it was the intrigue of it all," Leroy said in a patronizing tone of voice. "The Vamp from KC trying to unmask the mysterious Dr. Double-X!"

Leroy was a huge, muscular man, with longish bleached-blond hair that fell to his shoulders, but Leona jerked his arm off her like a twig and spun herself toward the popcorn machine. "It was a business lunch," she said to Sussman, then pointed her thumb backward at Leroy. "That's all *our* first date was, but as you can see, I was won over by his sophisticated wit and charm."

"It's the truth," said Leroy, grabbing Leona by the waist and turning her back toward him. "Leona's the most completely honest woman I've ever met—even when she thinks she doesn't mean it."

"So tell me all about this 'date' with the Doctor," Sussman said. "It's not like I mean to pry or anything, but I am trying to do this story, as I'm sure you know—"

"Of course," Leona said, in a prissy voice. "And Ben Garrison says we should do everything possible to accommodate you." She paused for a second, took a gin and tonic that Leroy had poured for her, and smiled sweetly. "Not that I give a rat's ass about Ben Garrison."

"He'll be positively shocked to hear that," Leroy said.

"Pity," Leona whispered, then took Sussman's hand and continued. "I'd been considering this wrestling thing for a couple of months, you understand, and the WFA was where the action was—all credit to Ben. He's a weasel, but he knows how to promote. And of course I'd followed all this since I was a kid, really—in Kansas City it's a big deal. I knew who Crash Kopeck was, he used to own the town, and when Double-X beat him and jumped to the WFA—whoa there! That was *mucho* patatas fritas, baby. The man was either gonna be a superstar or he was gonna end up in concrete pajamas somewhere, you know?"

"Now, hold on," said Leroy. "Look, Andy, this is an

honest business—in its own way, of course. No Mafia, no underworld. Guys like Harvey, they're sweet as can be."

"In their own way, of course." Sussman turned to Leona. "So you approached Dr. Double-X, with the thought of developing this 'business relationship'?"

"I met him after a match. He didn't even wait till the card was over, you know? He was heading for the parking lot ten minutes after his bout ended. It was up in Oakland. But he knew who I was, and I gave him a card and told him to call me when he got to LA, he had a match here the next week—"

"He didn't give you a phone number or anything?"

"Nope. He barely talked. He grunted."

"The most eloquent he ever got was on the wrestling promos," Leroy said. "I think he managed a few complete sentences during *Celebrity Superteams.*"

"I never did talk on the phone with him," Leona said. "I got a message on my answering machine. Some fleabag hotel in El Segundo, out by the airport. I should've known it was trouble, just from the looks of the place."

"You didn't take anyone with you?" Sussman asked. "Just in case?"

"I'm a big girl. I can take care of myself."

Leroy Wedbush flashed Leona a disapproving look.

"Well, I'm surrounded all the time by security guys and record people and paparazzi, sometimes it's just a little challenge to get away from it all. Anyway, what could happen, he was a famous guy." Leona tossed a kernel of popcorn high in the air and caught it seductively in her mouth. "I was wrong. He was a rotten man. A truly nasty man. And I deal with a lot of truly nasty people in the record business." She reached into the cooler and grabbed an ice cube for her drink. "But he scared me," she whispered. "He did."

Downstairs, they could hear the television people setting up their cameras. The voice of Ben Garrison came bellowing through the stairwell, informing everybody that the show would start in fifteen minutes. But Sussman and Leroy didn't say a word, they both sipped quietly on their gin and tonics and waited until Leona continued. "I told him what I wanted to do," she said. "All the theatrics, maybe I'd be just like his manager, you know? Like Wireless, sort of. I told him about the possibilities for the crossovers into concerts and MTV and all that."

"Was he interested?" Sussman asked.

"How could you tell? He had that goddamn mask on, of course, and his eyes were always kind of glazed anyway, and he just grunted something about considering it. And I asked him, what's with the mask, cutie pie, for God's sake, we're in a crummy little dive in El Segundo, who does he think's gonna recognize him?

"So he says, look, this is where he's stayin', how about if I just come upstairs for a moment, we can get out of this sleazy spoon, we can talk. So I figure, well, maybe he's shy, maybe he's got some terrible scar or something on his face, maybe he's overwhelmed by me approaching him like that."

Leroy cleared his throat and scrunched his face into a look of disbelief.

"What! I'm a big star, musclehead! Guys dream of me walking up to them, they got my posters in their bathrooms."

"Leona," Leroy whispered. "We're in the presence of journalists."

"Excuse me," she said to Sussman, "how indiscreet. My posters are in their dorm rooms. Anyway, I went up there and I walked in, just the cruddiest dive you've ever seen, the bed wasn't made, a tiny little desk. A bag of pistachio nuts on it, shells all around, beer bottles. And I was just a little scared right then, honestly, and I say, 'Okay, Doc, let's just be friends'—and the scumbucket *grabs* me! Jesus Christ! He tosses me on this disgusting bed, it sagged so much you couldn't get out of it—and I grabbed for his mask and he knocked my arm away, nearly broke it! Fortunately I've got these beautiful long nails and I poked him good a couple of times, I thought I got him once in the eye—"

"Did the room have a phone in it or anything?" Sussman asked.

"Are you kidding? Not that I had time. I rolled off the bed and he's rubbing his eye with one paw and he's got a goddamn beer bottle in the other and he smashes it and I am out the door, señor—all that dancing around on stage's got me in shape, you better believe it. And the Peugeot starts first time, thank God, I'd just got it out of the shop, and I am *gone*, baby. Vamos." Leona turned back to Leroy, put her hand softly around his waist.

"Good thing I was next on the list," he said.

"He was nasty," whispered Leona. "I don't know who he was. But let me tell you, Mr. Press Guy, this was not the type of man who dies of a heart attack. Guys like him do *not* stick around long enough to die of natural causes."

So he wasn't the only one having suspicious thoughts, Sussman mused as he drove back from the Sports Arena to Redondo Beach. It was nearly ten o'clock, the memorial service was over. It hadn't been quite the unqualified disaster he had assumed it would be, or maybe it was just his low expectations that made the whole thing bearable. There were seven or eight wrestlers present, the ones that weren't on the road performing somewhere, plus some extras Garrison had added to fill the ringside seats. Leona had brought along her keyboard player, a skinny crew-cutted kid named Toby, who had hooked up a synthesizer and played a funeral dirge as the wrestlers filed in.

There had been nothing revealing in Garrison's eulogy, just the "young champion cut down in his prime" type of thing, performed as only Garrison could do it. Leona followed him, singing a slow version of "I Only Need All of Your Loving," one of her hits. Sussman had never heard it performed before without the benefit of three ear-shattering guitars, and he did have to admit that she had an appealing voice—a little on the throaty side, not exactly Beverly Sills, but more than adequate for the occasion.

Garrison had, of course, provided Andy with bodyguards. The Mad Elk and Rough Reggie Randolph had done the honors, Sussman barely had room to hold his microphone and wedge his way in front of the camera. "Ladies and gentlemen," Garrison had said, "here stands a brave and fearless man: a *profile in courage!* His life threatened by the very tenacity of his *personal inquest* into the sad and shocking death of a champion. And I want you to know, ladies and gentlemen, that as long as Mr. Sussman allows himself to be *my guest,* on *my show,* then he has *my personal guarantee* of safety!"

Of course, Sussman thought on the way home, nobody who was a regular viewer of Ben Garrison's wrestling shows was actually going to believe that his life had been threatened. They might believe that he, Andy Sussman, was a blithering idiot—he had long since realized the inevitability of that. All he could do was implement Damage Control. Fortunately, The Thing had given him a semiliterate interview about mortality and the fickleness of life, and the illusory strength of a young athlete. It had taken up a good five minutes; Sussman definitely owed Leroy one. Tomorrow he would get Cliff Trager in the editing room, they would review the tape and see if the ten-minute *Sports Spectacular* segment could be assembled in a way that would make Andy look as unridiculous as possible.

There was only one thing that struck Sussman as odd about the whole night, and that was the absence of Dr. Double-X's manager, Wireless. "He was just too totally struck with grief," Ben Garrison had said, resting a palm on Sussman's CBS blazer. "He's an emotional man, Andy; they were like brothers. I'm sure you can understand his reluctance to get in front of the TV cameras so soon after this terrible tragedy."

But of course, thought Sussman, those were exactly the reasons why Wireless *should* have been there, bawling his head off, stomping around in the ring. Why wouldn't he be there? Maybe he'd already been assigned to another wrestler, Sussman theorized as he parked his car at the Sheraton. Maybe he was off in Denver or Tucson with Lennie Weintraub, breaking in a new act. Or maybe he was on a special assignment from Ben Garrison, of some sort of unexplained nature. And what could that be?

Sussman stopped off at the desk to check his messages. There was no threatening nursery rhyme this time, nothing from Cliff, just a note that Susie had called. Sussman had tried to reach her at work several times that afternoon, but she was completely unavailable, she'd left word through her secretary that she was buried under a Great Wall of Chinese depositions. Sussman considered calling her back, but it was midnight back in Chicago and she'd be getting up at six. She probably needed to sleep more than she needed to talk to him.

So Andy Sussman locked the door, fastened the bolt, and plopped into the king-size bed that had seemed much too large for him lately. As plush and luxurious as the suite at the Redondo Beach Sheraton was, when the lights were out it was just another hotel room in another town, and he was just as alone as he'd been in Green Bay and Reno and New York after Susie had left. He closed his eyes and listened to the hum of electricity and the occasional sound of a car going by, and he fell off into deep sleep.

He awoke with a start. It was the middle of the night, and someone was in the room—that much was unmistakable even in his sleepy fog. Sussman forced one eye open; he didn't see anything, but he heard someone creeping around.

He smelled something.

He tried to peek through half-closed eyes; he didn't want the intruder to know he was awake. He thought he heard more than one person—no, it was just one. There was a smell, it smelled Mexican. Tacos, enchiladas. He heard the sound of a wrapper being crinkled up and tossed into the wastebasket.

Someone was walking toward the bed.

Sussman reached under his covers as the person got closer—what did he expect to find there? A gun? A knife?

The person walked over, he was tall and lanky. Sussman could make out the silhouette as the intruder swallowed the rest of whatever he was eating.

Andy held his breath for a moment, then let it out slowly. The man walked right up to him, he sat down next to his pillow.

"Murray?" said Andy Sussman. "Is that you?"

"You better fucking hope it is," said Murray Glick.

10

"Andy, I'd like you to meet my friend Bree," Murray said, pointing to a slim figure in the back of the room; Sussman had been right, there had been someone else there all along.

"Hi," giggled Bree; she had a sweet Southern drawl. "Sorry to barge in like this. Murray said y'all wouldn't mind."

"Bree was a guest on my Caribbean cruise," Murray explained, chomping down the last bites of an enchilada. "She solved the mystery on the second-to-last day. Figured out it was the ship's cook, I don't know how she did it."

"Clairvoyant, I'm sure," Sussman mumbled. "Murray, it's two in the morning—"

"I got here as soon as I could, Hoops. We just got back to Miami last night, I had to be a good host and make sure everybody got their luggage from the boat, and there was a farewell party—"

"We saw your interviews on the basketball game." Bree giggled again, the condition sounded terminal. "We had one of those satellite antennas. Wow, I'd be scared getting that close to those big ugly gorillas—"

Semiconscious as he was, it occurred to Sussman to inquire as to how Murray had managed to get into his double-bolted suite, and why he hadn't just found his own room and called in the morning.

"You got any soft drinks in here?" Murray asked,

searching in the dark for the refrigerator. "Those enchiladas really leave you thirsty. And I think Bree needs
to use the bathroom."

"Murray, where are you staying? I don't think the
couch folds out and there's only one bed in here—"

"Suite right above, Hoopsie."

Sussman looked at the balcony to his third-floor suite.
The patio door had been left slightly ajar to let in the
ocean breeze; outside, a rope was dangling from the
balcony above.

"Just your basic rappelling, like we learned at Boy
Scout camp."

"I thought I was going to fall *right* in the pool," Bree
said. "And I'd just had my hair done—"

"And not the greatest security in the world, either,
Andrew. They wouldn't let me phone your room, but
they gave me the suite right above."

"You could have knocked."

"It's a good thing you gave the suite number to Peggy,
I'd never have found you."

"Do you have anything diet?" asked Bree, bending
over the small refrigerator.

"There's water," mumbled Sussman. "Which you'll
also find thoughtfully provided in your own luxury suite."

Murray rubbed Sussman's sleep-tousled hair and pulled
the sheet back over his head. "Glad to see you're safe,
old buddy! Looks like we made it just in time. C'mon,
honey," he said to Bree, rubbing her backside. "Andrew
needs twenty more winks. We'll talk in the morning,
Hoops."

"Late in the morning."

"Work to be done, pal. I've got some angles on this
thing already."

"Nighty-night," said Bree. "Nice meeting you, Andy."

"Pleasure," groaned Sussman as Murray and Bree exited through the more conventional method.

"Mañana, Hoops," shouted Murray as he closed the
door behind him. "Don't forget to put the bolts on!"

*   *   *

Murray and Andy sat by a table out on the balcony of Sussman's suite, silhouetted by the bright morning sunlight that poured into the room. They were an asymmetrical pair: Murray sloping over the table, wearing sweatpants and a dinner jacket left over from his cruise; Sussman, a good six inches shorter, unshaven and in his bathrobe, a slightly pudged belly cushioning him from the glass tabletop. "So I think we can start narrowing down the suspects in a day or two," summarized Murray, gobbling down a Denver omelet that had been brought up by room service.

"Suspects? Murray, I was really hoping we could just identify this guy and go home."

"Andrew, where's your sense of theater? This is your big shot! A chance to make a name for yourself."

"That's what I'm afraid of."

"Hoops, listen: here's a guy who's already got at least two people happy to see him dead, maybe three if you count a jealous boyfriend, and I haven't even got to my bacon yet."

"Mur, Crash Kopeck was a hundred and fifty miles away when it happened, and I hardly think Leona Z would tell me that whole story if she'd just offed the guy."

"Maybe it's exactly what she'd do. Maybe she needed to reassure herself that the guy'd deserved it. Listen to me, Hoops, I know the criminal mind."

"But the police did an autopsy—"

"Andy, hear me out." Murray reached for a piece of bacon; he had managed to devour nearly the entire omelet before Sussman had gotten to his third bite. "Autopsies don't pick up everything. Now, I saw what they showed on TV, it was a little snowy out there on the high seas, we're going to have to check the videotapes just to be sure—but I can see at least two ways that a murder could have been committed. Drowning, obviously, for one."

"Murray, I was there—"

"The boat was capsized on top of three of the swimmers, Hoops! The camera was switched off for a while. They could have easily held him underwater."

"Hal and Carol? The Bobbsey Twins versus Dr. Double-X?"

"Some people are much stronger in the water. And there's poisons, Andy. There's all sorts of things that don't show up in an autopsy if you don't look for them. And remember, this guy had no family or friends. No one's clamoring for another inquest. And wrestling's kind of a twilight thing, you know."

"What do you mean, Murray, it's a ratings boffo smash, just ask my producer—"

"But the newspapers aren't really covering it. The sports pages don't consider wrestling legit—if that ice skater had drowned, you don't think it'd be headlines for a month? You don't think they'd be pressing an investigation?"

"It's possible," Sussman admitted.

"And the magazines don't know what to do with it either—believe me, Hoops, *Time* will *not* devote two covers to pro wrestlers in the same decade. It's a curiosity item, they're freaks. And as long as the wrestling people aren't treating it as anything more than an accident, neither will anyone else."

"But we will?"

"You already are, like it or not. And unless we start coming up with some hard facts, Andrew, you *are* going to look like a buffoon, so let's get on the stick." Murray swilled down the rest of his orange juice and helped himself to Sussman's toast. "What time does your buddy Cliff Trager check in with his office?"

"He should be over at KCBS by ten, we were going to cut the rest of the *Sports Spectacular* segment—"

"Good, we'll drop in as soon as I get dressed."

"We?"

"Well, I have some ideas for a few things."

"What kind of ideas?"

"Good ideas. About how to spice up your program a

little, Andrew, give it some pizazz. You're looking a little stilted out there, which I can't blame you for, but there's ways of making that story work. And Bree's all excited about seeing a TV show."

"I almost forgot. Murray, how old is that girl, she looked about fifteen."

"Old enough. And rich enough, she paid for the cruise."

"Uh-huh. So what does she do?"

"Anything I want," chortled Murray. "Boy, you oughta try running your own cruise sometime—"

"Glick," said Andy, "you are a true sleazoid. You just better hope there aren't any truant officers around."

"Not to worry, Hoops, everything checks out. Her daddy owns a big tobacco farm in North Carolina. They didn't think she was quite ready for college, so she decided to take a year off and build up a few experiences."

"Like hanging around a semiretired private eye for a few weeks. Who, incidentally, if I'm getting your drift, is now volunteering for active duty again."

"I was never retired. And I didn't volunteer, Andrew, you called."

"Murder-wise, I mean."

"Time to run, Kimo-Sabe," said Murray, grabbing the last piece of bacon from Sussman's plate and heading for the door. "I've got to get Bree moving. Meet you in the lobby at ten o'clock sharp."

Sussman listened to Murray's programming innovations as they drove to the KCBS studios on Sunset. Glick rambled on for almost the whole trip, pausing only long enough to allow a few adoring comments from Bree, who was lying in the back seat of the car with her bare feet sticking out the window. Murray's latest had short blond hair and a waifish smile, she wore faded denims with a light yellow blouse. She managed to interject a few tourist requests in her soft Carolina drawl, she couldn't wait to go to Disneyland and Rodeo Drive and Universal Studios and see King Kong. Murray assured her that they would get around to it, as soon as all the proper network negotiations had been worked out.

Those negotiations began in earnest once they reached Cliff Trager's office, although Trager was not sure exactly whom or what he was negotiating with. "Now, Cliff," Murray explained, leaning back in Trager's swivel chair and pointing an unlit cigar at the row of television monitors in the front of the control room, "what I'm proposing is sort of an analyst-type thing. Like a John Madden. Or a Jimmy the Greek."

"Um . . ." Trager glanced back at Andy Sussman, who was watching all this with complete seriousness; he had even worn a tie for the occasion. "Well," said Trager, "we *are* investigating a death here, there's a certain gravity expected—"

"Exactly," Murray said. "Now, Andrew is a reporter, and a damn fine one. I hope you appreciate the legwork he's done on this case already, Cliff, he had absolutely nothing to work on—"

"Of course, Mr. Glick—"

"And I, Cliff—I am a world-famous detective." Murray winked at Bree, who beamed, wide-eyed, at him from across the room. "Now, what could be a better setup for *Sports Spectacular* than to have a world-famous detective right on the set, analyzing the murder investigation every Saturday afternoon as it progresses? It'd be a smash!"

"Well, it would be different," Trager allowed. "Andy, perhaps we could discuss this . . ."

"I think Murray has a little demonstration all arranged," Sussman said. He was enjoying this meeting immensely and was happy to let Trager squirm for a while. "If we could set up the videotape of the drowning and turn on the Chalkboard for Murray, I'm sure this'll just take a few minutes . . ."

Cliff cleared his throat. "Oh, all right—we'll go over to 6B. But we've got to get the Saturday thing set up this morning, so let's try to be, uh, efficient about this."

One of the engineers took a couple of videotape packets and led the four of them to the studio. It was a sports anchor set, used occasionally when football or basketball broadcasts originated from Los Angeles. The engineer turned on the houselights and organized the set; there was a desk with several chairs around it and several monitors which Sussman and Murray stood behind. Murray was given a grease pencil that he could use to make markings on the "Chalkboard" TeleStrator in front of him. There were no cameramen present; the only functioning equipment was the preview monitors, which were cued to the tape of the fatal paddleboat race.

"Now, first of all," Murray said, pushing his desk over a few inches, "we'll have to arrange the studio a little more logically. I want the Suspect Board right behind me, in red and white lettering—and it's got to have room for everybody that was in that boat race, because they all had access."

"Suspect Board?" Trager turned to Sussman.

"For the people in the CBS boat," Andy explained.

"Plus Wireless, he was right there," Murray added. "And I'll need room underneath each name for motive and method. Then there's the Accomplice Board for people who weren't there but wanted to see Double-X dead." Murray moved a blackboard behind him to demonstrate how he would refer to the proposed graphics. "Now, already that's a much spiffier arrangement, don't you think, Cliff?"

Trager was standing in the shadow of a camera taking notes. He had a bemused smirk on his face. "Dandy. Go on, Mr. Glick."

Murray cleared his throat and pointed his cigar at Sussman. "Now, Andy, here, describes the videotape and gives a summary of progress up to this point, just like before—but here's where we have the 'CBS Murder Chalkboard.'"

"Murder Chalkboard . . ."

"Roll the tape, Jack."

The engineer turned on the video recorder and the tape of the raft race started. When it got just to the point where the CBS boat started to tip, Murray shouted, "Freeze it!" and the engineer stopped the tape. "All right," said Murray, rapping his pencil on the monitor, "right here we see the boat go over, but was it an accident?" He took the grease pencil and drew a circle around Hal Barron. "Watch how he leaned, Andy. He could have intentionally caused the craft to go underwater. Now, roll it . . ." The tape moved ahead to the isolated shot of the raft turtled on top of Hal, Carol, and Double-X, with Cindi Beamon struggling to free them. "Freeze it!" said Murray, and the tape stopped again. "Now," he said, drawing a little square on the bottom of the screen, "we should have a little clock underneath, here, counting the seconds. Those seconds underwater are vital, Cliff."

"Mr. Glick," said Trager, looking at his watch. "Perhaps—"

"And we should have all the footage that was shot prior to the start of the race, so we can see who was milling around. I assume you guys have that, I know you edit a lot."

Cliff Trager stood with his hands on his hips, alternating his gaze between Sussman and Murray.

"And I think maybe we should have a 'Clue of the Day' feature too. Maybe we could get a corporate sponsor for it, like the 'Rolaids Relief Pitcher' spots or 'Alcoa Fantastic Finishes.' Corporate sponsors are the big thing now, Cliff."

"Of course, where have I been?" Cliff Trager shot Sussman a poisonous glance; he turned off the monitors as the engineer removed the tape. "I suppose it'll be a shame if we ever solve this thing. The sponsors would never forgive us."

"And someone would have to go hunt yaks," Sussman reminded him. "Can you get those tapes for us, Cliff?"

"I'll work on it, Andy. But Saturday's segment goes as planned. We don't have time to set all this up and we obviously can't organize a new feature in such brief time."

"I could do a guest appearance," suggested Murray, following Trager back toward his office, with Bree clinging to his arm.

"And of course I need clearance from my superiors," Trager said. "Look, fellas, we're late already, let's get that tape from the memorial service edited. We'll organize this new concept next week."

"Fine, Cliff."

"Ten minutes, okay? Why don't you take your friends back to the front, Andy, they're taping some game shows today."

"Oh, wow, Murray!" said Bree. "I wonder which ones they're gonna do?"

"*Twenty-Five-Thousand-Dollar Pyramid*, I think," Sussman said.

"Oh, how *neat!* Do they ever pick contestants from the audience? That would be *so* exciting."

"I don't know, Bree," Sussman said, leading her and Murray to the front lobby. "I've never seen it. Why don't you ask them—"

"Oh, I will!"

"Well, good luck," Andy said, leaving Murray and Bree in the hands of a tour guide. "Have fun." He went into the studio with Cliff to edit the *Sports Spectacular* segment, and shouted back at Murray, "Maybe you'll win a cruise."

11

On Friday morning the check came by Federal Express; it was tucked into a white business envelope with the International Wrestling Association insignia on it. "Hope this helps, Andy," said the small note accompanying it, scrawled in red ink. "Best, Harvey Kopeck."

"Here, this ought to be the beginning of the end," said Sussman, handing the check over to Murray, but Murray seemed less than thrilled about the whole thing. He gave the check a cursory inspection and stuck it in the pocket of his beach shirt.

"Maybe, Hoops. At least it's a Chicago bank. First Lakeshore's near north, I'm sure I know someone in there." First Lakeshore was the bank where Kopeck's IWA check had been deposited, in the account of "Dr. Double-X, Inc." Sussman had assumed that it would be a fairly simple bit of spookwork to get inside the bank's files and find out who the officers of the corporation were and whose signature was authorized to draw money out of the account—presumably it would be Dr. Double-X himself; he had to have a way to get to his money, after all. But Murray was skeptical. "It's too easy a shot," he said, taking a draw from a Corona beer. It was eleven in the morning, and they were back on the patio of Sussman's suite. "Look, Hoops, this guy went to a lot of trouble to hide his identity. If I can get inside a bank's charter file—and I can, fairly easily—then so can someone else."

"But doesn't he have to have his name on the account?"

"Nope. Could be a trust, or he could just assign someone else to be president and secretary—it would be their names on the charter."

"How would he get paid, then?"

"Lots of ways. He could just have one of the signers take the money out in cash and give it to him."

"That would assume he had a girlfriend or confidant, someone he trusted, somewhere—and no one here thinks he did."

"Or he could have set up a phony ID, Hoops. If he was really determined, he could have left a dead trail. I'd have to see the checks and account records for Dr. Double-X, Inc."

Sussman sank back into his deck chair and guzzled some beer. He had been so excited about getting the check; now he was trying to keep from getting depressed. "Well, he couldn't have been perfect, Mur—if he was, he'd probably be alive now. Assuming he was murdered, of course."

"And assuming that the murderer was after the man behind the mask, not Dr. Double-X. Remember, Kopeck and Leona both had reasons to hurt the Doctor, even if they didn't know who he really was—"

The phone inside the suite rang and Sussman started to make a move for it, but Murray was closer to the balcony door and rushed inside. "Murray, please don't," Andy implored, but it was too late, Murray had already picked it up.

"Good morning, Andrew Sussman's suite," said Murray. He stood silently for a moment, then put the phone down. "They hung up."

"Murray, I'd really appreciate it if you wouldn't—" The phone rang again and this time Sussman answered it. "Hello?"

"He's there," said the voice at the other end.

"Who's there?"

"Don't give me that," said Susie Ettenger. "The Sultan of Sleaze. Andy, you could have at least told me—"

"Susie—"

"Andy, what possible good is Murray Glick going to do you out there?"

"C'mon, Suse, think about it. I've been stuck for a week with this thing, people have been threatening to break my neck."

"I brought that up with the company lawyers—they can't force you to work on a life-threatening assignment, Andy."

"Oh, sure, that'll look great. I back out of a story involving professional wrestling because I've been threatened, people'll really take me seriously." There was a silence between them for a moment, then Andy said, "Look, Suse, I just want to get this over with, and Murray's the best guy I know, he can get things done that you and I can't." There was still more silence. "Susan, are you there?"

"I'm here. But I'm going to be there tonight."

"Hey, great!"

"Aw, Andy, is he really going to be hanging around us the whole time? I've got a few days off, the Chinese thing got delayed a week. I was hoping we could have some time together."

"We'll have plenty of time, except when we're working on the story. And anyway, Murray brought a girl with him."

"Another one of his famous bimbettes?"

"Hoops," said Murray, elbowing his friend in the stomach. "Is that Susie?"

"Yes, Murray. She gives her highest regards."

"Tell her I said hi!"

"Murray says hi," Sussman said into the phone.

"Tell him I hope he gets eaten by a shark."

"She says she hopes you're having a good time at the beach," Sussman said. "Suse, what time are you coming in?"

"Nine o'clock, LAX. American 231. You'll be there?"

"At the gate, sweetheart."

"Looks like a hot weekend," said Murray as Sussman put the phone down. "Maybe we should make reservations for somewhere Saturday night. Bree'll be really excited to meet Susie—"

"Murray," began Sussman, but it was just no use trying to explain to him how anyone as pretty as Susie could despise him so completely. He dropped the subject, turning his attention to a large piece of white cardboard, a sample "Suspect Board" on which Murray had scrawled out the names:

> HAL BARRON
> CAROL VIVIAN
> CINDI BEAMON
> WIRELESS

"The trouble is," Andy said, "everyone's spread all over the country, people just came in for the *Superteams* thing and then split. I don't know where Wireless is. Hal and Carol are back in New York—you don't seriously suspect them, do you, Murray?"

Murray admitted that he didn't; Hal and Carol were national celebrities, murdering a pro wrestler on network television seemed like a lot of trouble to go through just to boost the ratings. Still, they were in the fatal boat. Murray instructed Sussman to put a call through to New York, just to sound them out again.

"Sussman, you dog, you!" said Barron. He was just about to take off for a weekend skiing trip to Vermont. "You're still in LA! I bet you've known who the Doc was all along."

"Sure, right, Hal. Listen, I was wondering . . . if you don't mind, and I don't mean to be prying and everything, but I'm doing a little background on this whole investigation thing, and, uh . . ."

"I didn't do it," laughed Hal over the phone line. "I'm an innocent man, honest Injun."

"C'mon, Hal, 'fess up," said Carol Vivian, picking up an extension. "I saw it all, Andy. He gave him three real hard nuggies and tickled him in the pupik and that was it."

"Lies, all lies," said Hal.

"It's his new macho image," Carol said. "Merle Summers called last week, he wants Hal to go *mano a mano* with a six-hundred-pound three-horned white rhinoceros bull—"

"Good-bye," said Hal Barron. "I'm going skiing. I'm moving to Switzerland. If you want any more information, call the public defender's office."

"Well, I guess that means we need a guest host," Carol said. "Andy, how about coming on next week with The Thing and Leona Z?"

Sussman respectfully declined and the rest of the conversation did not produce any startling revelations. He said good-bye to Carol and hello to a corned-beef sandwich and another bottle of Corona.

"You're a relentless interrogator," said Murray, who had been listening in on the bathroom extension. "What do you think of their alibi, Hoops?"

"I think they're in the clear, unless you can murder someone with cuteness."

"Could just be a clever ruse."

"Now, why do I doubt that?"

Murray shrugged. He took the Los Angeles *Times*, which had been dropped off at their door, and opened it to the sports section. "Let's move down the list, Andy. The Olympic volleyball team practices right here in town, isn't that what I read—"

"You're thinking Cindi Beamon? I thought she was the one that wasn't in any position to drown anyone."

"But she was there, she can tell us some things. Call her up, tell her it's a follow-up story. Your friend Cliff must have some number where she can be reached. And try to do it this afternoon. I think they're going on some sort of exhibition tour."

Sussman finished his beer and did as he was instructed, even though he was growing slightly aggravated at following Murray's marching orders. It was against his nature to be bossed around; before CBS he'd been a sports director at several small stations, and even in Chicago he'd had a good deal of autonomy over his own broadcasts. But Murray was the expert. And he was right. It *would* be helpful to interview Cindi early in the afternoon—Andy wanted the day's work done well before Susie arrived. It turned out Cliff Trager did know where Beamon could be reached; she was practicing for the last game of an exhibition series with a team from Red China. Cliff set up a fifteen-minute conference at three o'clock; they would meet in the press room at the Forum, where she would just be ending a practice.

"Now, there's one other thing," Murray said. He was about to go back to his suite upstairs. He had promised Bree a few hours at the beach together and she still wanted to go to Disneyland and Universal Studios. "Just something to think about. It's about Dr. Double-X and his agent."

"He didn't have an agent, Murray. Not with Garrison or Crash Kopeck."

"Well, isn't that a little unusual, Hoops? Isn't that how most of them get started?"

"He didn't need one for Garrison—he was champion of the IWA, after all. And according to Harvey, when he showed up at his doorstep two years ago, it was all by himself, and he looked like he knew the ropes."

"But what about when he started? With that league that folded?"

"Allegedly. No one seems sure about that."

"Well, let's make some assumptions. Let's assume that Dr. Double-X did get his first shot in that league—the MWA, wasn't it?"

"Right."

"I'm thinking he must have had an agent. Pure speculation. If there was some reason why Double-X dropped out of sight for a couple of years, that agent might know it."

"And," Sussman said, "he might be interested to know

that his ex-client became a big gate attraction three years later."

"*If* he knew who it was," Murray said. "Double-X sat out a couple of years—that's what Kopeck thought. He puts a mask on, let's say he gains fifty pounds, builds up the muscles."

"I suppose if he found out, he could have got pretty pissed," Sussman said. "Depending on the terms of the contract. He may have thought Double-X owed him."

"Owed him plenty."

"Of course, it would be pretty stupid to kill the guy, Murray, if that's what you're thinking. He'd want to get his percentage and keep him performing, wouldn't he?"

"Just speculating, Andrew. There could have been more to it."

"Well, we'll see. Take care of that check from Harvey, okay? I think if we could just figure out who Double-X was, we'd have a better idea why someone wanted to kill him."

"Could be," said Murray. He drained the last few swallows out of his Corona and headed for the door. "Could be. Just remember, though—the killer started with a motive and went forward. We start with a murder and go backward."

"So?"

"So, Andrew, we may not figure out who Dr. Double-X really was until we find out who killed him. And why."

12

The Los Angeles Forum was where Andy Sussman had wanted to be all along; it was the reason, really, that he had joined CBS. This was where the Lakers played basketball, this was where the NBA championships had been contested five times already in the eighties, this was the top of the pyramid. It was not just the glamour, although there was nothing wrong with being seen with Jack Nicholson or Tom Cruise or the Laker girls. It was being with the best: the best players, the best broadcasting team—and no one could appreciate that as much as Andy Sussman, who had spent three years covering one of the worst teams in professional basketball.

But it wasn't basketball that Andy was covering this warm winter's morning in Los Angeles; the Lakers were off in Seattle, the basketball nets were stored away. Sussman was sitting in the stands with Murray Glick, watching the U.S. Women's Volleyball Team practicing for their game that night against an all-star team from mainland China.

"I don't understand why this isn't a more popular spectator sport," said Murray, looking at the competitors through binoculars. "They're all gorgeous, especially your pal Cindi—I'm tellin' ya, Hoops, if that girl ain't Endorsement City, I don't know who is."

"Sorry, Mur, somehow major-league volleyball hasn't captured the imagination of the American public yet. Maybe people just need to be educated—"

"Whattaya talking about—everybody plays volleyball. They play it in gym, they play it at picnics. More people play it than tennis, I'll bet, and there's six beautiful girls on each side instead of one or two. I bet if you guys promoted it the right way—"

"You mean like female mud wrestling?"

"Save me the lecture on sports culture, Andy. Truth is, people watch car races to see crashes. They watch hockey to see fights. They watch women's tennis to see Chrissy Evert in a short skirt. And I'm tellin' you, give volleyball a little network prime time, I bet Cindi Beamon'd be on more magazine covers than Vanna White."

Somebody blew a whistle on the court and the practice broke up; a few of the players milled around, practicing sets and firing serves, but most of them headed for the locker room. Sussman and Glick walked down from their seats toward the pressroom, where they waited about five minutes before Cindi Beamon joined them.

Cindi had her warm-ups on, navy-blue pants and a sweatshirt with red-and-white piping and a field of stars around the shoulders. Her sun-bleached hair was tied in a ponytail and she wore no makeup. She carried a large plastic cup of Gatorade with her. "Hi, Andy," she said briskly, looking around for the television cameras. There weren't any. She looked surprised by their absence and Murray's presence.

"How ya doin', Cindi?" Sussman shook her hand and patted her on the back. She seemed friendly but businesslike, just as she had on the *Superteams* competition. She'd made only a token effort to mix in with the other participants; once or twice during the week she'd joined some of them for a beer, she'd gone out for dinner once with Hal and Carol, but otherwise she'd gone her own way. "This is Glen Murray," Sussman said. "He's working with us on the production end. We're trying to finish off this whole *Superteams*/Dr. Double-X thing."

"Well, I'm sure it's been a big hassle for you. All that hard work you did, and they're not even going to run the show now. The team was a little upset, we could have used the exposure."

"Well, they've been showing a few of the tapes, of course. The interview we did—"

"I know," Cindi said, "I've been hearing all about it. The Chinese girls saw it, they all want to hear about 'big U.S. wrestlers.' Did you see the story in the *Herald* this morning?"

Sussman hadn't, he had only seen the *Times*, but there were copies lying around in the pressroom and Cindi showed it to him: "VOLLEYBALLER BEAMON TRIES TO FORGET MYSTERIOUS DEATH RACE."

"It's unbelievable," she said. "The guy called me up about tonight's match, he never even asked me about volleyball. Do I have nightmares? Can I ever get it out of my mind? Good grief." She tapped a closely manicured fingernail on the table. "Thank God the Forum's running this event, they're too classy to start promoting it like that."

"I suppose that wasn't the only media contact you've had since last Saturday?" Sussman asked.

"Well, fortunately I was out of town most of the week. We had matches in Santa Barbara and San Diego, and next week we're going to the Midwest. Chicago, Minneapolis, Detroit. Some people called the team offices the first couple of days, but once they established it was an accident, it kind of faded off. Except the wrestling fans, of course."

"You're hearing a lot from them?"

"We had dozens of letters sent here. Maybe almost a hundred."

"Were any of them threatening?"

"Are you kidding?" Cindi said with a thin-lipped smile. "All but a couple said he was a dirty SOB and had it coming. Two guys said they were frogmen who'd swum underwater and drowned him. Three of the worst claimed to be his mother. And a couple of guys sent along marriage proposals."

"Who said wrestling fans were all morons?" Murray smirked.

"I sent them an autographed picture. This team can't

afford to dissuade any potential supporters; we may have to take a tugboat to Barcelona in ninety-two."

Cindi sipped on her Gatorade; she was thirsty from the practice and drank about half of it while Sussman tried to reconstruct some of the events leading up to the fatal race. "Did the Doctor talk much to you or Hal or Carol during the week?" he asked.

"Nope, not at all. I don't think we got a complete sentence from him the whole time, except when he was standing there with The Thing and Leona and his manager. During the practice heats he just sat there with that Wireless guy, they looked like they were talking sometimes, but when you got right up to them, they just seemed to get real quiet."

"What about his routine for the races?" asked Murray. "Warm-ups, that type of thing. Did he have some kind of predictable habits?"

"I think he warmed up before he got there. Once, earlier in the week, when we were doing the relay races, I saw him up the beach, maybe a half-mile, doing his stretches. Then before the race he'd stretch some more and hyperventilate, and Wireless would give him this massage for about ten minutes."

"Any other oddball habits?"

Cindi shrugged. "Well, he was just pretty odd to begin with."

"What about the preliminary heats?" asked Sussman. He hadn't seen them all; several of the prelims had gone on at the same time.

"Well, we won our races, if that's what you're asking."

"Did you guys talk about strategy much? How did you figure who took what position in the raft?"

"Carol did all that," Cindi explained. "She was running the whole show. I don't know how Hal can work with her, if that's the way she is all the time. I felt like shoving her overboard once or twice myself."

"It was her idea to put Dr. Double-X alone in the bow?"

"How else could you do it? He was so much bigger

than anybody else, if you put him on one side, we'd tip right over."

"Did you tip in practice?" Murray asked.

"Oh, sure. Everybody did at first, the boats were so flimsy."

"But not during the heats?"

"No. There were two boats from each network, remember. If we'd tipped, we wouldn't have made it to the finals."

"And when you did tip," Sussman asked, "in the actual race, did you notice anything unusual while the boat was over?"

"Unusual? I was a little busy . . ."

"I mean shouts for help or anything. Nothing unusual going on out there?"

"Just that there were four people struggling like crazy, trying to get out of the Redondo Beach Harbor. That water's cold this time of year, you guys. You don't see many people swimming at the beach in February, except in wet suits. I was a lifeguard, I've seen a few hypothermia cases."

"What about before you tipped?" Murray asked. "Any sign that anything was abnormal with anyone in front of you?"

Cindi let out a deep breath. "I heard Hal say he thought maybe the wrestler jerked or something, but really, we were hardly watching for anything like that, we were just paddling like hell. I wanted to win, you know, I'm not ashamed of it. The competition may have been just a stupid, contrived thing for you guys, but we figure that every thirty seconds I get interviewed on national TV, it might raise ten or twenty grand for the team. And it's not easy raising money, it's not like when the Olympics were here in LA."

"How's your brother Steve doing?" asked Murray.

The change in the line of questioning was abrupt, tactlessly so, Sussman thought, as he watched Cindi's mouth drop and lines draw on her forehead.

"We're both from Chicago, you know," Sussman ex-

plained as Cindi stared at Murray and swallowed some
more Gatorade. "I used to broadcast basketball games
there, so naturally I knew that he got hurt and everything."

"He's doing fine," Cindi said softly. "He's doing about
as well as he could, considering . . ."

"It was a swimming accident, wasn't it?" Murray asked.
"Diving or something?"

"We really haven't discussed it publicly."

"But he isn't going to play ball again?" Murray asked.

"We, uh . . . don't think so. No. He's been in rehabilitation for almost a year now."

"At the Rehab Center in Chicago?"

"He was there for a long time. He's almost ready to
come home full-time now." Cindi's voice had dropped
almost to a whisper. "We really don't want a big publicity thing with him, if you don't mind. He's going to
go back to school this summer."

"They left him his scholarship?" Sussman asked.

"Yes, they did."

"What about damages, that kind of thing?" asked
Murray. "Anything to help pay the bills?"

"It was an accident. You can't sue a river bottom. He
had good medical insurance at least." Cindi tapped her
plastic cup on the table and stood up. "Can I go now?"

Sussman rubbed Cindi gently on the back. "Sure. Sorry
to bring all that up, Cindi. Good luck tonight."

"Thanks, Andy," Cindi whispered, and hurried out the
door.

Afterward, as they drove back from Inglewood down
the Pacific Coast Highway to Redondo Beach, Sussman
wanted to know why Murray had been so interested in
the medical progress of Steve Beamon.

"It's an X factor," Murray said. "Probably means
nothing. I'd just like to know how he got hurt."

"What could it possibly have to do with the death of
a professional wrestler?"

"You never know. College kids go to those things a
lot. We went all the time at Madison—"

"I never did."

"Well, those of us who weren't worried about being seen by a spy from network television. And we drank a lot and we got rowdy, Hoops. Maybe Beamon goes with some friends, maybe there was some kind of a confrontation. Maybe the swimming thing's all a big cover-up."

"Pretty farfetched, Mur."

"Maybe. You know, Hoops, when I was looking over that tape, the one of the race and right before? Seems to me I saw Dr. Double-X chewing a big ugly gob of chewing tobacco, it was dribbling right down his face."

"One of his more disgusting habits. I think he used to aim the stuff at our blazers. The guy was a pig, I'll admit."

"So don't you think Cindi would remember that?"

"What do you mean?"

"I asked her about odd habits."

"Well, I thought you meant something out of the ordinary. Something different from usual. I don't think I would have noticed."

Murray lowered the window of the Chrysler LeBaron and leaned back in his seat. "Right," he said. "Next time I'll ask you first." Murray opened the sun roof, found an oldies station on the radio, and turned up the volume. He didn't say another word to Andy the rest of the way home. When they got back to the Sheraton, there was one message apiece waiting for Murray and Andy.

Bree had checked out.

And Wireless had left a message, scrawled personally on the back of a gasoline-credit-card receipt. The number he had left was the hotel switchboard.

13

Sussman wondered why none of this could have happened earlier in the week, when he didn't have to worry about picking Susie up at the airport and planning a romantic weekend. Murray, for his part, did not exactly seem crushed that Bree had left him. He could live without Disneyland and Universal Studios, and had evidently told her as much. She had left a note saying that she had discovered an old boyfriend up in Malibu, maybe she'd see him on another cruise sometime. Murray looked at the note for about two seconds, crumpled it up, and tossed it in the ashtray by the elevator; he was already entertaining ideas of going to the volleyball match tonight.

Wireless was another matter. Sussman would have preferred to plop into the Jacuzzi with a margarita until Susie's plane arrived, but the wrestler was apparently somewhere in the hotel and Sussman did not want any more unannounced visitors in the middle of the night. So he called the switchboard and gave the extension number on the note. He got connected to a room and heard the rasp of Wireless on the line.

"Sussman, 'at you?"

"Yes it is, Wire—"

"Don't say the name. I ain't here."

"Where are you?"

"Don't get smart. Get up here, room 934."

"Sure. Mind if I bring a friend?"

"Bet your ass I do."

"He works for me. And the network."

Wireless was quiet for a moment, then said, "Look, this ain't a threat. I'm the one in trouble."

"Just the same, I'd prefer if—"

"Fine. And bring a six-pack, I'm gettin' thirsty up here."

Sussman stopped over at the bar. They wouldn't let him take any beer out, but he arranged for a room-service waiter to accompany them up to the room and leave three beers by the door. When Wireless finally let them in, Sussman introduced Glick as Glen Murray again; with all the notoriety in Chicago, there was always a chance that people would recognize his real name. "So what's the problem?" Sussman asked, surveying the hotel room.

Wireless was wearing a light blue sport shirt and slacks that looked like they had been slept in; there was a tangerine-colored sport jacket slung over the chair. The bed was rumpled. He hadn't shaved; a small Dopp kit rested by the pillow. "I was robbed," Wireless said.

"Mugged?"

"Not mugged! I look like the kinda guy gets mugged? I was robbed, my apartment was broken into."

"Uh, well, I'm sorry. I hear it can get pretty bad in LA—"

Wireless grabbed a bottle of beer and swallowed half of it in one gulp. "No, no. The place was ransacked. Turned upside down. Furniture knocked over, mattresses knifed up. Drawers, cabinets, plates tossed all over the place. It was a mess."

"What was stolen?" asked Murray.

"I don't think anything. I got lotsa jewelry, none of it was taken. Checks, insurance stuff. Didn't even take the change lyin' on the kitchen counter."

Sussman paced around the hotel room. It was antiseptically clean, except in the places where Wireless had sat or lain down. "So why come here? Why not go to the police?"

"The police wouldn't be interested."

"And we would?"

Wireless swilled down some more beer. "If the police was interested, I'da heard from 'em by now."

"And why is that?" Murray asked.

"Don't be a wise-ass!"

"Believe me," Sussman said, "we're considerably less wise than you give us credit for. Now, let's take it for granted that all this has something to do with a certain masked wrestler you once handled."

Wireless sat on the foot of the bed, hunched over like a troll, and pondered his bottle of beer.

"Let's further assume," Sussman said, "that said competitor's death was less than accidental."

"I dunno," Wireless mumbled. "They ain't got no proof."

"But you have your doubts," said Murray.

"Not at first. I followed the autopsy. If 'at's what they say, then I believe 'em."

"But not now?"

"Still coulda been. But, let's face it," Wireless said, "this was a man a lotta people weren't unhappy to see end up where he ended up."

"And why is that?" asked Murray.

Wireless shrugged. "Some people have a hard time makin' friends, I guess."

"I don't suppose," suggested Sussman, "that his unpopularity had anything to do with his not always performing in the ring the way he was supposed to?"

"I don't catch your drift."

"C'mon, Wireless. He won a belt he wasn't supposed to win. Against Crash Kopeck in the IWA. I assumed you knew that."

"It was a helluva upset," Wireless said, finishing his beer and grabbing another in one fluid motion. "Helluva upset. A young, unpolished grappler—'at's what brings the fans out, fellas—the unexpected."

"Right. It sure as hell caught Harvey Kopeck by surprise. Would you say, Wireless, that Dr. Double-X had one less friend after he won that match and jumped to the WFA?"

"Look," Wireless growled, "I ain't here to discuss things like that. We gotta honest show. Ten years in the game, I ain't never seen a fan ask for his money back. You wanna see a fight that's fixed, go to a hockey game. And lemme tell you, Sussman, professional wrestlers are the greatest athaletes in the world. You see the pounding we take? Three-hunnerd-pound guys put ya in a flyin' mirror, toss ya off the ropes, land right on toppa ya? You think some candy-ass baseball pitcher can take that? A *golfer?* You know how many hours a day I spend at the gym—"

"Wireless," Sussman said, "you came to us. Now, if you think this had something to do with Dr. Double-X, then cut out the bullshit—"

"It ain't got nothin' to do with competition! I don't want you sayin' that all over CBS, that we ain't honest." Wireless got off his bed and stalked over to the balcony. The door was closed and he gingerly pushed the curtain aside and sneaked a look at the pool below.

"Wireless," Murray said gently, "we're not here to dispute your integrity. What do you say we begin at the beginning?"

"Where is that?"

"His name. What was his name?"

"I dunno, guy."

"But you traveled with him, you ate with him. When he went to a hotel room, how did he register?"

"I never stayed at the same place with him, 'cept for once. He stayed in dumps. I'm a class athalete, I ain't gonna share a room in no dump. An' no one asked his name in those places, 'at's for sure."

"Did he always wear the mask?"

"Never saw him without it."

"Even in public? Even when he went shopping?"

"I never saw him in public, outside the ring."

Murray reached for a beer, but there were none left, Wireless had just started on his third one. "All right, fine. All this was strictly professional." He walked over to the closet, looked in, peeked into the bathroom, then walked back toward the balcony. "Incidentally, Wireless, would you mind telling us *your* real name?"

"What's it to ya?"

"Well, we are investigating a murder."

"Sez who?"

"And you were at the scene of the crime."

"So was fifty other people. My name's Wireless. I had it legally changed."

"Uh-huh. From what?"

"Hey, what do you care, faggot?" Wireless slammed the sliding balcony door closed, but Murray put his hand on the lock and twisted it back open. "Whadissit, are you guys gonna help me or not?"

"Maybe not," Murray said. "Truth is, I got better things to do in LA on a Friday night. Another wrestler gets bagged, it's all the same to me." He slipped his spidery frame onto the balcony, then came back inside and closed the door. "Last chance, Wireless. What was your name?"

"Gregory Peck."

"Right." Murray took Sussman by the hand and escorted him toward the door. "C'mon, Andrew. Waste of time, we could be at the beach."

"I'm not kidding!" shouted Wireless, bolting from the balcony door. "It was! My mother's idea, she loved the movies." He blocked Sussman and Glick as they started to leave. "Lookit, you guys, how could I wrestle with a name like that? You know what kinda crap I used to get, a guy lookin' like me, name of Gregory Peck?" He lowered his voice to sound like a ring announcer. "In this corner-r-r . . . at two hundred eighty pounds . . . Gregory fucking *Peck?!* So I changed it, what's it to you?"

"Let's just say that it's good to get in the habit of telling the truth," Murray replied. "It won't hurt so much from now on. Now, what about Dr. Double-X?" Wireless had sat back down on the bed; he took out a pillow and jammed it under his head. "He never mentioned anything to you about his past, not even once?"

"Never talked about it. I asked a few times, all I get is a growl. He was a nasty mother, y'know, type a guy doesn't give a goddamn 'bout nothin'. 'At's why I stayed away from him."

"How did you know he was so nasty if he never talked to you?" Sussman asked.

"Jus' the things he did. Jumpin' leagues like he did. Way he was with Ben. Thought he owned the goddamn league."

"Is that why Ben assigned you to him? Because he was, let's say, unpredictable?"

"You could say that. 'Course, what the guy does with other people, 'at's his business, and theirs. But what he does with Ben Garrison, 'at's Ben's business. And mine."

"So Ben wanted to make sure that Dr. Double-X had no doubt who was in charge," Murray said.

"You could say that."

"Did the Doctor get the message?"

Wireless shrugged. "Much as he got anything. The message was given."

"Did his performance in the ring indicate that he'd gotten the message?" Murray asked.

"The man was a great athalete."

"Wireless," Sussman asked, "did he get the message? Or did Ben have to give him another message?"

"Look, guy! I ain't afraida Ben; if I was, you think I come to you? I work for him, you think he'd have any reason to trash my place? You think *Ben* had any reason to grease Double-X, a guy was makin' him money?"

"Maybe Ben was sending another message," Murray suggested.

"Helluva message."

"Wireless," Sussman asked, changing the subject, "how come you weren't at the memorial service for Dr. Double-X?"

"I was grieving."

"Right. Where were you?"

"Hey, look, what's with the third degree? Someone just tore my place to hell. You think I come to you if I got something to hide? I had personal things to do that night, I got a personal life too, ain't none of your business."

Sussman looked at his watch; he had wanted to make some reservations for a late dinner when Susie came in, but he was beginning to think they'd both be too tired to do anything but rack out. "Wireless," he said, "think for a moment. You were Dr. Double-X's manager. Now, certain people might presume you were close, even if you weren't. If Double-X had something that someone wanted, and they couldn't locate him, they could presumably locate you. And it's not unreasonable to think that whatever it was they wanted, you might have it or know what it is. Right?"

Wireless grabbed an empty beer bottle and thumped it on the bedspread. "I dunno exactly."

"You don't know exactly?" Murray asked. "What about vaguely?"

"Look, he was a hard-ass. He didn't take nothin' from nobody."

"And which nobody did he not take nothing from, Wireless? Any specific nobodies?"

"I dunno, I dunno. It was in Chicago, maybe six months ago." Wireless tossed the beer bottle into a wastebasket. "We had a match at the Horizon, he was late, maybe a half-hour. Barely made it for the match, the crowd's startin' to get rowdy. Afterward, in the locker room, he's about to duck out like always. I collar him, I say whatsa problem, you gonna show up late you gotta let me know. Ben ain't gonna like it, you don't show up."

"So what'd he say?" Sussman asked.

"Oh, he grumbled something, something about some old relationship. Thought it might be a woman, but you know I gotta look after business things for Ben. Guy with a nothin' past like Double-X—we'd talked before, Ben and I."

"Talked about what?"

"Old contracts. Maybe promoters, agents. We'd checked the IWA thing, he was clean. Naturally, I asked him; I say: look, Doc, any a this gotta do with business, you tell me, we clear it up, unnerstan'?"

"And?" asked Murray.

"Aw, he jus' spat tobacco juice at me. Says he handles his own problems. Says he got everything under control."

"What do you mean, under control?" Murray asked. "What did he say? What was under control?"

"I dunno. All he said was, 'This guy won't bother me no more,' that's all I know."

"Who?"

"I dunno."

"Why wouldn't he bother him?" asked Sussman.

"I can't tell ya." Wireless got off the bed. "Alls I know is, Double-X, he says, 'I got the SOB. I got him by the balls. Ain't nothin' to worry about.'"

"That's it?" Murray said. "That's all he said?"

"Most I ever got out of him. Then he looked at me like he never shoulda said that even. And he grabs his old parka, ratty old army-surplus thing, the guy dresses like a hobo . . ." Wireless got up slowly from the bed and walked toward the door.

"And?" said Sussman.

"And," said Wireless, "he puts on his old blue stocking cap, and he's out the door. And the next time I see him, we're in Tucson."

14

"Murray wants to go for a *boat* ride?" Susie Ettenger flopped herself down on the bed. She'd just put on her swimsuit but now she pulled the covers over her long brown hair and spoke to Sussman through the comforter. "Andy! In the first place, I do not want to be anywhere on the same ocean with that slimeball. And I certainly don't want to be confined with him in a boat."

"Not a boat, Suse. A raft."

"Don't even think about it."

Sussman turned off the VCR, a new feature thoughtfully provided by the wonderful folks at the Sheraton. He had been looking at a tape of his appearance the day before on Saturday's *Sports Spectacular*—his interviews with Ben Garrison and The Thing at the memorial service and his analysis of the search for Dr. Double-X's identity. He had stayed away from any direct insinuation that Double-X had been murdered, at Cliff Trager's suggestion. Since no one would publicly admit anything irregular about the late Doctor's behavior, they both felt that anything along the lines of an "exposé" would be premature and laughable—"exposing" wrestling as a hoax would not exactly be a scoop. But the audience, according to Cliff, remained fascinated by the story. He seemed certain that new evidence would break within the week: Sussman had told him about the canceled check from Crash Kopeck and the encounter with Wireless. So Trager had made the *Sports Spectacular* segment just long enough to titillate the viewers, and had scheduled another fifteen-minute report for the following week.

Meanwhile, Sussman had his girlfriend to placate. "Look who's sulking now," he said, pulling the covers off her. "We're only talking an hour, babe, on the outside—"

"Well, I'm entitled to sulk! In the entire United States of America there's only one person I'd go to all this trouble to avoid, and this is my vacation time and it's a beautiful Sunday morning at the beach and—"

Sussman kissed Susie on the cheek and slid next to her on the bed. "Aw, Suse, he's not so bad."

"I just don't understand why you had to schlep him all the way in from Chicago—"

"Honey, you have no idea what nobility Murray is capable of exhibiting in the proper situation."

"You can say that again."

"And this is strictly business. Crucial to the case, which we all want to solve so I can go home. Right?"

"Uh . . ."

"Right?"

"Well . . . I'm off through Tuesday," Susie said, kissing Andy on the tip of his nose. "It snowed three more inches in Chicago yesterday. It's not exactly as if—"

"Out of the sack, woman!" shouted Sussman, ripping the comforter off Susie.

"Hey! Just a joke—"

"There's work to be done!" Sussman pulled Susie off the bed and tossed her a pink-and-blue beach bag. "Beachward, wench!"

"You sexy Neanderthal, you," muttered Susie, but she slung the beach bag over her shoulder and they were off for the Redondo Beach Harbor.

Lennie Weintraub had returned from Tucson the previous night at 2:30 A.M., after another drubbing—his fourth on the road trip, this one at the hands of the Mad Elk. "Crazed Elk is more like it," he said, yawning into the ocean breeze. "He missed his fall and came down right on my knee. I'm lucky it was only a bruise. And of course it didn't look too great when my forehead started bleeding out of nowhere.''

"He couldn't have gone for a quick eye gouge?'' Sussman asked, staring into Lennie's bloodshot eyes.

"I'm afraid the whole match was pretty well muddled by then. It was hopeless, I went right into the death scene.''

"Don't you ever get to win a match?'' asked Susie. They were standing on the pier in the harbor, in front of a large fishing boat called *Redondo I,* munching on some popcorn and waiting for Murray. "It hardly seems fair, Lennie. Even the good guys win once in a while.''

"The fault lies not in the stars, but in ourselves,'' Lennie pronounced, placing a solemn hand on Susie's shoulder. "Actually, it's Shakespeare's fault, he wrote all those tragedies, the hero always dies in the end. And I can hardly do scenes out of *A Midsummer Night's Dream.* I do have a new concept, though, I've been trying to sell Leroy and Leona on it.''

"The Thing and Leona Z,'' Sussman explained to Susie. "What is it, Lennie?''

"I was thinking of a mixed tag-team match. Romeo and Juliet versus Antony and Cleopatra. It'd take a little work, of course, integrating the plays, and lots of practice. And I'd need to recruit a partner, of course.''

"Of course.'' Sussman crunched some popcorn. "You don't think that's stretching the concept a little thin, O Renaissance Man?''

"No such thing. It *is* professional wrestling, after all. And no one's ever done mixed tag teams, not that I've seen. Think of the whole new audience it would reach, Andy. It'd be perfect for *Friday Night Videos.*''

"But who would win?'' Susie asked. "If I remember my college Shakespeare, all four characters die at the end.''

"It'll be a double disqualification!'' bubbled Lennie. "What great theater! A battle royal, four great orations, then four deaths, all four wrestlers prone on the canvas. The crowd will absolutely love it.''

"I think you should mull that one over for a while," suggested Sussman.

"Yo, team!" shouted Murray Glick, jogging over to the boat slip. He was struggling with a large red inflatable raft; it was the one that the NBC team had used during the fatal race. "Geez," he said to Sussman, "is it hard trying to pry a piece of equipment from you guys."

"I called Cliff, I told him you were coming."

"Had to sign my life away—hey, Susela!" Murray took Susie's hand and kissed it like one of King Arthur's knights. "Suse, you defy time, sweetheart, you get prettier every day."

"Uh, thanks, Murray. You defy science in your own way too."

"See, Hoops? See, I told you she'd come around." Murray presented Susie's hand to Sussman, then turned to Lennie. "And you're Lennie, the Renaissance Man. Gee, I'm sorry I woke you up this morning. I hope Wireless isn't too big an inconvenience."

"I'm sure we can manage for a few days, we're used to guests. The Condo in Redondo, as my wife calls it."

Wireless had spent a restless Friday night at the Redondo Beach Sheraton; he was convinced that whoever had ransacked his apartment was following him. Sussman felt slightly guilty about leaving him on Lennie's doorstep; it wasn't in his nature to take advantage of friends (it was Murray Glick who had eventually made the phone call). But it was a logical move; Lennie was the one wrestler he was sure he could get information from, he was the perfect person to accommodate Wireless for a few days.

"So what exactly are we doing here?" Susie wanted to know. "I'm an entire shade away from the perfect tan, and a certain client of mine is dying to take me shopping."

"Ah, Rodeo Drive, right, Susela?" Murray slid an arm around her waist. "Vogue, Giorgio's. And you're worth every penny of it, sweetheart."

"Speaking of flimsy propositions," Sussman said, "let's get that raft in the water."

"Not so fast," Susie whispered into Sussman's ear. "You can afford it, I happen to know."

"Let's go, troops," Murray said. "Before the beach gets too crowded." He dragged the raft over to the section of the pier where the *Superteams* race had started and dropped it in the water.

"Now, what are we supposed to be accomplishing?" Susie asked. Sussman had not explained anything. At Murray's request he had been intentionally vague about the whole exercise.

"Well, obviously, we're going to recreate the *Superteams* race," Murray said. "But I don't want any more questions, it'll ruin the experiment. Now, Lennie, I want you in the bow, just like Double-X was. Susie, you'll be Carol in the middle on the right. Hoops, you're Hal."

"And you're Cindi Beamon?" Sussman asked.

"Fact is, Hoops, I did go to her match the other night. Tried to get her to come play with us, but she's on her way to Detroit. Anyway, we're both tall, even though she's better-looking, but who's to notice?"

"Do we have to do the jump-in start like they did in the race?" asked Susie.

"Nah. Just follow my instructions." Murray held the raft steady while Lennie got in the front, and Sussman followed. Before Susie got in, Murray whispered something in her ear, then helped her into the raft, following her into the rear position.

"Just give us the word," said Lennie, and Murray did; they were off, paddling through the harbor with their hands, toward a single red buoy that bobbed in the center of the harbor. Lennie was double-windmilling like Dr. Double-X, oblivious of what was behind him; Sussman and Susie were just trying to stay afloat. When they reached the red buoy and started to turn around it, Susie, on Murray's instruction, leaned to starboard—not an overt attempt to tip the boat, just a subtle shift in body weight. Sussman seemed to catch the shift instinctively and leaned the other way, and Murray adjusted. The raft proceeded without incident, circled the buoy, and returned to the dock.

"Now what?" said Sussman, wiping a few drops of salt water off his shoulders.

"Switch positions." Sussman started to protest, but Murray had already started to move toward his seat in the middle, and Andy made the switch before the boat flipped over. "Okay, folks. Test run number two."

Sussman, now in the stern, pushed off again and they started dog-paddling once more into the harbor. This time, as they began the turn around the buoy, Murray, who was in Hal Barron's position, leaned slightly to port as the boat went into its pivot. "Whoa," said Andy, shifting his weight to starboard. "Careful, there, Mur. Water's cold." He ruddered the rubber craft around the buoy and back to the pier.

Lennie, who had been windmilling furiously during both sprints, sat up straight in the raft and took a deep breath. "This is harder work than I thought. I can see how somebody could have a heart attack if they weren't in the proper condition."

"Could be," said Murray. "If the circumstances were right. All right, crew, one more lap. Hoops, back in the middle."

"Aye, aye, captain." Sussman crawled through Murray's legs back to the center. "Pitcher of margaritas at the end?"

"Sounds like a fair proposition." Murray stared ahead for a moment, making sure everybody was in position, then pushed off from the pier. "Let it all out," he shouted as Lennie crouched forward and went into a maniacal windmill. Sussman and Susie dog-paddled a little harder than before, and the raft progressed in its herky-jerk way toward the red buoy. This time, as the boat curved for its leftward arc around the buoy, Murray, sitting in the stern, leaned ever so subtly into the turn.

"Jesus *Christ*," shouted Sussman, trying to counterbalance by shifting his weight to the right. "Dammit, Mur—"

But it was too late. The raft filled with water, then flipped over. The four paddlers were left flailing around in the Redondo Beach Harbor, three of them cursing furiously at Murray as they swam back to the pier.

15

"The problem," said Cliff Trager from his temporary office at the KCBS studios in Los Angeles, "is that he's not exactly what we'd call 'network type.'"

"Cliff, this whole assignment isn't what you'd call 'network type.'"

"But we're handling it with the dignity befitting CBS, Andy. And frankly, your friend, although I find him highly entertaining and possibly even competent—"

"Cliff, he's more than competent. He's way ahead of us on this case already, and I don't want to lose him."

"Andy," Cliff said, lighting up a pipe, a habit that Trager had when he was making a last-ditch effort to look scholarly, "look at this from a network standpoint. Did you listen to him? Suspect Boards? Murder Chalkboards?"

"I'll admit he sometimes gets carried away."

"Sometimes? Andy, I'll admit I like the guy, but he's definitely cable material. Maybe good cable material."

"Cable material?"

"Sure, you know. Like the guy that does the basketball on ESPN, the bald guy? Six games a week, all that lingo that no one understands except real basketball junkies. I think Murray's a detective junkie, Andy. He'd be great with a specialized audience, perfect for cable. But we're a network, we have a broader constituency, we have certain standards to keep."

"Cliff, is it my imagination, or does this dignity argument only seem to work when I'm on the wrong side of it?" Sussman did not think it was his imagination, he thought that just about every argument he had been in lately seemed to work only when he was on the wrong side of it. But Cliff Trager did not see the issue in terms of life's general inequities. The decision had been made. It was left to Andy to relate to Murray Glick the termination of his career as a network murder analyst.

Murray, as Andy well knew, was not a person used to dealing with rejection. Offhand, he could not remember Murray being turned down by anyone about anything—except Susie, of course, and Murray still hadn't given up on her. When Sussman finally did manage to track Murray down, he was lounging in the Jacuzzi, sipping on a piña colada, his arm around a pretty blond flight attendant whom he was regaling with an account of his Caribbean murder-mystery cruise.

"I don't suppose this can wait, Hoops," Murray said as a waiter arrived with a tray of salsa and corn chips. "Even a great detective needs sustenance once in a while. Take a load off your feet, give Suse a call."

"Murray," Sussman said, leaning into the whirlpool and stealing a sip from his friend's drink—he had a feeling he was going to need it—"bad news. You've been canceled."

"I think you're overreacting, Mur," Sussman said, but he seemed to be talking to shadows. Murray was pacing through the hotel suite with long, loping strides, puffing on a cigar, spewing bursts of smoke out over the balcony. He had packed his suitcase like the Russian Army was closing in on him; the suite was already empty except for his winter jacket, a box of videotapes, and a pair of panties that Bree had left behind in the bathroom.

"Overreacting? Hey, I'm off the case, Andrew, out the door. Think I can afford to pay two hundred and fifty bucks a night at this place—overpriced, for Chrissakes. The piña coladas were out of a can."

"Murray, you never were exactly employed by CBS. I'll cover the expenses, exorbitant as they may be."

"Cable material? Is that what he said? What the hell is that, Hoops? Look at the yo-yos they've got on your network. Hal Barron? Carol Vivian? Dignified? Please!" Murray took a last look at the medicine cabinet in the bathroom, grabbed a few Sheraton towels, and stuck them in his suitcase.

"I just don't think you should take it so seriously, Mur. You want a list of people who've been rejected by the networks? Ever hear of Bill Cosby?"

Murray walked back over to the desk and tapped the pile of videotapes. "I'm on the trail, Hoops. Believe me, I'm putting it all together."

"I do believe you. Which is why I don't want you to quit. Which is why I will continue to pay you, Murray, even to the extent of putting you up at this luxury hotel."

"Quit?" Murray opened up his Dopp kit, pulled out his brush, and gave his hair a once-over-quickly, tapping the cigar ashes in the sink. "Did I say quit?"

"Uh, I thought I heard 'out the door.'"

"I'm taking the videotapes with me, Andrew. You've got copies, right?"

"Yes, I do, Murray."

"Well, you're going to have to do a few things on your end."

"I didn't know there was any other end."

But there was; there was a Chicago end, as Murray explained while Sussman drove him up the Pacific Coast Highway to the airport. "There's the check, of course. I called around, I've got a former client with a brother at First Lakeshore, he'll photocopy the corporate charter for Dr. Double-X, Inc. We'll see who signs on the account and go from there. Then, of course, there's the Wireless story."

"Pretty vague, Mur. Some guy threatened Double-X, he threatened back. What's there to go on?"

Murray opened up the sun roof on the LeBaron and lit up another cigar. "Oh, I gotta few ideas. I'll check 'em out."

"I don't suppose you'd like to share them with your benefactor?"

Murray flashed a Cheshire-cat grin and puffed a smoke ring out through the sun roof. "I dunno, Hoops. May not be of national significance. Could be it's just cable material."

"Cut it out, Mur. I need all the information you can get."

Murray looped a long arm around Sussman's shoulder. "You need Double-X's identity, which I'll get one way or another. By the way, how's things goin' with Suse?"

"I'd say the situation just dramatically improved with your departure."

"Yeah, yeah. I'm feeling very unappreciated, I'll have you know. I expect to be best man, Hoops. Anytime now."

Sussman choked for about twenty seconds, but not with great sincerity.

"C'mon, there, Hoopsie. Time's catchin' up with you, don't let this one slip away."

"Oh, sure, Murray. How about you? When are you getting married?"

"Me?" Murray pulled down the mirror on the sun visor, as if to make sure there was no one else in the car to whom that question could have been addressed. "Me? Why should I get married? I can get it anytime I want it."

"Oh, and I can't?"

"But you don't want it anytime you can get it, Hoops. You're in love, baby. One girl, doesn't happen every day, despite what the song says."

Sussman was approaching the entrance to LAX, he hadn't bothered to ask Murray what airline he was taking, he didn't think Murray had even made a reservation. "Mur," he said, turning off the PCH, "we have big problems. Susie's put threee years in at Chavous and Birnbaum, she can hardly just walk out. And I need to be in New York, for a little longer at least—"

"United Airlines," Murray said. "Last terminal. Don't make excuses, Hoops. She'll come to New York for a few years, no problem. Soon as you pop the question."

"Sure. Kiss off three years of work. What'll she do for a career?"

"Have a baby."

"Pardon me?"

"She'll have a baby, Hoops. Maybe two babies."

"Murray, that's disgustingly chauvinistic."

"Hey, what can I say? I'm an old-fashioned guy."

Sussman turned off at the United terminal and pulled up to the departure doors. "Well, it's good having these discussions, anyway—just to remind me why I never listen to you."

"Of course you listen to me, Hoops. Who told you to ask her out in the first place?"

"The intention was already there."

"Sure it was. The road to hell is paved with good intentions, Andrew."

"Murray!"

"Labor Day's a great time for a wedding, you know. All your friends can get there."

"Murray," Sussman said, opening the lock on Glick's door. "Mr. Detective: call me as soon as that checking-account info comes in, okay?"

"Andrew, Andrew. I'm telling you, put your faith in true love. You'll thank me, years from now—you and Susie, in your split-level house in Highland Park with your two lovely children. 'Oh, Andy, if it hadn't been for that wonderful Murray . . .' "

"Who, no doubt, will be somewhere in the Caribbean with a boat full of babes and a cargo hold full of caviar and Dom Perignon."

"Andrew," Murray said, extinguishing his cigar in Sussman's ashtray, "the future looks golden." He grabbed his suitcase from the back seat and slid out of the passenger seat. "Ciao, fellow wanderer."

"Talk to you later this week," Sussman shouted, but it was too late. Murray had already disappeared into the crowd. He was on his way back to Chicago.

16

Murray Glick stood just inside the entrance to Glick Investigations, on the second floor of the Northbrook Court mall, watching as a quiet Monday-morning crowd filtered its way through the shopping center. It had been nearly three weeks since he had last been in his office, there had been the Caribbean trip and then the week in Los Angeles, and the mail had piled up. Most of it was about his mystery cruises, there were two more planned for the summer, and a Christmas cruise down to the Yucatán peninsula. Registration was nearly full already. There were a few inquiries about some actual casework, a few old customers who had remembered his work in the Highwood days when he had specialized in industrial espionage. He would refer them to someone else. A few Northbrook Court shoppers had filled out forms while he was gone: a man from Glencoe wanted a golfing buddy's handicap investigated before they left for Palm Springs, a lady from Winnetka wanted to know who had knocked up her prize-winning dalmatian.

It all made Murray reconsider whether he really needed this whole Dr. Double-X thing. It was snowing outside. Four inches had piled up already and it was supposed to get worse, the street salt was chewing up his Maserati. He'd forgotten how miserable Chicago could get in February. Why would anyone want to leave the mall, where it was always a comfortable seventy-two degrees, where he had merchandise credits everywhere? Not to mention the suburban housewives who were crazy about him—he hadn't paid for a lunch in over a year.

But Murray was restless. He had to stay sharp, one genuine assignment a year didn't seem to be asking too much. And if he *was* going to do a case, it might as well be one with plenty of publicity. Solving the Lester Beldon basketball murder had been the best thing that ever happened to him, commercially speaking—he really was thankful that Sussman had brought him into it. Now, if he could somehow find out who killed Dr. Double-X and take advantage of all the television hoopla, there was no telling where business could go.

And it *was* a murder; about that Murray had no doubt. He'd been sure from the beginning, when he'd seen Andy stumbling around on television. How could it possibly have been an accident, a guy like that, at the top of everybody's hate list? A heart attack? Geez!

Now, admittedly, arranging for the threatening letter was of questionable ethics—Murray hoped he hadn't put too bad a scare into Andy. If he'd known CBS was going to stick with the story anyway, he'd never have sent it. But after the autopsy report he'd been afraid they would drop the whole thing, and there he was, stuck in the Caribbean for two more days, he had to keep things stirred up. He'd make it up to Hoops. He'd find out who the guy was, and he'd find out who killed him and why. But you wouldn't hear about it on CBS, you could bet your sweet ass on that.

"Murray, there's a report on your desk," said Peggy, his receptionist. She had just returned from the junk-food center with a half-dozen sweet rolls and two orange juices. Murray took a doughnut and an OJ. He had promised himself to cut down on sweets but the truth was he never put on any weight. It was his metabolism, he guessed. His only interest in diets was as a conversation piece with the hundreds of girls who always seemed to be on one.

"Thanks, babe," Murray said as he wandered back toward his office. "Hold calls, I've got work to do."

"Bob Graber said he'd come by—he was the one checking about the golf handicap."

"Right. Tell him to get me a country-club history on this guy, where he's belonged. I'll take it from there." Murray closed the door behind him and walked behind his long mahogany desk. He was just about to unwrap a cigar when he noticed that there was another person standing in the far corner of the office, a portly man with a walrus mustache who was wearing the uniform of the Lake County Sheriff's Department. "Augie?"

"Hey, Murray!" Augie Fratengello waddled over to Murray, carrying several large manuscript boxes, which he plunked on the desk. He picked up a cruise application and said, "Will ya getta loada this! Northbrook Court, Mystery Cruises! To think I taught you everything you know, helluva lotta good it did ya."

"It did me large amounts of good, Augie." Murray lit his cigar and offered one to Fratengello. "You taught me everything I needed to know about hard-core detective work."

"Yeah, like how to avoid it."

"Hey, it was valuable instruction. I'll always treasure those hours spent together during the Handleman Jewelry Caper, you were a true mentor for a young detective." That was five years ago, Murray remembered. He'd been fresh out of college. Augie had been one of the investigating officers on a string of jewelry thefts.

"Yeah, yeah. I got you a date with Sam Handleman's daughter. He ever finds out it was me who introduced you, I'll be pullin' hedge-cuttin' duty in Libertyville."

"Now, now, the young lady had the most exciting three nights of her life. And anyway, how were you supposed to know she was only seventeen?"

"Hell, she told me she was twenty-three, been divorced twice." Augie took Murray's cigar and put it in his pocket; he sat down in one of Murray's leather guest chairs. The office was neat and bright, Murray's criminology degrees and licenses were on the wall, along with posters for his cruises and newspaper clippings from the

Lester Beldon case. It was about as comfortable as an office could be, considering there were no windows and the nearest fresh air was two football fields away. "Thirty-seven years, Murray. Can you believe it? Thirty-seven years, tomorrow."

"Augie, pal, you don't look a day over thirty-five."

"On the force, Murray! Thirty-seven years on the force, they're about to retire my number, you know that?"

Murray stared at Augie Fratengello, his uniform pudged at the belly and sagged at the armpits, he looked more like the Maytag repairman than a county policeman. "Augie, no one deserves a joyful retirement more than you."

"Retire to what? My kids are off all over the place, I got one in Boston, one in Frisco. My wife's sellin' real estate. What am I gonna do?"

"I don't know, Aug. Go fishing? Write your memoirs?" Murray looked at the pile of manuscripts sitting on his desk. He lifted the cover of one. The title page read:

Murder in the Skokie Lagoons
by
August G. Fratengello, Cop

"Augie, you're an author! I never would've dreamed it."

"Neither would anybody else." Augie pulled his manuscript back. "I been doin' this for five years, Murray. First I tried the novel, then I tried some TV. I did episodes for *Hill Street Blues, Columbo, Cagney and Lacey.*"

"Augie, I'm impressed, if not downright stunned. I don't watch the tube much, but get me the tapes, I'd love to see 'em."

"Tapes, are you kiddin'?" Augie opened another one of the packages, took out a screenplay, and dropped it on the desk. "Hell, I ain't sold a thing. Can't even get a phone call returned. You'd think a real-life cop, they might at least call me back."

Murray leaned back in his chair and sent a smoke ring

into the ventilating system. He could see that Augie was looking at him with imploring eyes, he could sense the impending obsequiousness, which would be awkward for both of them.

"See, Murray, what I was thinking was, you got these mystery cruises of yours, right? And I figure you'll be needing plots, you're a busy man. So just think, wouldn't it be great to have a real cop writing them?"

"Uh, well, Augie, I thought I was doing okay—"

"Murray, just listen! I got some great ideas. I got thirty-seven years' worth of cases. I got innovations, I was thinking maybe we could split the boats into teams: the Cop versus the Private Detective, just like in the movies. I bet the passengers would really love that."

Wonderful, Murray thought. He had a genuine affection for Augie Fratengello, but what would he do with him on his Yucatán Christmas singles' cruise? A bartender, maybe? But he knew Augie, the old man would want to run the show.

"Whattaya think, Mur? Give 'em a read-through, huh? I mean, it ain't Hollywood, but it's a start. And it's better'n what ya see on the tube, I guarantee."

Murray took a deep puff on his cigar. He didn't have it in him to reject Augie outright. What if this Double-X thing broke, after all—there'd be business all over. He could expand to all sorts of cruises, maybe Augie could lead a polka tour of Dubrovnik. That, of course, was contingent on his solving the case, and Murray figured it was time to get back to business. "Augie, I'll tell you what. I can't promise you anything—"

"No problem, Murray. Just read the material, okay? Think about it? Think how easy it'll be, me handlin' all the casework, leavin' you to take care of the social aspect of the cruises."

"It's an alluring thought. And it's nice to know you're always thinking of me." Murray gave Fratengello a warm handshake and ushered him out of the office.

"Call me at home, okay? Not at the office. This is kind of a secret—"

"Absolutely, Aug. Gimme two weeks. Take care of yourself." Murray bid Augie farewell and instructed Peggy to hold off any intruders for a while. He returned to his desk, pushed Augie's manuscripts onto the far corner, and picked up a single manila envelope that was marked "MG: Private."

Murray opened the envelope. Inside was the information from First Lakeshore Bank; his ex-client's brother had come through. It had been easy enough to open up the file, check the microfiche for some canceled checks, and take a picture of both; even a fairly adventurous teller could do that much. Not surprisingly, the folder revealed very little. There was no Dr. Double-X in Dr. Double-X, Inc., unless the wrestler was a transvestite. The president was a Shirley Adams, the treasurer a Carol Quincy. They were the only two signers on the account; their signatures looked very similar. The address was a PO box in Elk Grove—bogus, Murray assumed. There was a hold on the file, indicating that the canceled checks and deposit slips were not to be mailed out.

Murray's source had enclosed photocopies of several months' bank statements, along with a photocopy of several checks that had been written out to cash and endorsed by Shirley Adams. Dr. Double-X had evidently withdrawn his money by means of these checks. Murray could envision the wrestler disguising himself as an old babushka and trundling into run-down currency exchanges; he guessed that the locations of the receiving banks on the backs of the checks would match Double-X's wrestling itinerary. It might cost him money on every check he cashed, but that was the price he paid for complete anonymity. The canceled checks, Murray was informed, had never been picked up at the bank. The current balance was $14,303.93.

So it was not much to go on. He would have to call Andy and tell him that there was still no positive ID, unless he wanted to go on national TV and claim that Dr. Double-X was really Shirley Adams. He would hold on to the copy of the canceled checks; the signatures could be of some use to him later on. He would call his source at First Lakeshore and ask him to keep tabs on the remaining balance, in case anybody made a withdrawal.

But Murray was still convinced that the way to solve this case was to work backward from the murder. He thought about his experiment with the rafts. It had been pointed out, principally by a sopping-wet and frothing Susie Ettenger, that it made no difference what Hal Barron or Carol Vivian or Cindi Beamon did in the boat; if a huge wrestler like Dr. Double-X had had a seizure and toppled over, he would take everyone down with him. But if you were going to kill someone, Murray reasoned, and you wanted to make it look like he'd had a heart attack and drowned, then you'd want to make damn sure he fell in the drink. And if anyone could have done that, it was Cindi.

Why? wondered Murray as he went through his files, trying to pull some data from the Caribbean cruise. What possible connection could there be between a deliciously attractive volleyball player and a disgusting pig of a professional wrestler? Murray found what he was looking for; it was the applications for the cruise, with home and work telephone numbers. One of the women on the cruise was a physical therapist at the Rehabilitation Center of Chicago; she and Murray had conversed amicably several times on the trip, but had not had what you might call an instant magnetism toward each other.

Her name was Terry Tollison. She had not been especially enthusiastic about the mystery aspect of the cruise, she was more interested in lying on the deck and drinking strawberry daiquiris and listening to Bach on her Walkman. That was okay with Murray; he had dated therapists before, he knew there was a burnout factor among people who worked so many hours with patients who were handicapped or crippled—a cruise in February seemed just the right idea. He had talked with

Terry briefly, out of entrepreneurial concern, but he hadn't pushed things, he was getting along quite adequately with little Bree at the time.

Now he was glad that he hadn't antagonized her; he wasn't unaware that he had that effect on certain women at certain times, although he guessed it wasn't his fault—hey, most people liked him. He found her work number and called her there; he was his usual cheery, flattering self. True, Terry Tollison wasn't exactly blown away at the prospect of seeing him again, but she wasn't doing anything for lunch, and she agreed to let Murray pick her up at work.

It was a long shot, Murray thought as he sloshed through the snow that was piling up in the Northbrook Court parking lot. It was a hunch. But he figured it this way: Dr. Double-X may have been damned good at covering up his identity, but he wasn't a professional, he had to slip up somewhere. And his murderer probably wasn't a professional either—just someone pissed off beyond redemption.

On the other hand, Murray said to himself, I, Murray Glick, *am* a professional, albeit slightly out of practice. And I *will* crack this case.

There were, after all, standards to be met, and reputations to keep, and cruises to fill.

17

It was snowing harder by the time Murray reached downtown; you could barely see Lake Michigan from the Rehab Center and it was only a few blocks away. The traffic on Michigan Avenue was jammed, people were heading home early, but Murray knew that Terry Tollison would stay for the duration of her shift. He parked the Maserati on Erie Street and slogged his way down the block and a half to the entrance.

The Rehabilitation Center of Chicago was about as cheerful a building as you could ask for, considering its purpose; it was a treatment center for some of the most debilitating injuries a human being can endure. Even in the middle of the snowstorm its glassy entrance was warm and clean, the floors polished. Murray walked past the restaurant and gift shop. He took the elevator up to the fourth floor, where Terry worked. Her floor was a halfway house, as she'd described it to him on the cruise. The patients there had almost finished their stay, which might have ranged anywhere from three weeks to a year or longer. They were getting ready to integrate themselves back into the community.

Murray passed all sorts of people in wheelchairs— they came in all shapes and sizes, many suffered from paralysis of some sort—some managed to walk on walkers. Murray had a smile for all of them, he said hello to everyone he saw, and they all smiled or waved. Murray knew that some people felt queasy in situations like this, they didn't like to look at the horrible damages that could happen to people in the twinkling of an eye, in car accidents or football games or swimming pools, changing their lives forever. As for his own unremitting friendliness, Murray figured it was an inherent quality of his; he didn't work at it consciously. He supposed that as a detective, he had to treat everybody equally; everyone was a potential perpetrator—it was a kind of general suspicion that had its flip side in a common respect for people.

Murray stopped outside Terry Tollison's office. He could see her standing by a small desk, next to a model skeleton that had a Walter Payton warm-up jacket draped over its back and a Cubs cap tilted on its cranium. She wore a light blue dress that appeared to be a uniform, although it looked good on her. She had a nice figure, Murray had seen her in a swimsuit; her amber hair had been cut short since the cruise—too short, Murray thought, she could do a little more with it, but he wasn't going to suggest it over lunch. She was talking to a little boy in a wheelchair, she was tapping on the skeleton and then on the boy's legs, moving his knees up and down as he protested weakly.

"We did those downstairs," said the little boy. "They don't help anyway. Can't I go play catch now?"

"Craig, we're going through the whole routine. You're going home in two weeks, I'm not going to be standing there looking after you. And I don't want you trying to talk your Mom and Dad out of finishing your exercises every morning."

Murray knocked on the open door; he assumed Terry had not seen him standing there but she had, she flashed him a tight smile and waved him inside. "Hi, Murray," she said as the boy in the wheelchair pushed away. "Craig, say hello to Mr. Glick. He's a world-famous detective—like Sherlock Holmes!"

"Hiya, champ!" said Murray, tousling the boy's thin blond hair. "How ya doin'!"

"Fine," said Craig. He looked to be about ten years old; he had rosy cheecks and wiry arms, but his legs appeared lifeless. He wheeled up to Murray, almost close enough to touch him, and stared right at his chest. "You're Sherlock Holmes?"

"A modern adaptation," said Terry with a sardonic grin.

"Sure—where's your gun?" The little boy leaned over in his wheelchair and reached inside Murray's wool-lined trench coat.

"Careful, pardner," Murray said, leaning backward. "Men have died for less than that."

Craig stuffed his hand into Murray's coat pocket. He searched for a pistol, but found only a four-color brochure for the Yucatán cruise. "C'mon, you're not really a detective."

"Watch it, kiddo, that'll give you a nasty paper cut." Murray poked the boy in the ribs and snatched the brochure back, then tickled him in the belly button and wheeled him toward the door.

Craig laughed; he warmed up right away to Murray. Even after Terry dismissed him, he loitered by the door for a few minutes, bantering with a secretary as the two adults exchanged more formal greetings. He was still there when Murray and Terry walked away to lunch. He hung on to Murray's hand as they headed for the elevator. Murray laughed and joked with him all the way, asking him about the Cubs' chances next year, whispering to him a few things about little girls that Terry probably hadn't told him.

"You get along well with kids," Terry said softly after they had boarded the elevator. "I wouldn't have guessed that from the cruise."

"Hey, there weren't any kids on board."

"By decision of the cruise director, I take it."

"Next time I'll have a family boat," said Murray, helping her on with her down ski jacket. "Can I count on you to be social director?"

Terry admitted that he probably couldn't. She wrapped a scarf around her neck and followed Murray down the street to Gino's East for a Chicago-style pizza. It was only a few blocks away; with the snow raging, it didn't make much sense to drive anywhere.

"What I meant," Terry explained, "was that you just didn't seem, uh, the parenting type."

"True, but I *am* a perpetual adolescent, according to some that claim to know me well, so kids and I get along just fine." He was doing pretty well, he figured, he was softening her up. Murray hated to be so cynical about his performance; after all, it wasn't like he was faking it or anything. He *did* like people, kids especially, he knew they wanted to be talked to and joked with and looked in the eye. And he liked Terry too; after three weeks with Bree he was in the mood for someone with a brain bigger than a pterodactyl's. Just the same, he had a job to do, and by the time the pizza had arrived, he had managed to steer the conversation to the subject of Steve Beamon.

"Aha," Terry said, "a special interest in a patient. I knew there was a reason for all this."

"Hey, gimme a break, Ter. There's plenty of ways I can get patient information without taking a beautiful girl out for lunch in the middle of a blizzard."

Terry flashed a disbelieving smirk. "Just tell me you're not working for the insurance companies, that's all. If you're trying to find some way to stick some poor kid with a six-figure hospital bill, which in reality *we* would be stuck with—"

"Terry, Terry. Does a world-famous detective who leads cruises to the Caribbean—and incidentally Yucatán next Christmas, you don't want to miss it—does he need to find employment from shady insurance companies?"

Terry nibbled on her slice of deep-dish pizza and stared at Murray through a glass of Diet Pepsi. "So you're just a concerned basketball fan, is that it? You're a pretty tall guy, looks like you might have played a little."

"Third-string forward in high school," Murray said; it wasn't often that he admitted he was third-string at anything, but he needed a little sympathy. "Never played except when we were thirty points behind. Look, Terry,

I don't need to consort with hoods. I represent only the side of truth, justice, and the American Way—"

"And I represent my patients, confidentially of course."

"Well, I'd hardly expect you to betray that for me, Ter." Murray leaned toward her. "So just shake your head yes or no. If anything I ask is confidential, give me a nice hard slap right in the kisser."

"I bet a few girls would love to trade places with me right now," Terry laughed.

"I'll ignore that. Now: Steve Beamon was injured in a swimming accident. Correct?"

"Okay."

"He took a ten-foot dive in an eight-foot river, I think that's what I read."

Terry choked on her pizza. "You could say that."

"But. There were certain things about this accident, Miss Tollison, that, let us say, were not thoroughly reported. Am I right?"

"No. What kind of things?"

"The time, date, circumstances of the accident."

"I thought it was reported pretty completely, Murray. The *Tribune* had a whole Sunday feature on it. They went up to the Wolf River in Wisconsin, talked to the doctors and the paramedics, talked to the kids from his fraternity that were rafting the river with him. It wasn't easy for Steve, either; at that stage of his hospitalization he was still coming to terms with his paralysis and he had to read about what a jerk he was right in the Sunday newspaper."

Murray sipped on a beer. "I can imagine. Any chance of recovery?"

"No."

"Of even walking?"

"No. I mean, you can always hope for a miracle, but that's not our job. We have to cope with reality."

Murray wolfed down some more pizza and looked into Terry's eyes—she didn't seem to be hiding anything, she seemed almost disappointed that he hadn't presented a greater challenge to her integrity. "Terry, if I'm out of bounds here, let me know. But was there anybody at the scene of that accident other than college kids? Anybody that might have precipitated an altercation that would have made that accident less accidental?"

Terry shook her head. "Honestly, Murray, no one. Believe me, this is all information you could have gotten from the papers. It was a stupid accident; most of the accidents that leave people with us are. They were rafting down the river, they were drunk. Steve Beamon took a swan dive out of the raft, he didn't realize the river was only a few feet deep. It's a hell of a price to pay for one too many."

"Can't argue with that," Murray said softly. "So the insurance company paid?"

"After their usual foot-dragging."

"And now, I understand it, he's going back to school?"

"Starting in the summer. He was never much of a student, basketball was everything. But all he's got right now is that scholarship, he has to get the education. You never know how a kid'll turn out, but he has a chance."

Murray leaned forward; he noticed that his hand was touching Terry's. "Ter, is it possible I could talk to him for a few moments?"

"Um . . . it would help if I knew what for."

"I'm not sure. I've got confidentiality problems too. You'll just have to trust me. And I promise, Steve's best interests will in no way be compromised."

Terry drew her hand back. "Well, it's a free country. There's nothing I can do to stop you, Murray, unless he asks you to leave. Just remember, it's a nervous time for him. He's got to go back out there and start a new life. So far, he's only made it a couple of blocks."

"I'll be good. I'll tell you all about it over dinner Saturday night," Murray heard himself say. "How about it?"

"I don't know," Terry said with a wink. "Am I putting myself in peril's way, associating with such a known scourge of master villains?"

"Life's a gamble, baby." Murray took her hand again. "But just to be safe, we'll do something downtown, where nobody knows me."

"Someplace like Rush Street, where we'll be safe from the criminal element?"

"Maybe even dinner and the theater. Trust me, Ter, I'm a classy guy."

Terry coughed, took a deep breath, and let it out slowly. "Oh, sure, why not?" She slipped her hand in her purse and paid for half the bill, over Murray's protests. It was not, he figured, the most enthusiastic acceptance of a date he'd ever had, but what the hell, yes was yes.

When they had finished lunch, the snowstorm had gotten worse, it had all the makings of a classic Chicago blizzard. Murray had the feeling that he would end up spending the night downtown, although he guessed that spending it with Terry would be too much to ask. He assumed that finding Steve Beamon would be easy enough, he would talk to the kid for a few minutes, then hole up at the Drake for the evening. But he was wrong, Beamon was nowhere in sight.

"You might try the Rail," Terry said as she hurried off for a therapy session with some lower-back patients. "It's a bar down the street, a half-block before Michigan. We passed it on the way to Gino's."

"A bar?"

"Well, he's not confined to quarters. If he's going to have a beer now and then, at least we know about it, we can work with it. It's a place to go for an hour or so. He's supposed to be back at four, if you want to wait."

Murray didn't; he had visions of his Maserati ending up beneath a twelve-foot snowdrift and not thawing out until June. He waved at Terry and started to say good-bye, but it was too late, she was already walking down the hall with one of the doctors. Murray winced; he thought he had sensed a spark of romance, but maybe he was wrong. He headed for the elevator, then stopped and looked back. Terry had turned around too; she was looking over her shoulder. They stared at each other for an instant, then both of them turned back as if the moment had never happened.

Murray grinned, tossed his keys up in the air, and caught them behind his back. He zipped up his trench coat and headed for the Rail.

Murray sat inside his Maserati. He had not gone directly to the bar, he'd decided on a little makeup adjustment first. He felt slightly silly, fastening a fake mustache and sprinkling a little powder on his hair, but all the advertising and media exposure had made it necessary. Not that he wanted to hide anything from Steve Beamon, who might not be in a condition to recognize him anyway. There was just this thought gnawing inside him that something was amiss, and Murray Glick trusted his instincts.

Once inside, it occurred to Murray that he had seen all sorts of bars before: bikers' bars, gamblers' bars, most recently yuppie bars. But he had never been to a "chair" bar before—practically all the customers at the Rail were patients or former patients at the Rehab Center. The bar was lined with wheelchairs; some of them were clustered around small tables at the back, others were folded against the wall, their owners sitting on special bar stools, there was an assortment of canes and walkers lying around.

Murray considered his next move; he decided to just walk on in, appearing slightly tipsy, which wasn't too hard—he had had a couple of beers at Gino's and he was falling in love again. He threaded his way through the haze of cigarette smoke, the jumbles of conversations. If anyone was looking at him funny, he couldn't tell. He didn't gawk, he grabbed a stool at the end of the bar, ordered a beer, and looked around for Steve Beamon. Beamon wasn't hard to find; he was six-foot-three and lanky, even in a wheelchair it was obvious that he had been a basketball player. Beamon sat at a

table a few feet from the other end of the bar with two
other men in wheelchairs. He didn't look drunk. He had
a loopy smile on his face and appeared to be telling a
story.

Murray was about to walk over and introduce himself,
when he saw another figure who looked slightly familiar,
a stocky middle-aged man with black hair that had a
few gray streaks in it and muttonchop sideburns. The
man was sitting a table away, in a wheelchair. Murray
rubbed his eyes. Could it be? Had too many years gone
by? Murray squinted through the smoke; he was looking
for a scar under the man's left ear. He thought he found
it. Barney Hennesey?

Five years ago, when Murray had just come out of
college to work as a security-systems analyst, he had
been involved in a case of industrial espionage. Someone
had been stealing the codes to security systems and selling them to a burglary ring; it was Murray's first real
case and he watched as his superiors did most of the
work. One of the culprits had been Barney Hennesey,
who had been working for the security-systems company, but was being paid off by the burglary ring. When
he was finally caught, he was able to plea-bargain in
return for his testimony; as far as Murray could tell, he
had served a few years in Joliet. He was obviously out
now.

It wasn't exactly shocking that Barney Hennesey might
end up in a wheelchair. There certainly might have been
a revenge factor among his former compatriots, certainly in his line of work it wasn't unusual to sustain a
disabling injury. Still, Murray was a suspicious man.
He picked up his beer and staggered across the room.
"Stevie!" he blurted. "Steve Beamon! Hey, buddy, how
ya doin'?"

Beamon raised his head and stopped his story. He
shrugged and waved. "Hey, how ya doin', pal? Have a
seat."

Murray stumbled over. "Stevie, babe, I'm a fellow

alum, ISU 'sixty-four. Damn shame, Steve-o." Murray tripped over a chair and fell, pitching his beer forward. It spilled all over the table next to Beamon.

"Hey, careful, buddy. Take care of those wheels, never know when you'll lose 'em."

Murray lay on the floor, watching the beer ooze off the table, dripping onto Barney Hennesey and another fellow sitting next to him. "Aw, geez," he said, pulling himself up. "Aw, Steve-o. I just cried when I heard what happened to you. I sure hope they're takin' care of you."

Beamon looked around self-consciously. This was what he came into the Rail to get away from. "I'm doin' fine, buddy. Damn fine. Looks like you need a little help yourself, though."

"Aw, hell no," Murray said. "Hell no, jus' a few business setbacks. Thought maybe we could sit back, talk a little hoops, thought you might like to do that. Hey, bartender," Murray shouted, "how 'bout a replacement?"

The bartender walked slowly from behind the bar; he flashed Murray a broad smile. "Hi there, buddy, what can I do ya for?"

Murray pulled himself up from the floor. The bartender was definitely a healthy man, but Murray wasn't looking for a demonstration. "Well, I thought I might have a beer and go over old times."

"Well, old-timer, I'll tell you what. It's a terrible blizzard out there, and it's gettin' worse, and I bet you've got a long way to go."

"Uh," Murray said, "jes to Northbrook, that's all."

"That could take you all afternoon, fella. And you've had enough to drink. How about hittin' the road and leavin' my friends to themselves?"

Murray stood up straight; he smiled at Steve Beamon, who smiled back.

"Thanks for droppin' by," Beamon said. "Really. Call me when you're feelin' better. We'll talk hoops. Okay?"

"Sure," said Murray as the bartender led him out the door. "Nice kid, ain't he?"

"The best," said the bartender, escorting Murray back into the snow.

But Murray did not go far; he made it back to the Maserati, shoveled the snow off the windshield, and stared out across the street, keeping an eye on the Rail as its patrons wheeled in and out. It was three-thirty, Beamon would be leaving pretty soon, but it was Barney Hennesey that Murray was thinking about. The old spilled-beer trick was pretty elementary, he almost felt ashamed that he'd used it, but he had a job to do. He was not sure of the results, though. When the beer had trickled off the table onto Barney's legs, Murray had thought he had seen him flinch; it was hard to tell.

At a quarter till four, Steve Beamon left the bar. He wheeled out into the snow, it was tough going, but he made it into the street and wheeled his way down Erie, toward the Rehab Center, followed by the two men that had been sitting at the table with him. Murray remained in his Maserati, shifting his glance from the Rehab Center to the Rail.

At 4:20 Barney Hennesey wheeled out of the Rail, powering the chair with his swarthy arms. He didn't head back to the Rehab Center, though, he headed west toward Michigan Avenue, turning right at an alley.

Murray started the Maserati, keeping a few feet behind and stopping where the alley began. He pulled a pair of binoculars from his glove compartment and peered through them. He saw Hennesey wait in the alley for a few moments; then a van pulled up beside him. The door of the van opened and a ramp descended. Hennesey wheeled the chair toward the ramp, but he got stuck. The snow had accumulated, it was hard to tell where the curb was. The wheelchair had tottered off the curb, snow had gotten into the wheels. The driver, a smaller man, got out and tried to help Hennesey, but he couldn't budge him.

Murray, still looking through the binoculars, saw the two men exchange words. The snow was falling harder, he couldn't see as clearly. But there was no doubting what he saw next. Barney Hennesey looked around him and pushed the driver away. He raised himself out of the wheelchair. He picked it up, shook the snow out of it, and placed it in the van. Then he walked into the van, crawled into the passenger seat, and shut the door behind him.

It was a miracle.

18

It had been a while since Murray Glick had done this sort of hard-core detective work; it harked him back to his pre-mall days, which were also his pre-Maserati days. Following a van in a raging blizzard in his little sports car was not exactly out of the detective's handbook, but hey, you made the best of what you had. At least the van was easy to spot; the Maserati, by contrast, was nearly invisible and Murray doubted whether Barney Hennesey had the slightest idea he was being followed.

Murray tailed the van across town to the Kennedy Expressway and sat there, stalled in traffic, for almost an hour; it seemed like all of downtown had decided to abandon work for the day and head for home. The van exited at Tuohy, which was also jammed; Murray was barely able to keep an eye on it, he was several cars behind and had to dart through whatever openings he could find. The snow was getting heavier and if the van got more than a block in front of him he would lose it.

Finally the van turned off Tuohy onto a side street, Murray couldn't even tell which one it was, the signs were covered with snow. He slipped past a bakery truck and made his turn just as the van was veering west again, fortunately for the last time. It stopped off at an apartment building. The passenger door opened; Barney Hennesey and the driver got out and walked upstairs.

Murray left his Maserati a block away and slogged up the street; he was parked illegally, but five years of living in Chicago had taught him that the snowplows would not be along anytime soon. He trudged toward the apartment building, he could see that the driver and Hennesey were conversing by the door. He didn't have much time. He approached the van from the rear and gave the bumper a kick; the snow dropped off the license plate and Murray wrote the number down. He looked around for any writing on the sides, but there was none. He saw the driver make his way back toward him, so he turned around and walked back down the block.

When the van had left, Murray returned to the apartment building. Barney Hennesey's name was right on the mailbox; he didn't appear to be running away from anyone. Murray thought about going up and paying him a visit, but he didn't want to overplay his hand. He suspected there were a few things he could find out about Barney's life that would make a future meeting more productive, and besides, the Maserati was beginning to look like an Indian burial mound. Murray retreated to his sports car, lit up a cigar, and headed back for Tuohy Avenue. There was a certain excitement to being back on the trail again, but enough was enough—there was a whole stack of cruise applications waiting for him at the office, lest he forget what was paying the bills these days.

Northbrook Court had certain fortresslike qualities about it; to Murray Glick's knowledge the place had never closed. One day and thirteen inches of snow later, it was not about to set a precedent. Murray doubted whether many suburban shoppers would fight their way along Edens Highway, which had been down to two lanes all morning, or try to negotiate the snow-clotted arterial streets which fed into the mall's entrance. But Northbrook Court's corporate operators had little sympathy, they expected all their stores to be open for business, whether there was any or not.

As it turned out, Murray's receptionist, Peggy, had little sympathy either—she had held down the fort for three weeks while her boss was soaking up the sun in the Caribbean and Los Angeles; she didn't think it was asking too much for Murray to occupy his own office for a while, at least until she found the owner of the snow-plow who had rammed her Honda Civic from a perfectly legal parking space in front of her apartment and deposited it on someone's lawn a block and a half away. So Murray was marooned in Peggy's swivel chair, his feet propped up on her desk, puffing smoke rings into the ghostlike walkway; there were so few people in the mall that their footsteps echoed all the way from Neiman-Marcus to Sears.

Murray had spent the first hour of his day plunging through old records of cases he had worked on several years back, when his office was in Highwood. Was it really this long since he had actively pursued a criminal? The Lester Beldon case hardly counted, Andy Sussman had done all the legwork on that one, and there were police assigned to that case from the start. He was alone this time, and he needed a friendly police officer who might help him out. He'd been trying all morning to find an alternative to the solution suggested by the pile of manuscripts he was now using as a doorstop, but he was out of ideas. He picked up the phone and called up the Lake County Sheriff's Office.

"Murray!" said Augie Fratengello. "Hey, kiddo, I didn't think you'd get back to me so soon—"

"Listen, Augie, I don't mean to interrupt you there, I've just got a—"

"Hey! Ixnay on the ookbays, okay? Didn't I give you my home number? The walls have ears."

"Aug—"

"You talk, I'll listen. Boy, I didn't think you'd get through the stuff so quickly."

"Augie," said Murray, retrieving one of the manuscripts from the floor and opening it up, "I'm not exactly through the ookbay yet. I'm up to page ninety-two here, in *Murder in the Skokie Lagoon*. The part where the carp fisherman sees the Mafia guy—"

"Good, good, Mur. That was based on a real case,

1963." Fratengello dropped his voice. "Looks like I got visitors. We'll talk about it later, okay? Call me at home. So long, pal—"

"Augie! Wait, don't hang up. I need your help on something."

"Gee, Murray, I'm on duty here. Try 555-3232 after six—"

"It's police work, Augie. I'm working on a case."

"A case?" There was a moment of stunned silence, then Fratengello said, "What the hell, Murray? What's the point of being in the goddamned shopping mall with your cruise brochures and everything if you're gonna do roadwork again?"

"Just temporary, Augie. I'm not quite ready to be put out to stud."

"That I could handle, if it wasn't too late. Listen, Mur, I got a pension comin' in six months, maybe you're asking the wrong guy."

"Nah, Augie, not to worry. Small job, license number and a parole report."

Augie chuckled into the telephone. "That's it? Christ, Murray, are you a lazy bum. Ain't you got a computer? We got high-school kids gettin' that kinda information outta their bedrooms."

"Well, Aug, after you dropped in the other day, I just thought it would be nostalgic to rekindle an old relationship—could be the last chance before you hang up the holster." Murray searched his legal pad for the license number. Computers? He supposed he could have wandered over to the Radio Shack on the first floor, bought some software, and tried to figure it out, or he could always ask Peggy—for all he knew, she did that type of thing every day. But Augie Fratengello was much more user-friendly, and besides, Murray had gotten used to letting his fingers do the walking.

"Hang on," Augie said after Murray read him the number and filled him in on Barney Hennesey. "Won't be a moment." And a minute later he said, "You're still gonna read the ookbay, though, Mur? Be honest, you get the info anyway."

"Sure, Aug. Have it all done by the weekend. Send me some outlines for the cruises, while you're at it. Come back to the mall next week, I'll treat you to some tacos, piece-a-pizza, dog-on-a-stick, you name it."

"Murray, you better watch yourself, that stuff ain't no good for ya—I got an earful from my doctor last week—"

"All in the metabolism, Augie. I'm in primo condition."

Fratengello cleared his throat, then said, "Okay, Mr. Glick, here is it: Barney Hennesey served three years of a three-to-ten for burglary and conspiracy to defraud, released on parole two years ago."

"Still on parole?"

"You bet. Four more years."

"If he violates?"

"Back in the can."

"What a shame. The license plates?"

"Just a second . . ." Murray thought he heard the clicking of a keyboard, then a whir. "Here we go. Winner's Circle, Inc. First National Bank Building, Chicago."

"Winner's Circle? What the hell is that, Augie?"

"Beats me. Suite 840, go look 'em up."

"Thanks, Augie, I will. Take care now, buddy."

"You'll still call in a couple of weeks?"

"Absolutely."

"And be careful, Murray. I bet you're rusty, you could screw up. You need any help, you know where to turn."

"Sure thing, Augie." Murray jotted the address down and said good-bye to Augie Fratengello. He was glad to hear that Barney was out on parole, cooperation would be much easier that way. As for Winner's Circle, Murray had several options, and none of them seemed very wise at the moment. He decided not to call and ask who they were or what they did—he didn't want to arouse the slightest bit of suspicion that someone was snooping around. He was not crazy about schlepping downtown to peek in their office, either—he needed to keep his own headquarters open and it would take him most of the day just to get to the Loop and back.

On a hunch, he decided it was time to call Andy Sussman. "Winner's Circle" had a sporting ring to it, it sounded like Andy's territory, and he hadn't informed his friend about the check info yet. Besides, it was time the client got some reassurance—and enough information to keep the Dr. Double-X story on *Sports Spectacular.*

19

Andy Sussman was sitting in the steam bath with Susie Ettenger when the call came; they had just finished a brisk set of tennis, and the combination of fatigue and a blanket of steam heat had soaked most of the ambition out of him. As he lay prone on the wooden bench, absorbing a massage from his girlfriend, it occurred to Sussman that it was not just the tennis that had drained him; in the several days since Murray had left, the intensity level with which he had been fighting off the whole *Superteams*/Double-X predicament had been trickling away. He had come to the realization that there wasn't anything he could do about the fifteen-minute segments airing each Saturday. He had done all that could reasonably be expected to cooperate with Cliff Trager; all he could do now was try not to look too ridiculous, hope that Murray came up with something, or wait for the story to fizzle out.

In addition, Sussman realized that the resentment that he had built up toward the wrestlers was melting away. Stranded as he was on the Left Coast, it didn't hurt to have his old friend Lennie Weintraub around. When Susie went back to Chicago, Lennie would be just about his only friend left, with the possible exception of Cliff and the bartender at Pancho and Wong's. Lennie and his wife had invited him over for dinner tomorrow night, and even though the company would be The Thing and Leona Z and Wireless, who was still taking sanctuary at the Condo in Redondo, Sussman found himself preferring their company to Trager's.

In the meantime, Andy had one more day with Susie, and he meant to take advantage of every minute of it. They had woken up at seven to play tennis; as soon as the sun poked its way through a few more inches of South Coast haze, they would exit the steam bath and head for the beach. Sussman was absorbing the last tender touches of Susie's back rub when the Mexican attendant knocked on the glass door, wiped away the steam, and showed them the telephone.

"It's Murray," Susie said after opening the door a crack and slipping outside. She listened for a few seconds, then stuck her head back inside. "He says it snowed thirteen inches there yesterday."

"Did you give him our most profound sympathy?"

"What sympathy? I've got to go back there tomorrow. Here."

Sussman took the phone and switched places with Susie, grabbing a glass of grapefruit juice from the spa attendant. He listened as Murray first explained that the canceled check from Crash Kopeck was not exactly the light at the end of the tunnel and then described the encounter with Steve Beamon. Andy wasn't sure he was happy to hear about it all; it shook him from his hard-earned complacency—he might have to do some actual reporting after all. The name Winner's Circle did ring a bell, though. "I think it's an agency," he told Murray. "Sports agency. There was a guy, I think his name was Buddy Beddicker, he made a lot of money five or six years ago, then incorporated . . . Hold on." Sussman tapped on the door to the steam bath and Susie opened it a crack; the steam poured out of it like a boiling teakettle. "Suse, heard of Winner's Circle, sports agency in Chicago? Isn't that Buddy Beddicker?"

Susie stepped outside, moist with steam and sweat. "That's exactly who it is. Why?"

"They've had a tail on Steve Beamon, according to Murray."

Susie walked over to a nearby shower head. She jerked the chain and doused herself, then walked back over to Andy and sat down, playfully spritzing him with water. "The sleuth's been hard at work, I see. I suppose this is relevant in some completely unsupportable way?"

"Hoops," said Murray, who was listening to the conversation over the phone, "ask your adorable attorney-friend if Winner's Circle has any history of brushes with the law."

"Suse, are they legit?"

"Never been convicted," Susie said. "All you can ask of someone in the eighties."

"Hoops," Murray shouted into the phone. "Any indictments?"

Sussman passed the question along and Susie shrugged, flicking a few more drops of water into his juice. "I'm not a walking encyclopedia of legal trivia," she said. "Look, Andy, the only sports contract I ever negotiated was yours. Bernie Chavous did a few basketball guys, I don't recall any big skirmishes with Buddy Beddicker. But it's easy enough to find out. Have Murray look it up in the Civil Index—if he can pull himself out of the mall and get over to the Daley Center, he'll find everything he needs. Tell him if he comes up with anything listed under Winner's Circle or Buddy Beddicker to call me at work tomorrow, I'll look it over."

Sussman repeated all that to Murray, then said, "And while you're at it, you might give Dwayne Reddick a call—they're on the road right now, but they'll be back tomorrow, I think." Reddick was a power forward on the Chicago Flames basketball team; he and Andy had been close during Sussman's play-by-play years. "Dwayne's tuned in to all the agent gossip, Mur. If there's anything juicy about Beddicker, he'd probably know it."

"Fine," Murray said. "And I want you to know, Hoops, I've been doing some serious wilderness trekking for this case. Tell Susie I'll look forward to thawing out with her at lunch when she gets back."

"Don't push your luck, O Great Sleuth. You find a new love yet?"

"Hoops, I could extol the virtues of the sensational young lady I'm having dinner with Saturday night for hours upon end, but I don't want to run up your long-distance charges."

"*My* long-distance charges?"

"Hey, I work for you, right? Remember, I could be staying at the Sheraton."

"I almost forgot."

"And one other thing, Hoops. None of this information goes to CBS, okay? Strictly between us."

"Murray, you just told me you were working for me. What good does all this do if I can't use it?"

"You can use it. Eventually. But let's you and I be the judge of that, okay? Not the yo-yos that employ you."

Sussman was about to launch into a gallant defense of the yo-yos that employed him, but that, too, would be a waste of his nickel. He would rather hear about Murray's new girlfriend. He promised Murray that everything would remain deep background, said good-bye, and gave the phone back to the spa attendant.

"Surf's up, moondoggie," Susie said as Sussman stepped back toward the sauna. She wrapped a towel around his neck, dragged him a few feet backward, and pointed at the ocean. The sun had burst through the haze, the breeze had dwindled to nothing, the beach was beckoning. "I've only got a few more hours, Andy, let's hit it."

"I don't suppose," Sussman said as he led his girlfriend away from the spa cabana and out of the Sheraton, "that you've given this living-arrangement business any further thought."

"You think we should buy a place in Redondo and spend all our weekends here until Memorial Day?"

"That wasn't what I was referring to." Andy and Susie dodged a Porsche and a VW bug as they crossed the street. They cut through the parking lot, it was nearly empty, and headed toward the arcades and foodstands at the Redondo Pier. "I was thinking more along the lines of—"

"I know what you were thinking, Andy." Susie stopped beside a stand that was selling sunglasses and considered a pair of blue-framed reflectors.

"Don't buy those, sweetheart. I want to see those beautiful eyes of yours."

"All the time?"

"More than just weekends."

"Andy," Susie said, "I tried New York. I can't work for C and B there, they're strictly Chicago. I'd have to pass another bar exam, I'd have to start at the bottom, with complete strangers. It won't work."

"Who says you have to work at a law firm?" Sussman bought a large pink lemonade, stuck two straws in it, and took Susie's arm as they strolled past the shops and boutiques and out toward the beach. "There's lots of firms that need legal consultants. Not to mention entertainment agencies—you've already got me as a client, that should be enough clout to get your foot in the door somewhere."

"Maybe I don't want to be strictly an agent," Susie said, taking her tennis shoes off as they reached the sand. "I like the variety of cases we get at Chavous and Birnbaum. I like doing a pro-bono case every once in a while. And I know Chicago, I can deal with the people there. It's not just a new firm I'd have to cope with in New York, it's new judges and prosecutors and city officials."

"Well, it wouldn't be forever. Look, Suse, as soon as I get where I want to at CBS—"

"Andy, why is it that *I'm* the one that's supposed to do all the sacrificing?" Susie grabbed the lemonade away from Sussman. She stopped in her tracks, about twenty yards from the ocean, and sat in the sand.

"Well, *somebody* has to do it. It's either you or me, we can't compromise and move to Cleveland."

"And I'm the one whose career is more flexible?"

"For the time being. We've gone over that before."

"And there's nothing that I should expect in return

from you, Andy? If I quit my job and take up permanent housekeeping in New Yawk—"

"Of course, there's plenty you should expect. Love. Friendship. A shoulder to cry on. All the reasons we want to be together in the first place."

"Commitment?" Susie whispered as she spread out her beach towel and tilted her face toward the sun.

"Of course commitment. If we weren't committed, we'd have split up long ago." Sussman hesitated, as if he were playing the last sentence back to himself; even he didn't believe that. "Susie," he said, "would you really come to New York?"

"Did I say that?"

"If I, uh, committed?"

"Are you?"

"Would you?"

"I don't know." Susie winked and kicked some sand in Sussman's direction. "I think it's one of those things that you never know for sure until the situation actually arises."

"No hypothetical answers?"

"Forget it, bub. Pays your money, takes your chances."

Andy sat down in the sand and focused on Susie's sparkling brown eyes. He took out some suntan lotion and splashed it on her back. "Well, I guess it's something to think about. In the meantime, I suppose I should try to extricate myself from one tricky situation at a time."

"Meaning?"

"This Double-X business."

Susie laughed and turned sideways toward the ocean, her hair brushing against Sussman's knees. "Right, right. Well, keep me posted."

"Of course. And you'll be keeping tabs on Murray back in Chicago?"

"Exactly, sweetheart. Maybe that *will* drive me to New York." Susie shook her hair, put on some lip balm, and sank her head back on Andy's legs. "In the meantime, can you do me one immense favor?"

"Name it, Suse."

"Oil my back. If it's not too much of a commitment."

"Can you roll over a little?"

"No."

"Not even an inch?"

"Not even."

"I'm sure glad you're my agent," Sussman muttered. He took Susie's bottle of coconut oil and smeared a handful all over her back. He rubbed it on gently, massaging her shoulders, then lay down on his back and rested Susie's head on his thighs.

Decisions, decisions.

He put on his sunglasses and let the sun pour over his pale, slightly pudgy stomach. He took Susie's hand and caressed it. He sank into the sand and closed his eyes, determined to block out network aggravations, dead wrestlers, and stalled romances from his mind, at least for a few more hours.

20

By Wednesday morning Chicago was returning to a semblance of normalcy. The good thing about snowstorms in late February was that they didn't stick around long. The temperature had shot up to a toasty thirty-eight degrees, the sun was out, and the snowbanks were already starting to dissipate. Still, Murray had decided to leave the Maserati in the garage of his Northbrook town house. He thought of the buckets of salt that had undoubtedly been emptied onto the streets; he was afraid that by the time he got the Maz downtown there'd be nothing left of it but the headlights, the motor, and his sheepskin-covered steering wheel.

So he had pulled together his maps and train schedules, he had carefully planned his trip into Chicago like an intrepid explorer steaming up the Yangtze. He could have used a couple of Sherpas to get him through the snowdrifts, but he settled for Peggy, who dropped him off at the train station in Glencoe. From there he took the train to Evanston, switched to the el at Davis Street, and commuted to his first stop, Alumni Hall, on the campus of De Paul University.

The Chicago Flames professional basketball team had not improved dramatically since Andy Sussman had left them to join CBS. Last year's starting point guard, Sly Thomas, was now playing in Spain. Their first draft pick, a six-foot-ten center from Louisville, had held out and reported to camp out of shape. The team proceeded to lose eleven of its first fourteen contests; by this point in the season they had barely won twenty games. Murray had not paid much attention to them since Christmas, when it became evident that they would miss the play-offs for the third straight year.

As usual, the Flames were second-class tenants in their own building; with the hockey team in town, they were forced to find someplace other than the Stadium to practice. Today they were at De Paul, in the small gym that the Blue Demons themselves had abandoned several years ago in favor of the Rosemont Horizon, out by the airport.

"Lordy sakes alive, look who they let out of the mall," rumbled Dwayne Reddick, who was practicing his favorite baseline jump shot as Murray wandered onto the floor. "What happened, the ceiling collapse in there?" Reddick was the one legitimate star on the Flames, a six-nine power forward from Michigan. His gray-flecked goatee gave him an appearance of eminence among this team of rookies and castoffs; in fact, he had achieved two semesters' progress toward a law degree at Michigan.

"Yeah, yeah," said Murray, walking over to Reddick and giving him a soul shake. "So happens we all need a little fresh air now and then."

"Man does not live by Chocolate-Dipped Banana Pops alone?"

"Yo hey," shouted Jack Bryce, jogging across the floor. "Look who's back." Bryce was the team's center, a curly-haired six-foot-ten white man with a vertical leap of about three-tenths of an inch. "The great shamus! Doin' some recruiting for your cruises, Murray? I read about that trip to St. Thomas in May, maybe I'll put down a deposit."

"Bryce," said Reddick, "the playoffs are in May."

"Gee, how could I forget? Well, just on the off-chance that by some incredible twist of fate we don't qualify this year . . ."

A whistle blew in the back of the gym and Ted Weaver, the coach, shouted instructions for the players to meet downstairs in the locker room in five minutes.

"You know, Murray," said Bryce, "I've got this idea—you ought to charter a team cruise with us. Lots of pro teams do it, the fans eat it up. Maybe we could go up to Alaska this July, I bet you'd fill up in a week."

"Bryce," replied Murray, "didn't I hear your coach calling you?"

"Hey, I'd be social director. SRO, no shit. We'd rake it in."

"Bryce, who would possibly pay money to go on a cruise with you guys? For the betterment of the NBA, they'd probably never let you land again—you'd be floating around from port to port like that New York garbage barge."

Bryce glared at Murray; he looked to Dwayne Reddick for some moral support, but Reddick waved him away. "I believe Mr. Glick has some personal business here," Reddick said. He swished a jumper from the three-point arc and led Murray back to the fold-out bleachers, where Glick filled Dwayne in on the nature of his visit.

"Poo-o-o-or Andrew," Reddick moaned. He had been Sussman's best friend on the team. "I can just see him steaming on the beach out there. He works all his life to get on the network, then they put him with those bumblebrained wrestlers."

"Hey, it ain't so bad, Dwayne. Redondo Beach sure beats the hell out of Chicago this time of year."

"I know that and you know that . . ."

"Yeah, yeah. Look, I got two names for you, tell me if they ring a bell: Winner's Circle. Buddy Beddicker."

A deep-throated cackle emanated from the chest of Dwayne Reddick. He shook his head and slapped Murray on the shoulder blades. "Glick, you are after a ba-a-ad-assed dude this time. I thought those Caribbean cruises were keeping you out of trouble—you ought to take Andy on one, it'd be good for his nerves."

"Believe me, Dwayne, I've tried; the man does not know how to relax. Now, tell me all about Buddy Beddicker. He represent anyone you know?"

"Not anymore. I'll give you a hint, though. You check

the standings, you'll see an inverse ratio between the number of Beddicker's clients and the won-lost records."

"And why is that?" Murray said, bouncing a basketball around to drown out the conversation.

"Class athletes stay away from him. Class teams stay away from his clients."

"I don't suppose you could elaborate on that?" Murray knew about Reddick's law background; he supposed that Dwayne shied away from unsubstantiated allegations—that was where lawyers and detectives parted company.

"Well, there's two things. Briefly—I gotta get downstairs. The first is managing investments, which Buddy Beddicker tried to do once he got a stable of athletes."

"Without much success, I take it."

"He ran with a fast crowd a few years back, lost a lot of his clients' money on real-estate schemes and restaurants. But there was some whispering around that Beddicker made out a lot better than his clients, that he got kickbacks on some of the investment schemes, that some of the money never actually got invested, except in Buddy's bank account."

"Any of that proven?"

"It's still in the courts. May get settled, he'll stay in business. Let's just say it made the situation uncomfortable for attracting new clients."

"Interesting," said Murray, although he doubted that Beddicker had been cheating Dr. Double-X. More likely it was the other way around. "Second point?"

"Regarding the attraction of new clients. Beddicker has a reputation for homing in on poor black kids on the playgrounds, getting 'em signed on with promises of big NBA contracts, sometimes while they're still in high school."

"Legally?"

"No way. I've talked to guys that've played here, they tell me Beddicker advanced them money, hundreds of dollars a month, cars, girls. Selling their souls for a shot at the big time. There's one guy here, you can talk to him—"

"Nah, I don't want him running back to Beddicker. Any of that ever end up in court?"

"Not yet. The NCAA's more interested in drugs right now, and Beddicker's stayed away from that. As long as all of his clients test clean, no one much cares what else he does."

"Except for the investment schemes."

"Different arena," Reddick said. "NCAA's not involved in that. Well, I gotta get goin'. Hundred-dollar fine for missing a meeting." He let go with another cackle; it was no secret that his annual salary made a hundred dollars look like pocket change. "But listen, Murray, you better watch your butt. This dude ain't like all those country-club guys you've been hanging out with."

"Dwayne, I appreciate your concern."

"Seriously. Rough customer. I talked to a few of his former clients. It turns out Mr. Beddicker doesn't appreciate it when his clients decide to take their services elsewhere."

"Is that right?" Murray felt a little pang of hunger; he had been reserving lunch for an Irving's hot-dog stand at his next stop. "And how did Buddy Beddicker express this lack of appreciation?"

"Oh, he threatened to disconnect some of said clients from their major producing assets."

"Such as?"

"Such as their legs." Reddick took the basketball from Murray. "Got to go, my man." He took a long, looping hook shot from the out-of-bounds line that clanged off the rim and rolled to the other side of the court. "Regards to Andrew. And be careful. Come out and see us, Glick, we've won two in a row."

Murray promised he would come and see the Flames play sometime. It was a promise neither of them expected him to keep. He checked his watch; it was 11:30. He left the gym and hopped back on the el at Belden. His next stop was downtown.

*   *   *

Murray got off the el at Randolph Street and took a brisk walk through the center of the city. He blended in among the hordes of business people marching along in their suits and overcoats; he felt awfully common. He was tempted to put on his phony mustache again, just to protect his reputation. He thought about stopping off at the Rehab Center to have a cup of coffee with Terry Tollison, but there was no sense in overplaying his hand; he'd let her romantic passion simmer until Saturday night. He stuck to his original plan and walked over to the Daley Center, stopping outside for a few seconds to admire the Picasso statue.

Murray had not spent a whole lot of time downtown since he had moved his business to Northbrook Court; he couldn't recall the last time that he had just stood and stared at the Picasso. He couldn't remember what exactly it was supposed to be; it was either a big snowy bird that hadn't flown south for the winter, or some type of a beautiful woman—that was more to Murray's liking. But he couldn't stand by it for long, the snow was melting off it in huge wet glops and falling on the heads of unsuspecting gawkers, so he walked inside and addressed the task at hand.

The information he needed was in a little room marked 801; it was open to the public and contained a computerized index of circuit court cases involving amounts of fifteen thousand dollars or more. Murray had only a vague idea what he was looking for, but he had been kicking around his theory about agents ever since he had first mentioned it to Sussman, back in California. Winner's Circle was a sports agency; he wondered if they had ever represented Dr. Double-X. It wouldn't have been anytime recently, of course. Subtracting Double-X's six months in the WFA, and his year and a half in the IWA, and the year or two he had sat out, Murray guessed it could have been three to five years ago. And if there was a lawsuit involved, who had sued whom?

Murray had worked out this scenario: Double-X, in

his original identity, signs on with Buddy Beddicker. For some reason, he breaks off the contract, goes into hiatus, and comes back as Dr. Double-X. When would Beddicker have figured him out? Probably not at the beginning. Possibly when he defeated Crash Kopeck. More likely when he defected to the WFA and started getting more national cable attention.

Murray decided to start at the present and work backward eighteen months. It turned out that Winner's Circle was no stranger to litigation; in the last year and a half they had initiated eight lawsuits. Murray recognized some of the names of the defendants; one of them was a nationally ranked tennis player, two of them were shoe manufacturers. There were four names he didn't recognize; one was a woman—he skimmed over that one. The index gave a brief account of the contents of the lawsuits, and Murray studied them for clues. One had to do with royalties for television commercials; he didn't think that looked relevant. But the other three were listed as breach of contract and Murray took the names down: Alvin Sassler, Edgar Tuck, and Jerry Bonner. On a hunch, he looked for the names of Steve and Cindi Beamon, but he didn't find anything.

By this time it was 12:30. Murray was definitely getting hungry. He knew there was an Irving's hot-dog stand a few blocks away, it was a treat he had been looking forward to all morning, you couldn't get a quality hot dog at Northbrook Court, not to mention Los Angeles or the Caribbean. But he wasn't quite finished. Out of curiosity he went back to the index and looked up cases in which Winner's Circle or Buddy Beddicker had been a defendant. There were over a dozen such cases in the same time period. Murray again recognized many of the names as well-known athletes; two of the plaintiffs had already been sued by Beddicker.

Murray skimmed through the defendants to see if any of his three breach-of-contract names appeared as plaintiffs. None of them did, which set Murray to wondering. If Dr. Double-X had broken a contract, would Buddy

Beddicker take him to court? From the litigation records, Murray guessed that he would. But if Beddicker
was cheating Dr. Double-X, would the wrestler coun-
tersue? From what Murray had heard, that was not the
masked man's preferred method of patching up dis-
agreements.

Murray started to taste the red hot with his name on
it. He walked back out into the Daley Center and strode
with great purpose toward Irving's, Last of the Red-Hot
Lovers. Thinking back to his conversation with Dwayne
Reddick, he wondered how a young, impressionable athlete might react if Buddy Beddicker threatened to break
both his legs.

He wondered how Dr. Double-X might react if Buddy
Beddicker decided to break both of *his* legs.

He had a feeling they would be decidedly different
reactions.

21

Murray sat behind his menu at the Cape Cod Room in the Drake Hotel, surveying the elegant restaurant's New England decor and poring over the selection of fresh seafood, no doubt deliciously prepared. This was poor planning on his part; if he had known that he was coming here he never would have snarfed down the cheddar dog and french fries for lunch. Then again, lunch at Irving's did wonderful things for Murray's thought processes; there was something about a hundred-percent pure-beef kosher hot dog rumbling around in his stomach that got his mental juices all stirred up.

Across the room, Buddy Beddicker was placing an order with the waiter. Beddicker was accompanied by two men, one of them in his sixties and balding, wearing a gray banker's business suit. The other was younger, with greasy black hair. The suit he wore was much less expensive. He looked like the bodyguard type.

Murray guessed that Beddicker was the key to the Double-X murder, but approaching him was a ticklish proposition. He could have gone into the Winner's Circle office posing as a reporter, or as another agent, or even an athlete—he was tall enough and in decent shape. He could have asked a lot of questions about investments and college athletes and seen how Beddicker reacted, but why alert him that he was being watched? As far as Beddicker knew, the only person who was doing any investigating of the case at all was Andy Sussman, and nobody was taking that very seriously. Glick wanted to keep it that way.

Still, Murray wanted to get to know his suspect; it helped to see a man in his daily routine, to watch his little mannerisms, to see how he traveled around and what kind of an entourage he had. It was a tricky situation. He had called Winner's Circle and asked to speak with Beddicker, explaining that he was taking a survey for the Des Moines *Register* on incentive clauses in player contracts—he assumed he would not get through and he didn't. The secretary told him Beddicker was going out for lunch in a few minutes, he'd have to call back. So Murray had wandered over to the First National Bank Building. He had taken the elevator to the eighth floor and paced around, waiting for the door to Suite 840 to open. When the three men had walked out, he had taken a quick peek, then slipped downstairs via the stairwell. He was glad he didn't have the Maserati with him; it was easy to follow the men by cab. It was a gamble, of course—he didn't even know what Beddicker looked like: what if he'd tagged the wrong guys? But when he got to the Cape Cod Room, Murray peeked on the maître d's reservation book and saw the name; when the three men placed their order, the waiter addressed the smallest one as Mr. Beddicker.

Beddicker was maybe five-ten at the most, but he was well-built; he looked like he had done a little boxing. His arms seemed strong, he exuded the type of physical self-assurance that an athlete has. Murray guessed that he was in his early forties. He had a receding hairline and wore tinted glasses. When he spoke, he looked directly into the eyes of the person he was addressing. Sometimes he grabbed one of the two men by the coat sleeves; sometimes he made a point by slamming a fork to the table.

He wasn't drinking, Murray noticed, though he did smoke small, thinly rolled cigars. When the food arrived, Beddicker attacked his scampi with a fork, spearing the food with quick darts and gulping each shrimp down with one swallow.

Murray pondered all this as he enjoyed a bowl of Bookbinder soup; it seemed to mix in well with the hot dog and the fries. What was he able to extrapolate from all this circumstantial evidence? It was the intangibles, he thought, the type of thing that gave a clever detective such as himself an edge over the hoi polloi. He wished he'd brought a pen; it would be helpful to remember all this when it came time to write his memoirs. He guessed that Beddicker liked playing the tough guy on his own turf, with his own people around him. He guessed that he was capable of violence—perhaps not direct physical violence, more likely the type of violence carried out by others at his direction.

Murray checked his watch; it was getting close to three o'clock. He had one more errand to run today. He finished his soup and watched Beddicker order dessert. There was a long discussion with the waiter; it was obviously something that wasn't on the menu. Beddicker gave the waiter a pat on the rear and lit up another small cigar. He ripped apart a roll that was sitting on the side of his plate and chomped down a piece of it.

Murray resisted the temptation to walk over and say hello, introduce himself as the man who would preside over his demise. It had style, but it struck him as a little too much on the Greek-drama side. Murray paid for his Bookbinder soup and walked out; a few minutes later he had hailed a cab and was headed for Northwestern Station.

It was about this time that Murray was wishing he had taken his car after all, snow or no snow. Murray Glick was not a pedestrian kind of guy, he didn't even own a pair of overshoes, they were not the type of thing you needed often in Northbrook Court. The train was okay if you were just going downtown and back, but Murray had decided to pay a visit to Barney Hennesey's North Side apartment, and public transportation had left large gaps in the journey. The train had taken him nearly to Evanston, overshooting his mark by several miles, and he still had to head west on Tuohy. He had taken the bus; to his memory it was the first bus he had ridden since high school. He had no idea what the fare was; he didn't have exact change either. He had to stand there fumbling around with a ten-dollar bill, trying to get some help from a couple of old ladies who were in no hurry; they stood next to him running their hands over his London Fog overcoat until the bus driver threatened to kick them all off.

When he got off the bus, he still had to walk the five blocks to Hennesey's apartment. The salt and slushy snow had by now completely ruined his patent-leather boots, not to mention his slacks. He supposed he would charge some of that to Sussman, the rest to Uncle Sam.

When he arrived at Hennesey's apartment it was a quarter to four; he rang the buzzer, but no one was home. Murray was assuming that Hennesey was keeping a regular tail on Steve Beamon; he expected him to be home in a half-hour or so. That gave him plenty of time to break in; it was the one skill he had consciously kept sharp over the years.

Hennesey's apartment was a snap. The security-locked front door to the building was broken and Hennesey's apartment door responded to a combination of skeleton keys, a credit card, and a nail file; the whole procedure took about forty-five seconds. The inside of the apartment was not exactly a scene from *Better Homes and Gardens*: an old ratty couch, an easy chair, a rickety-looking coffee table. A few cheap pictures on the wall. There was a half-eaten sandwich on the coffee table, a half-empty bottle of beer on the kitchen counter.

Murray walked into the bedroom. There was just a bed and a night table, a shade was pulled halfway down, there were no curtains. Murray almost felt sorry for his suspect. After nearly three years serving exclusive North Shore clients, he had forgotten how the Barney Henneseys of the world survived from day to day. He rum-

maged through Hennesey's dresser, scrounged around
for any loose papers, but he didn't find anything. He
walked back into the living room and looked for something to read; there was nothing there. He turned on the
television, a twelve-inch RCA color portable. A UHF station was showing reruns of *McHale's Navy*; it seemed
like a good way to pass the time.

It was nearly five o'clock when Barney Hennesey got
home. He had noticed that his door wasn't bolted, he
had no doubt heard the television. There was silence for
about five minutes, he seemed to have gone somewhere,
but Murray was in no hurry. When Hennesey returned,
he kicked the door open with one swift motion. "All
right, hands *up*," he said, holding his pistol with two
hands. "C'mon, move it!"

"Barney, Barney," said Murray Glick, leaning back
on the couch. "A gun? That's terrible—wait'll the parole
board hears about that."

"They ain't gonna hear nothin', asshole, they'll find
your body in a sewer somewhere."

"Oh, I don't think so, Barney. You know, I'm a very
meticulous guy. I always let my secretary know just
where I'm going to be. Let's see: five o'clock, visit my
old pal Barney Hennesey. Make sure parole officer knows."

"What old pal? Who the hell are you?" Hennesey was
still waving the pistol, but he had closed his apartment
door and looked uncomfortable in his overcoat and boots.

"An old friend from the United Security System days,
Barney. Great times, weren't they?"

"Listen, buddy, I served my time. They was most happy
to return me to bein' a useful member of society. Now,
get the hell outta my place before I call the cops."

"Call the *cops*?" Murray got up and walked toward
the kitchen. "Barney, you don't have a thing to eat in
this place. A big guy like you, you could get malnutrition
or something. Maybe we should order a pizza, or get
some Chinese. We can have a couple of beers and talk
about your future."

"What about my future?" Hennesey dropped the gun

sight from Murray's eyes, but he still held on to the pistol.

"Maybe your future as a cripple. Faking a wheelchair, that's pretty low, isn't it? Any sense of shame at all, Barney?"

"I gotta job to do. I ain't breakin' any laws."

"Aw, Barney. A guy like you, on parole and everything, I'd think you'd ask a few questions before you took a job like that. Buddy Beddicker, not exactly a pillar of the community, asks you to get in a chair and spy on some poor paraplegic. What'd you think, Barney? Think that's strictly on the up-and-up?"

"Hey, listen, pal. There's nothin' says I can't go inna bar, listen what people say, tell an interested party."

"Of course! I'll bet employment opportunities must be tough for a man of your education and experience. Can't exactly get a job at First National, can you, Barney?"

"Fuck off." Hennesey took a step toward Murray, then backed away and walked into the kitchen. He found a can of beer in the refrigerator, popped the top off, and walked back to Murray. "What do you want?"

"I'd like a beer. Got any imports?"

"Budweiser, take it or leave it."

"Thank you, Barney, you're a gracious host."

Barney returned to the refrigerator, pulled out another Bud, and handed it to Murray. "What else?"

Glick popped open the can and took a sip of beer. He pulled out a cigar, tapped the end on the beer can, and lit it. "For starters, how come you're tailing Steve Beamon?"

"Dunno. Beddicker hires me, tells me to listen."

"For what?"

"I'm not sure. Loose talk, I guess."

"About what? Basketball? All the cute broads at the Rehab Center?" Murray paused, waiting for an answer, but Hennesey stood silently, slurping his Budweiser. "Barney, how often do you talk to Beddicker?"

"Not often. Usually his driver fills me in."

"Ever go to Beddicker's office?"

"A few times. When he wants to talk. When he hired me. Once or twice."

Murray rested his cigar on the edge of the coffee table. The room was rancid enough already without him polluting it with smoke. "Barney, when Mr. Beddicker or his driver debriefs you, do they ever ask you certain questions about Steve Beamon's conversations?"

"Like what?"

"Well, for example, do they want to know if Beamon talks about his sister?"

"They ask about his family. Not specifically about his sister."

"Are they particularly interested in his sister when he mentions her?"

"Could be."

"Think a little harder," Murray said, tapping his cigar on the coffee table. "Do they ever ask about professional wrestling?"

"They ask about sports. 'Course, the kid's an athlete. Was. Sure, they wanna know does he talk about sports. Basketball, boxing, wrestling."

"Did he?"

"Ah, mostly basketball. Oh, when that wrestler guy died a couple weeks ago, he said he saw it on TV. Now I remember, his sister was in the competition, it was one of them TV superstars things. He talked about that. Somebody kidded him, said the wrestler was crazy about his sister, had a heart attack."

"What did he say then?"

"He laughed. Said the guy wasn't his sister's type."

"What about Beddicker?"

Hennesey paused, gulped down some more Bud.

"What about Beddicker?" Murray repeated.

"Yeah, they were interested in that. They called me over to the office. Beddicker asked me personally."

"Asked what?"

"Asked what Beamon had said about the wrestler and

his sister. It was just a joke, what the kid said. Seemed like it to me."

Murray got up from the chair, picked up his cigar, and walked into the kitchen. He had a feeling that if there were any innocent people in all of this, Steve Beamon was probably one of them. It was too bad, he thought, that Beamon's life was the one that was irreparably damaged; guys like Hennesey got chance after chance. "Barney," said Murray, returning to the living room, "I think you and I have some business to discuss."

"Look, buddy, I don't even know your name."

"François."

"François? Funny, you don't look French to me."

"And you don't look like a free man to me, Barney. Waving a pistol at me, that'll put you right back in Joliet. And there's worse, Barney. Much worse."

"Like what?"

"Like accessory to murder. Obstruction of justice. Fraud. Conspiracy."

"How about rape and treason—you forgot that."

Murray relit his cigar. "Hey, Barney, a sense of humor. I like that, I like to have sharp guys working for me."

Hennesey took a deep breath and leaned against the television set.

"Because you *will* be working for me, Barney. I think we're going to have a mutually beneficial relationship."

Barney coughed, crushed his empty beer can, and sat down on the couch next to Murray. "I figured I'd have lots of employment opportunities when I got out. Whaddisit I'm supposed to be doing, François?"

"Nothing too complicated for a man of your skills, Barney. I'd just like you to pay a visit to Buddy Beddicker's office."

Hennesey nodded. He stared straight ahead at the TV.

"This is probably the type of visit best done after dark. I want you to go into his files and pull three contracts for me."

Murray described the assignment: he wanted Hennesey to pull the contracts of Alvin Sassler, Edgar Tuck, and Jerry Bonner and bring him photocopies; he had a hunch one of them was the alter ego of Dr. Double-X. Also, he wanted Hennesey to search for files or contracts under the names of Steve and Cindi Beamon. Murray supposed this was something he could have done himself—it was his specialty, after all—but why take a risk when someone could do it for you? More important, Murray wanted Hennesey to commit a neat little crime for him; it would be good to have something more concrete on him when it came time for a more difficult assignment.

"I suppose you want all this in time for tomorrow's papers?" Hennesey asked. He had graduated to a second Budweiser.

"Three working days, Barney, I think that's reasonable. Of course, if you want to get a load off your mind, why not just do it tonight?"

Barney said he would think it over. He asked for a phone number, but Murray decided it would be better to hold on to his sense of mystery. "I'll be back," Murray said. "Same time tomorrow. Get the information, maybe we'll go out for dinner. Maybe I'll take you to one of those fancy joints your ex-boss likes to frequent."

"I'll be sure and wear a tie."

"Sure. And shine your shoes. Ciao, Barney."

A few minutes later, Murray was back in the snowy Chicago streets, trying to stay out of snowbanks and potholes, navigating his way back to Tuohy Avenue. It was dark now, and cold, the wind had come up, the slush was turning to ice again. Murray pondered his trip home. Bus to the train station, train back to Highland Park, cab to Northbrook. It seemed awfully low-rent for a world-class detective. He stopped at a coffee shop on Tuohy. He had one quarter left; he called the Rehab Center and asked to speak with Terry Tollison.

"Terry," said Murray Glick, "sweetheart, I have a problem."

"About Saturday night?"

"No, no. It seems I have a transportation situation. My car is indisposed, and I'm stranded at a coffee shop on Tuohy Avenue, miles away from the comfort of my home and hearth."

"How perfectly horrid. I don't suppose you've heard of a b-u-s?"

"Would you believe it, Ter, I spent my very last quarter on this phone call? And I'm cold and wet, I could catch pneumonia."

"Gee, Murray, and here I thought you were the Mike Hammer type."

"We're all merely flesh and blood, Ter. I'm appealing to your professional concern for the weak and weary, as well as the personal warmth of your heart."

"I'm touched."

"And possibly a ten-percent discount on Yucatán."

"Ahem," said Terry. "So. Where'd you say that coffee shop was?"

"One-one-nine-two-eight Tuohy."

"I'll see what I can do."

"I'm glad I found the source of your compassion."

"Better quit while you're ahead," said Terry. "Listen, I've got one more patient. Steal a dollar from someone and get a cup of coffee. I'll see you at six-thirty."

They sat at a small corner booth at Francesca's, a family-owned Italian place buried somewhere in Chicago's near North Side. Murray had given up trying to keep track of directions as Terry zigzagged her VW Rabbit through the snow-filled side streets. It felt a little like he was being kidnapped—he half-expected to be spirited into a safe house somewhere and plied with antiestablishment dogma from some splinter religious group, such as Chicago Republicans. But Terry was not an Uzi-toting fanatic, she was just hungry and harried— even as they sat at the cramped table sipping on a bottle of Pinot Noir, she had a stack of papers in front of her; she was skimming some reports, initialing them, and slipping them into an accordion file.

"I don't suppose they have secretaries for that type of thing," Murray offered, pushing a loose strand of hair from Terry's eyes as he poured her some more wine.

"Nope. The people who fund us expect professional reporting—you wouldn't believe all the paperwork, Murray: the feds, the state, the hospital. Not to mention the insurance companies." A waiter came by and Terry ordered for both of them. Francesca's was a familiar haunt for her. She requested a special spaghetti dish with red-pepper-and-mushroom sauce that wasn't on the menu, she said something to the waiter in Italian, then went back to her reports. "I went overtime with my low-back patients today. The heater in the hydrotherapy pool went down, there's this lady from Toledo, she won't even *touch* the water unless it's ninety-two degrees minimum." She looked up at Murray, who had taken her hand and was gazing at her with sympathy. "Then I get a call from this helpless, self-pitying private eye."

"I was in mortal danger, Ter. Waves of bone-chilling slush were penetrating the outer defenses of my patent-leather Florsheims. Hypothermia was setting in. So I turned to the most beautiful physical therapist in Chicago—"

"Here," said Terry, shoving the bottle of Pinot Noir at him. "Drink up, Murray, it'll thaw you out."

"Miss Tollison, I happen to know for a fact that large doses of alcohol are not the proper antidote for plunging body temperatures."

"Nobody ever froze to death in Francesca's."

"Brr-r-r-r." Murray shivered. "Chills, frostbite . . ." He could see that he was finally forcing a snicker out of her; she put her reports down and gave his hands a brisk massage. "Much better, Terry. We have . . . circulation!" He kissed her on the hand.

"Careful, pal, my Swedish massage is next."

"A battered bod awaits thee, Ter."

"Taught to me by a black-belt Swedish drill instructor

of uncertain sexual leanings in the back room of an X-rated lounge in Stockholm."

"Um," Murray said, sitting up straight. "Maybe fifty cents and a Magic Fingers would do." He was saved from further embarrassment by the waiter, who arrived with a large bowl of salad and two plates. As the two of them turned their attention to nourishment, Murray admitted to himself that it was unlikely that Terry would soon be swooning in romantic rhapsody or directing him to the nearest hotel room. Still, it was only the second date; he could deal with a little conservatism and there was still Saturday night to look forward to.

"Incidentally," Terry said, sampling the salad in a ladylike manner, but with great purpose, "Steve Beamon's been acting a little nervous the last few days. He said there's been some funny people hanging around him—mentioned some tipsy ISU fan, came stumbling in the other day. Tall skinny guy. I wonder who that could have been."

"A concerned citizen, no doubt. Anybody else?"

"I don't know. He seemed a little skittish. He mentioned some people asking about his family." Terry pushed the salad away and sipped on her wine. "Murray, I've worked with that kid for almost a year now. It's no small achievement what he's done—we're talking about someone whose whole life was basketball and he had it cut away from him, just like that."

"Terry, believe me, I wouldn't do anything—"

"And he's going to make it, Murray. I've worked with hundreds of kids like him. It gets to a point, I can look in their eyes, I can see if they're going to get on with their lives—" The spaghetti arrived, but Terry ignored it. She stared directly at Murray for a few seconds, then quietly twisted a few strands around her fork.

"Clairvoyant," Murray said, "but I'll take your word for it."

"Years of practice. And whatever you're nosing around in—"

"I told you before, Ter. Steve Beamon comes out okay, I guarantee."

Terry held Murray's hand again. She smiled and twirled some spaghetti on her fork. "For some strange reason or another, I believe you. I actually think you're an honest guy."

"Dependability, Ter, it's the cornerstone of my business."

"In your own uniquely insincere way, of course."

"Terry," Murray Glick sighed as he chomped down a forkful of pasta, "did you know it's permissible to praise someone without instantly qualifying it?"

"No kidding?"

"Detectives have feelings too."

"Aw, what a teddy bear." Terry stroked Murray on the shoulder and looked at her watch. "Hey, Sherlock, it's barely eight o'clock. I bet we could still make Second City."

"Second City? In my near-cryogenic condition?"

"C'mon, I haven't been there in years! Since Belushi and Bill Murray were there, can you believe it?"

"Terry, baby, they haven't even begun to plow the streets yet, you'd need a dogsled to get into Old Town."

"For God's sake, Murray, they plow Wells Street! Worse comes to worst, you can walk a few blocks, it won't kill you. And we won't have any trouble getting in—"

"What about all your paperwork?"

"Order some dessert. I'll have it done by the time the coffee gets here."

Murray pondered his spaghetti. He'd hardly expected this, he wasn't prepared for such a burst of adventurism—truth was, he wasn't used to confronting a woman whose personality couldn't be summarized on the back of a cocktail napkin. "Of course, Terry, there is a slight problem—if we're going to stay for the improvisation and everything."

"What's that?"

"Well, I have to get home tonight. All the way back to Northbrook. Unless you were planning, uh . . ."

"On driving you back to the train station?"

"Right, that was it. Do they run that late?"

"I'm sure there's one or two that'll get you back to Highland Park."

"And then, of course, I've got to figure out how to get home from there."

"You're the detective."

Murray took a piece of garlic bread, broke it in two, and offered half of it to Terry. "You're an angel, Ter. I suppose I could take a cab. If I had any money."

"I'll pop, sweetheart. As long as you're getting dinner and the show. They take credit cards, incidentally."

"I think I knew that."

"But really, Murray, you should get in the habit of carrying along some mad money. You never know what kind of desperate situations you might run into."

"Nope," Murray said, pouring himself some more wine as he leaned back in his chair. "You never know."

And you never did, he thought as he watched Terry finish initialing her reports over spaghetti and cheesecake and coffee; they would make it, just barely, to Second City in time for the opening.

You never knew.

It was, he figured, the credo of his profession.

22

It was inevitable, it had to happen sooner or later, and it finally did, in Wednesday's Calendar section of the Los Angeles *Times*. "Wrasslin' Loony Toons Prevail at CBS," wrote the television critic.

> Sports journalism has reached new levels of infantilism with the continuing CBS "coverage" of the death of a masked wrestler named Dr. Double-X. Not satisfied that the police have found the death completely accidental, intrepid reporter Andy Sussman has been filing breathless reports each week about new developments on "the case."
>
> Who was Dr. Double-X? Was he Deep Throat? Amelia Earhart? D. B. Cooper? Walter Mondale?
>
> Why did this great champion leave us in his prime? Only Sussman, a one-man Woodward and Bernstein, seems to know. Certainly he's trod bravely to the story's sources, interviewing such "suspects" as The Thing, Wireless, cable huckster Ben Garrison, and rocker Leona Z.
>
> What suspects are next on Sussman's list? Will he be at Universal Studios interviewing King Kong and Jaws the shark? How about the Big Boy mascot? Or the Goodyear blimp?

"Well, there goes a promising career right down the sewer," Sussman mumbled, crinkling up the article and hooking it errantly toward an ashtray. "Maybe I can get a job holding the boom mike for Oprah Winfrey."

"Hey, the guy's a creep, whaddaya want," snarled Wireless. "Look, we been puttin' up with that stuff for years, think it bothers us? Hell, it's great press—every time some egghead writes a column like that, we get SRO crowds the next night, we get standin' O's, you bet your life on it."

"Refill time," said Jill Weintraub, mamboing over to Sussman to the tune of an old bossa-nova record, carrying a huge pitcher of liquid refreshments. "The blender's gone berserk, I can't do anything about it."

Sussman tried to get up, but the only thing that seemed to function with any kind of resolve was his right hand, which pushed his glass out a few inches, somewhere in the path of the margarita that was plunging out of the pitcher like Yosemite Falls. He was sitting on a beanbag in the corner of the Weintraubs' living room in the Condo in Redondo. It was Wednesday night. Dinner was rumored to be in the offing.

"There's some more chips and veggies over on the table," said Jill. She was a flaming redhead, with curly hair and freckles. She stood nearly six-foot-two in her bare feet. "Lennie, bring the chips over here, this boy needs a solid foundation if he's gonna make it through the night."

Lennie had tried to warn Sussman about his wife's locally famous "neutron margaritas"—they leveled all people within a seventy-five-mile radius and left only the buildings standing. Sussman hadn't cared, though, he was feeling spiritually abandoned. His life was a wreck, his girlfriend was in Chicago, his career was back in Des Moines somewhere. He pulled his harmonica out of his pocket and tried a few bars of "Goin' to New Orleans," but there was guacamole dip in the little holes and nothing much came out. "Let's go to Universal!" he shouted. "Screw the *Times*, I want to interview the damned shark! Call up Cliff Trager! Get a production crew over there."

"Oedipuss!" shouted Lennie, calling to a cat as he set a tray of carrots, celery, and onion dip in front of Sussman. "Oedipuss, get away from there. Go back and play with Aunt Leona."

Oedipuss was a brown-and-white cross-breed of some sort, with a fondness for onion dip and inebriated humans. She pounced on Sussman and curled up on his stomach, annexing one of his carrots and lapping up some spilled margarita.

"Aw, isn't she cute?" said Leona Z, who was dressed in a tie-dyed leotard and a psychedelic blouse left over from the original Earth Day. Her hair was tinted purple and orange, Sussman could barely look at her without getting the whirlies. "Andy, you're an absolute peach— I love it when men get their defenses down."

"Leona, please get the cat away from the food," said Leroy, dressed more conservatively in a black-and-white art-deco beach shirt and a tank suit. "She's getting in the dip, we're all going to wake up tomorrow with a craving for catnip."

"Here, Oedipuss. He-r-r-r-e, Oedipussy," said Leona, picking up the cat, who had fastened her claws onto Sussman's cashmere sweater. "C'mon, we'll let you play in Uncle Wireless's room."

"Great, I can sleep with all the cat hairs again—"

"You've had worse," said Jill. "Remember that dive Ben booked us into last fall in India-no-place?"

" 'At wasn't Ben's fault," Wireless growled. "It was recommended in the travel guide."

"Sure. 'Midwest Tanktowns on Five Dollars a Day.' " Jill pulled a pillow off her couch and sat down carefully on the floor next to Sussman. She was four months pregnant, just beginning to show. She had been abstaining from the margaritas—according to Lennie, the recipe seemed to have gotten stronger since she'd stopped sampling it. "Now, Andy," she said, sidling next to him, "we've got to stop this moping around. We've all had bad reviews now and then."

"I'm devastated, Jill. That guy won a Pulitzer prize, y'know."

"Well, he won't win any more for being such a sniveling jerk. C'mon, babe, you're in the bigs! Just think of all those aspiring young journalists who'd love to be in your position." Jill placed Sussman's drink on the carpet and rubbed him softly on the back.

"What? Drunk on the floor next to a beautiful pregnant woman who's married to a two-hundred-pound professional wrestler?"

"Hey, quit yer bellyachin'," said Wireless. "Lookit me: I got hoodlums followin' me around, I'm scared to go home to my own bed. Hell, I thought you guys were supposed to be investigatin' all that."

"Never fear, Wireless," Sussman said. "The intrepid reporter is on your side."

"Just remember, Andy," cut in Leroy, munching on a carrot, "when you *do* solve this thing, you can make the LA *Times* stick it up the ol' wazoo. How's your friend Murray doing, anyway? Did he come up with anything new?"

Sussman wrapped an arm around Jill and pulled himself to a semiupright position. He had meant to call Murray today, but he had been too upset about the *Times* article. He had gone for a long walk on the beach, he'd ended up halfway to Tijuana before turning around and hitching a ride back on the PCH. "Nothing new," he mumbled, settling back into the beanbag. "Too many loose ends . . ." Loose ends, he thought, he had been trying to sort out the loose ends while he paced along the ocean. He had no idea how he was going to tie any of them together for the next Saturday segment.

What was he supposed to say?

Murray didn't want him to mention anything about the Beamons or the check or Buddy Beddicker. And he had almost forgotten about the Wireless angle—that was one thing he'd hoped to unravel tonight, before he had unraveled himself. He made a mental note to talk with

Lennie before he went back to the hotel. After four days as a houseguest, Wireless must have left some clue as to what he knew, or what he had in his possession, or what someone *thought* he had in his possession that would make someone want to ransack his apartment.

"Lennie, how're the coals doing?" asked Jill. "Are we approaching Chicken City here?"

"Ten more minutes, my love." Lennie stood by the patio door, looking out at the Pacific Ocean. The condo had an unobstructed view of the harbor. "Fellow grapplers," he said, clearing his throat. "Wives, chanteuses, intrepid reporters, lend me your ears."

"And cats," said Leona. "Don't forget Oedipuss, she's on Wireless's bed but she hears everything you say."

"Hey, get her offa there. I wanna sleep tonight—"

"Siddown," said Leona, jerking Wireless back to his seat. "He's attracted to dumb animals—"

"And dear Oedipuss," continued Lennie. "As the coals burn down toward Chicken City here in our lovely Condo in Redondo, I'd like to introduce the birth of a new concept!"

"Bravo!" said Leroy. "The Renaissance Man adds to his repertoire!"

"Jill, dear," said Leona, "get the blender going."

"Grappling fans," Lennie said, "I've decided to add some Gilbert and Sullivan to the routine. I'm going to introduce a whole new character to the WFA. Are you ready?"

"Honey, how about marinating the chicken one more time?" said Jill. "Oh, and the corn, I forgot all about that."

"Voilà!" said Weintraub, pulling a black hood from behind the patio door. "The Lord High Executioner!"

"The what?" Jill said as she mixed some more tequila and Triple Sec into the blender.

"The Lord High Executioner. You know—from *The Mikado?*"

Jill poured in some ice cubes, while the other guests looked on in stony silence.

"But it'd be perfect! Listen, I stalk into the ring in my black robe and black hood, with my executioner's ax slung over my shoulder. And as my opponent swaggers in, I sing out:

"As someday it may happen that a victim must be found,
I've got a little list—I've got a little list
of society offenders who might well be under-ground,
and who never would be missed—who never would be missed!"

"Do we have any more of those Spanish olives?" asked Leona. "Leroy and I brought over a box of them."

"Aw, come on," said Lennie, "I've been working on this idea for weeks. Just try the chorus, okay: 'He never would be missed, he never would be missed . . .' "

The condo remained deadly silent, except for the blender. Then Oedipuss the cat let out a bloodcurdling cry from the guest room.

"That about says it all, I'm afraid," said Leroy.

"You're not trying," Lennie complained. "It's not fair, I've got it all choreographed."

The cat let out another cry, but this one was much weaker. "Oedipuss?" said Leona. "Oedipuss, are you okay?" She ran into the guest room to check on the condition of the pussy, while a disgruntled Lennie took the top off the barbecue and started spreading the coals out.

"Neanderthals," Lennie said. "Whatever happened to the spirit of innovation—"

"Ya-a-a-a!" shouted Leona Z from the guest room, with a scream that rivaled her live performances. This one, though, had no need for three electric bass guitars and a synthesizer. "Leroy! Lee-*roy-y-y!*"

"What now?" muttered Leroy Wedbush.

"The cat!" screamed Leona. "Oedipuss! The cat's *dead!*"

*   *   *

Wireless stomped around the guest room in a panic, several times approaching the cat, which lay indisputably dead on the bedspread. "It was meant for me!" he rasped. "They found me, they probably knew where I was all along."

"Oh, Oedipussy," whimpered Leona, showing considerably more remorse than either of the cat's owners. "Oh, Oedipuss! What did you *do?*"

"It was poison!" said Wireless. "Jesus Christ, we gotta check everything! It coulda been the dip or the carrots or the tequila. Call a doctor! Someone call a doctor!"

Sussman wandered in. He felt something gnawing deep in the pit of his stomach, but he didn't think he'd been poisoned; it was more likely the pitcher full of margaritas and the chips and the guacamole and the onion dip and carrots and celery and Spanish olives.

"Call an ambulance!" Wireless was shouting. "I wanna get my stomach pumped! Jesus Christ, somebody call 911!"

Lennie and Jill stood in front of the bed; Jill had stroked her cat a couple of times, but the animal was lifeless and her sentiment had run out quickly. "Go sit on the patio," Lennie said. "You've got another life in there, I don't want you anywhere near all this. Go call a vet or something." Jill had nodded silently and walked out, leaving Leroy and Lennie as the principal mentally sound humans in the room.

"I don't think it was the onion dip," Leroy said. "Couldn't have been any of that stuff, the cat died too all of a sudden. Look at this mess." Leroy waved his hand around the room. Wireless's personal belongings were spread from wall to wall, his silver duffel bag half-unzipped in the corner by the closet.

"Wireless, what've you got in there?" said Lennie, picking up a trail of socks and underwear. "You need your own personal maid—"

"Hey, 'at's my personal stuff—hands off!"

Lennie picked his way through a collection of shorts

and T-shirts and jeans, then lifted a small satchel that was lying on the carpet—it had been pulled out of the duffel by the cat. "What's this?"

"My corner kit," Wireless said. "For the matches. Massage balm, blood capsules, towels, all my stuff."

"Lemme see." Leroy picked up a canister of camphor; it was the balm that Wireless smeared all over his wrestlers' backs, prior to the matches. He worked the top off and sniffed it. "Whew!"

"Ain't as bad as it smells," said Wireless. "Loosens the muscles up, been usin' it for years."

"The smell alone could have killed her."

"Wait a second," said Sussman. He was trying to fight off the demons in his stomach and his head; he had focused his sights on the opposite corner of the room. Something had flickered in his brain. He sat staring at the bottom of a floor-length drapery that was open a few inches. "Hold it. Nobody move."

"We ain't goin' nowheres, pal."

"Wireless," said Sussman, "what is this?" He picked up a dark green pouch of chewing tobacco. It had been torn open and rolled closed, but it appeared as if the cat had managed to knock it onto the floor and claw it open again; a greenish-brown smudge was leaking out. "This was Dr. Double-X's, wasn't it?"

"Jesus, yeah," said Wireless. "It's his chewin' tobacco. Christ, I forgot all about that, it musta been stuffed way in the back there."

"You carried it around with you whenever he wrestled?"

"Ah, he used to stick it in there before the matches. Wasn't anywhere else for him to keep it. Lemme see—"

"Nope, don't touch it!" Sussman struggled to keep his balance. He stood in front of the spilled chewing tobacco, his arms stretched out like a traffic cop's. "Leave it right there."

"Hey, what're you, Dick Tracy all of a sudden?"

"I said leave it!"

Wireless backed off, and Leroy and Leona and Lennie stood silently, waiting for Sussman to tell them what to do next.

"Andy?" whispered Lennie Weintraub. "Can we go out and play now?"

Sussman shook his head; he didn't say a word, he just stood there, his arms now folded at his chest. He knew, finally, that one key to the puzzle had been found. "Just don't touch it," he said. "I don't want any more prints on it."

He picked up the telephone. He dialed the Redondo Beach Police Department and asked to speak to Captain Stevens.

23

"It was poison, all right," said Andy Sussman. He was lying in his king-size bed at the Redondo Beach Sheraton, a wet towel wrapped around his head; he had taken enough Tylenol to send the stock of McNeilab up a point and a half. It was eleven o'clock on Thursday morning and he'd just gotten the lab report back from the police department. He was speaking to Susie Ettenger on the telephone, after an unsuccessful attempt to reach Murray Glick. Murray had left word for Sussman to call Susie—if the two of them had actually spoken to each other, something serious must be going on. "They said it was a substance called aconitine," Sussman explained. "It comes from a plant called monkshood, Captain Stevens says it has pretty little purple flowers, but it's deadly as hell."

"I'll have to remember that on Valentine's Day—if certain people aren't in the proper graces. That's all it took to kill Lennie's cat?"

"More than enough. One milligram of the stuff can kill a human being." Sussman read from the report that Captain Stevens had personally delivered a few minutes ago. "Numbness, slow heartbeat, convulsion, and death through paralysis of the breathing muscles, or cardiac arrest. It can happen in as little as eight minutes, and that pouch of chewing tobacco was laced with the stuff."

"What else did the police say?"

Sussman poured himself a second cup of strong coffee.

It had been only a few minutes since Captain Stevens had left but the whole experience seemed surreal, Stevens in his spiffy blue uniform and his short blond hair—was this guy really a cop? He was much too polite, he couldn't have made it as a meter maid in Chicago. "Sorry to wake you up, Mr. Sussman," he'd said. "How's your headache? Would you like me to call room service and order some coffee?"

Sussman had done the entire police interview lying in bed, being served coffee in his pajamas by the interrogating officer. Stevens admitted that he knew exactly what a margarita hangover was like, he spoke softly as he filled Sussman in on the rest of the sketchy information that he'd been able to assemble. "The ironic thing," Sussman told Susie, "is that because no one claimed the body, it's still in the deep freeze at the hospital. Now they can do another autopsy. The poison wasn't something they'd necessarily pick up the first time, but if they're looking for it, they might still find a trace."

"In other words, whoever killed him—"

"Assuming he *was* poisoned by the chewing tobacco, and it wasn't meant for Wireless—"

"Or the cat," said Susie. "But assuming it was meant for Dr. Double-X, the killer could have claimed the body after the autopsy, and then there never would have been a case."

"It was a risk. They would have drawn attention to themselves. My guess is they tried to clean things up from the back end. They must have figured they could pull the pouch out of Wireless's corner kit while all the pandemonium was going on at the dock, or just grab the whole thing and split. But Wireless jumped into the ambulance with the body, he had his bag with him, they never had a chance. That's why they sent someone to tear his place up. That's what they were looking for."

"I don't suppose they found any fingerprints on the pouch?"

"They're still checking. They'll have to match 'em

against Dr. Double-X's, but they already printed Wireless, and he was clean."

"In other words," Susie said, "the chewing tobacco got in Wireless's bag without Wireless ever touching it?"

"Well, it figures, Double-X would have stuffed it in there himself after he took a chaw. If there are any other prints on it, I'll find out by the end of the day."

"So what do the police do now?"

"Oh, they'll probably start asking all the questions that I've been asking since he died. They'll talk to Wireless and Ben Garrison and everyone who was on the raft, and probably everyone else that was around."

"In other words, it'll take them about two weeks to get to where you are now. Unless you tell them everything we know and how we know it."

"Which is mostly speculation—mostly Murray's speculation, which I promised I wouldn't divulge." Sussman took the towel off his head and dipped it into the bucket of ice water at his feet. He didn't know how long he could hold back information from the police. He had told Stevens about Dr. Double-X allegedly un-throwing the match with Harvey Kopeck and about Wireless's apartment being ransacked; he could probably wait with the rest until Murray came up with something more substantial.

"Well, here's some more speculation," Susie said. "I'm holding a photocopy of a contract in front of me, obtained in some obviously clandestine way by the Sleuth from Sears."

"You can say his name, sweetheart, I won't tell anyone."

"The contract is between Buddy Beddicker, aka Winner's Circle, and an Alvin Sassler. It's a personal-services agreement signed in 1985—I won't bore you with the legalese. Beddicker is named as Sassler's agent, he gets a fifteen-percent cut of everything Sassler gets. The contract runs for five years. After that time, Sassler still has to give sixty days' notice if he breaks the contract."

"And Murray thinks Alvin Sassler is our man?"

"He compared the signatures on the contract with the signatures on Dr. Double-X's corporate checking account."

"Shirley Adams, or whoever it was?"

"There were two, but Murray's convinced that the same person signed both, and the contract. He ran it past a handwriting guy at the Lake County Sheriff's Office. Oh, and Winner's Circle filed a lawsuit against Alvin Sassler four months ago, charging him with breach of contract."

Sussman poured himself another half-cup of coffee. "So Murray figures that Buddy Beddicker had a pretty damned good grudge against the Doctor. But why wasn't he satisfied with the lawsuit? Was the contract enforceable?"

"In my judgment it was," Susie said. "It certainly wasn't an agreement I'd ever sign, but at the time, Sassler was an unknown. He must have figured he needed an agent to get bookings."

"Did the lawsuit ever get to court?"

"I'm trying to find out. I sent Murray back to the court files. He can find out the resolution of the case. If the suit was dropped, then we naturally have some more questions to ask."

"Well, at least I can tell Cliff I've got an identity for him. That was the original deal. Hopefully I can wind this thing up. I don't suppose you can get back out here for the last weekend?"

"Not a chance. Look, Andy, why don't you try to get another two weeks to the story? It's just getting interesting, really. I can't imagine Cliff Trager would want to drop it now. Maybe you can stretch it out until Passover. I'll come out for a beachfront seder."

"I'll call the rabbi," Sussman grumbled. "Maybe we can have it catered."

But Susie was right, of course. Cliff Trager was overjoyed at the turn the case had taken. "Andy," he said less than an hour later, "New York is thrilled, abso-

lutely!'' They were sitting at the coffee shop at the hotel.
Andy still hadn't gathered enough strength to get in a
car and actually drive somewhere. He had sloped downstairs in his shower thongs and tennis shorts and a Chicago Bears sweatshirt and was working on his fifth cup
of coffee. "We're going to show those yackos at the newspapers too,'' Trager went on, rattling his pen against his
clipboard. "Listen: we're going to promote this identity
thing the rest of the week, we'll have teasers on all the
station breaks, and we'll get the local news shows to
plug it every night. Then Saturday we're going to do a
live segment, we may get an entire half-hour.''

"Cliff, what am I supposed to say for a whole half-
hour?''

"What are you supposed to say? Andy! You start with
the videotape of the prerace interviews. We've got Dr.
Double-X spitting out that wad of tobacco juice—my
God, that's what killed him! Then you do the story of
his real identity—''

"Not proven.'' Sussman had not told Trager about the
contracts: Murray had been adamant about Buddy Beddicker's name not being mentioned yet.

"We don't need to prove it publicly, Andy—I'm taking
your word about the source. I'll have our people put a
tracer on Alvin Sassler; if he shows up anywhere between here and Saskatoon, we'll kill that part of it. But
I think we can go public with all that speculation about
Dr. Double-X and Harvey Kopeck and jumping leagues.
We've got a legitimate murder now, we're not going to
be laughed at. And we can do live interviews. Wireless
is news now, the poison was in his possession. And we
should round up everyone who was in the vicinity. We're
going to try to reassemble everyone who was in the final
race for a video hookup—hell, Andy, we could do a whole
hour.''

Sussman felt his headache start pounding again; he
suspected that it was time for a hair from the dog that
bit him. He let Cliff drone on for another fifteen minutes

about the possibilities of a prime-time report, or a *60 Minutes* segment, not to mention an Emmy. Then he signaled the waitress for a Bloody Mary.

It was not the most nourishing breakfast he'd ever had, but it would at least silence the bats that were buzzing around in his belfry for a while. Hopefully the sauna, the steam bath, and a healthy nap would do the rest. If his career was going to turn into a laughingstock before his very eyes, he was at least going to do it in style.

24

Murray Glick sat in his office in Northbrook Court with the door closed. He was not taking any visitors. He could not, in living memory, ever remember turning down business: he had not had an angry customer since he had moved into the mall. But Peggy had left a stack of messages on his desk, most of them from an irate Mr. Graber, who had no intention of setting foot in Palm Springs until he knew whether Sy Feldman's golf handicap was legitimate or not. Graber would have to take his chances.

The shame of it was, Murray thought, he might not even turn a penny on this case, unless he decided to bill Andy Sussman an exorbitant fee. And if Sussman wasn't going to be reimbursed by the network, he would probably have to keep the charges down—it was bad business, but a friend was a friend, and truthfully Andy was one of the best he had. Furthermore, as if one personal relationship on a case wasn't enough, there was Terry Tollison to consider.

Ah, Terry. Murray had always tried to keep his love affairs from getting entangled in his cases, but it was hard to avoid, it was such a convenient way of meeting women. And the other night had turned out to be a wonderful time, they had made it to Second City and then cruised through Old Town until the wee hours— Terry had been holding back, she had a few hours of vacation time left over and had planned to take the morning off. So they wandered in and out of the various

folkie bars, caught a few late acts, and dropped in on
several bookstores—Murray had a reservoir of plot sum-
maries in the back of his mind, he could get through
literary discussions as long as they didn't dwell on one
title too long.

Unfortunately, when the evening finally ended, Terry
was true to her word. At 1:30 she had dropped Murray
off at Northwestern Station, leaving him with a warm
kiss and twenty dollars to see him back to Northbrook.
It fell something short of complete rapture, he guessed,
but it was more than enough to see him through until
Saturday night. In the meantime, Terry had pointedly
reminded him of his promise: that nothing would happen to upset Steve Beamon's recovery. It was a promise
she expected Murray to keep.

So Murray sat alone in his office, drawing little dia-
grams on the legal pad in front of him. The murder
scenario was fairly clear in his mind. Dr. Double-X had
been killed by the poison in the chewing tobacco, that
much was obvious. Someone would have substituted the
poisoned pouch for the real one—Murray was convinced
it had happened right before the race. The switch could
have been made earlier, if the killer knew that Wireless
had kept the chewing tobacco in his corner kit, and if
the killer knew that Dr. Double-X was using a bag that
had already been opened. But Murray was convinced
that the whole plan had been set up to make it look like
a drowning and heart attack. If Dr. Double-X had merely
keeled over from the drug, they might have gotten him
to the pier and possibly saved him. Falling overboard
in the cold water just as the poison took effect would be
much more lethal, and it would make the crime almost
impossible to trace.

Murray looked back at his legal pad. There were two
questions written down. First, why did Buddy Beddicker
drop his lawsuit against Alvin Sassler? He knew the case
had been dropped—he had gone back to the court files,
as Susie had suggested. If the contract was ironclad, as
Susie thought it was, why let him off the hook? Murray

remembered Wireless's story about the incident in Chicago. Double-X had claimed to have someone "by the balls." That someone was undoubtedly Buddy Beddicker. He needed to know what Dr. Double-X had on him. He guessed the answer lay somewhere in the second question: What did all this have to do with Steve Beamon? Barney Hennesey had not found any evidence of a business relationship with Steve or Cindi, but Barney had only looked in the contract file, he was not going to spend one more minute in that office than he had to. Murray supposed that he could go back to the office himself, but he was certain that if there *had* been any link to either of the Beamons, it would not be lying around, not at this point in the case.

Murray was not without his own ideas, though. Buddy Beddicker had a reputation for signing athletes illegally, supplying them with money and cars. Steve Beamon had been a hot player with mediocre grades; his school, Illinois State University, would never generate as much publicity as the Big Ten or the eastern schools. Who could blame a young kid for thinking a big-time agent could help give him some exposure? Was it possible, Murray wondered, that Buddy Beddicker had been slipping Beamon "laundry money" before his injury? And what would happen if the NCAA found out about it? What would happen to his scholarship at ISU if the school discovered that he'd been blatantly abusing the rules before his accident? It was just speculation. And there was the promise to Terry, which he fully intended to keep.

But time was running out. Murray was convinced that the discovery of the poison and the ensuing murder investigation would no doubt shake Buddy Beddicker out of any complacency he might have had—assuming, as Murray did, that Beddicker was behind the murder. If Buddy was going to protect himself, it meant dealing with whoever else knew about the murder.

Murray picked up the sports page of the *Tribune*. The U.S. volleyball team's Midwest tour was finally making it to Chicago, they'd be at Northwestern's McGaw Hall

in Evanston tomorrow night. It was time to confront
Cindi Beamon with some hard facts—maybe not the
kind that would stand up in court, but enough to reveal
another layer of the truth. The problem was, how could
he get to Cindi in private? Steve Beamon would obviously be there to watch her, and Murray didn't want
him involved. He had a hunch that Steve didn't know
what his sister had been doing in his behalf. Furthermore, Beddicker would probably have someone tailing
both of them, and it wouldn't be Barney Hennesey; the
wheelchair would be too clumsy.

Murray picked up the phone, called the Northwestern
University sports-information department, and asked
them about the volleyball team's schedule. He was told
they were playing an exhibition tonight in Minneapolis—that was perfect as far as he was concerned, he
could fly there in an hour and be back in time for breakfast.

Murray put the legal pad down and leaned back on
his swivel chair. He looked around his office, at the two
lead slugs that were set in matching glass paperweights,
standing sentry on the front corners of his desk. They
were the last two shells that had been fired at him in
anger. They were there to remind him of the life he had
left behind, of the cold nights staking out philandering
husbands, of dimly lit warehouses and seedy business-
men. Murder was no longer Murray Glick's territory.
Death was not a marketable commodity this close to
Neiman-Marcus.

But now Murray was beginning to face the probabilities that some unpleasant things would have to be done
before this case was closed. He buzzed Peggy and instructed her to make plane reservations for the Twin
Cities, then leaned back and lit a cigar. It didn't relax
him at all. He skimmed over his legal pad once more,
but the conclusions were the same.

Murray realized that in all likelihood, someone was
going to die before this case was over.

He wanted to make sure it wasn't him.

25

It was a crisp, clear night in Minneapolis. The temperature was in the thirties, but the breeze seemed warm. People walked around the streets with their jackets open, their scarves wrapped loosely around their necks. The city had gotten more than fifty inches of snow over the winter, but the streets were plowed and the snow piles in the parking lots were starting to melt down. Spring was in the air, Murray thought—just another three months, for crying out loud, how did people make it through a winter here?

The volleyball match was at Williams Arena, on the campus of the University of Minnesota. It was an old barnlike structure; Murray had seen a few basketball games there when he was in college. The fire department had almost closed the place down a few years ago, but it was still a better spot to see a sports event than the antiseptic Metrodome a few miles away. It had atmosphere. The old wooden bench seats were close to the action. The place looked and smelled like a college gym.

Getting close to Cindi Beamon wasn't difficult. Murray had bought a ticket right on the floor. Getting a few words with her in private was another matter. He waved at her, she waved back, but she didn't appear eager to talk. She warmed up with her usual look of quiet determination. Murray couldn't really tell if she was looking at him or not.

There were still a few minutes to go before the match started, so Murray got up and wandered around courtside. When a warm-up ball squirted loose, he grabbed it and waved again at Cindi. She finally acknowledged him and walked over. She didn't look exactly overjoyed to see him. "I'll take that," she said, reaching for the ball.

"Nice to see you too, sweetheart," Murray said as he shook her outstretched hand. "I flew in just for the match."

"I'm thrilled. Thinking of becoming a corporate sponsor?" Cindi glanced back toward her team, which was starting to head for the bench, but Murray held on to her hand.

"We have to talk," Murray said as the PA announcer welcomed the fans to the University of Minnesota.

"About what?"

"About a murder."

"I don't know what you're talking about."

"I think you do. I know all about Buddy Beddicker," Murray said, squeezing Cindi's palm as she turned to walk back to the sideline. "I know about the poison in the chewing tobacco. I know how you got that raft to tip over with just a little nudge."

Cindi stared at Murray. She started to edge back toward the opposite side of the court, but he held on to her hand.

"You can talk to me," Murray said. "Or I can just let my friend Andy Sussman report the whole story on CBS. Or I can go to the police. It's your choice."

Cindi Beamon shook her hand loose. "After the game," she said. "Marquette Hotel. Room 432. Eleven o'clock, come alone."

"See you then," said Murray. "Have a nice game."

It was a small hotel room, about the cheapest you could get in the swank Marquette. There were two double beds that took up most of the space, and a small desk on the far wall with two chairs that Murray and Cindi sat in. There was a vending machine in the far corner; it had everything in it from champagne to toothpaste; you could help yourself and it would be charged to the room. Cindi Beamon was wearing jeans and a light blue turtleneck sweater; her down jacket was tossed on the bed. Murray had dressed in his formal wear: gray slacks and a navy sport jacket. His collar was open.

"Let's get a few things straight," Murray said. "I'm not the police. I don't do things by the book."

"I thought you were working for television. That's what you said in LA."

"I was misinformed."

"*You* were misinformed? I don't even remember your name. Glen something."

"Murray will do."

"Oh, fine." Cindi tapped her fingernails on the desk. "So who *do* you work for?"

"Depends. On who treats me right. Whoever wears the white hats."

"I don't know if I can help you then." Cindi's voice was shaky; she had lost some of her casual self-assurance. "I don't know who wears the white hats anymore."

"It's a tough call," Murray said, taking her hand. "I'm hearing about some very nasty people these days. I'm not sure what side they're on. One of them is dead." He paused. "I think you killed him."

Cindi jerked her hand back. Their eyes met for a moment, then she turned away and walked over to the vending machine. "That's crazy," she whispered, pulling out a Lite beer. "You saw the news. He drowned."

"You're way behind, Cindi. They found the poison in the chewing tobacco. The police are asking questions. They'll be looking at tapes of the boat race."

"They can look all they want." Cindi fumbled with the bottle cap, it fell to the carpet. The beer foamed up around her hand. "I was there. It was . . . it was a terrible accident. I didn't . . . I had nothing to do—"

Murray gently took the bottle from Cindi and set it on the desk. "Cindi, time's running out." He put his hand on her shoulder, but she pushed him away and stared out the window. "People are starting to ask around. They're going to want to know why a lizard named Buddy Beddicker hired an ex-con to tail your brother."

Cindi looked back at Murray. A tear was welling in her eye, she quickly wiped it away. "I have no idea. Maybe he had a special place in his heart for paralyzed athletes. Maybe he wanted to set up a trust fund for him."

"I don't think so, Cindi. He doesn't strike me as a philanthropic type of guy."

Cindi didn't reply. She wiped the foam off her hands and sat on the foot of the bed.

"Cindi, I know all about your brother. It was a terrible thing that happened, and I don't want it to get worse. Just ask yourself: what's going to happen when people find out that he was taking money under the table from Buddy Beddicker all through his first two years in school? What happens to his scholarship then?"

Cindi twisted her hands in her lap and stared at the floor. "Someone already asked me that."

They sat still for a moment. Murray walked over to the window. He tried to open it a few inches but it was locked shut. "Cindi, what did Beddicker tell you? What proof did he have?"

"Proof?" Cindi hesitated. She looked around the room as if expecting some type of divine intervention, then said, "He had records of every payment he'd ever made. He had a contract Steve signed when he was a sophomore. He showed it all to me."

"Why, Cindi? Why would a kid do that? He wasn't illiterate, he knew the rules."

"How the hell should I know why?" Cindi gripped the edge of the bedspread; she made no effort now to hide her tears. "He was nineteen years old, he was a terrible student. Basketball was the only thing he could do. No one was sitting there baby-sitting for him, I was halfway across the world playing volleyball. What do you think happens? Some slick guy rolls up in a Mercedes, tells him how great he is. Tells him how he could be as rich as Magic or Larry Bird, if only the great Buddy Beddicker would get behind him."

Murray sat down beside Cindi. He pulled out a handkerchief and dabbed a tear from her cheek. "Cindi, it's not too late."

Cindi bit her lip and watched the carpet.

"Talk to me, Cindi. What did Dr. Double-X have on Buddy Beddicker?"

"I have no idea."

"I don't believe it—"

"For God's sake, how would I know?" Her head snapped up. "I wasn't exactly in a position to ask. Beddicker came up to me, he said he was going to ruin Steve. He said the NCAA would force ISU to take away his scholarship, they'd throw him out of school."

"And you believed him?"

"He showed me the contract! What was I supposed to do, call his bluff? I know how the NCAA works. What was going to happen to Steve? Where would he get the money to go to school? What would happen to him afterward? My parents don't have money. How much do you think Olympic volleyball players get?"

"So you went through with it."

"I was blackmailed!"

"You killed a man, Cindi!" Murray held her by both arms. She shrank back on the bed. "You took a life—"

"I didn't have any choice!" Cindi was sobbing. "He told me not to go to the police. He said he'd have someone there watching me. I was terrified."

"So you switched the tobacco pouches. You made sure the boat went over—"

Cindi broke away from Murray and walked over to the desk. She reached for her beer and took a long draw from it. Looking Murray squarely in the eye, she spoke softly. "I didn't want to. I'm not a murderer. But I worked on that TV show for three days, Murray, and you know what I saw? This ugly swine grunting around like he'd just crawled out of a cave. I'd heard rumors about him too. About how he treated women. And I asked myself, if I have to choose between him and my brother, who deserves a break? Who deserves a life?"

"It's a hell of a judgment to take upon yourself."

"I didn't ask for it. I didn't." Cindi's voice shook. She sounded as if she was trying to convince herself as well as Murray. "So what are you going to do? Tell the police? Lock me up? Ruin my brother's life?"

"Whoa, Cindi." Murray reached for her hand but she pushed him away. "Hey, do I sound like that bad of a guy?"

"I think you're a slime."

"First impressions can be tricky. And speaking of slime, what do you think Buddy Beddicker's going to do now?"

"Why should he do anything?"

"Why? Because the police know that Dr. Double-X was murdered. And they're going to know that his real name was Alvin Sassler as soon as Andy Sussman breaks the story. And before too long they'll know that Buddy Beddicker was Alvin Sassler's agent, and that Sassler broke the contract, and that Beddicker took him to court, and then inexplicably dropped the suit. By the way, Cindi, do you know why Beddicker dropped that suit?"

Cindi answered in a near-whisper, "I have no idea."

"I do. I think Alvin Sassler had something on Buddy Beddicker. Illegal recruiting, investment fraud—whatever it was, it was serious enough that Beddicker wanted him dead. I'm going to find out what it was, Cindi. And you're going to help me."

Cindi Beamon stared at her Lite beer. "And why would I do that?"

"Because," Murray said, "you're the only one that can tie Buddy Beddicker to that murder. You're the link between Beddicker and Dr. Double-X. What do you think would happen if you were suddenly out of the picture?"

"I suppose," said Cindi, "that things would be a lot more comfortable for Buddy Beddicker."

"You bet your sweet petunia they would be. And the more the police unravel, the more danger you're in. Now, the way I figure, you've got two choices. You could go to the police and admit the murder. Tell them you were blackmailed, agree to turn state's evidence against Beddicker. I should point out, however, that there are certain risks inherent in that course of action."

"No kidding."

"They'd find out about Steve. The NCAA might be inclined to be lenient, of course. Maybe they'd figure he'd suffered enough already. Maybe they'd let him keep his scholarship."

"What do you think?"

"No promises. And that, of course, presumes that your story holds up in court, that you can convict Beddicker. He'll have the best attorneys money can buy. The main evidence will be your testimony. Risky proposition."

"Terrific," said Cindi Beamon. "I run out and confess. I could end up in jail, my brother could end up on the street, not to mention a certain hoodlum that'll want revenge." She took another sip of beer. "What's behind door number two?"

Murray got up and paced around the room. He wanted to light up a cigar, but there was a large no-smoking sign on the mirror. "Behind door number two," he said, "is what I would consider a gamble, but a good one. We need to get to Beddicker. We need to find out what Dr. Double-X had on him. We need to get him to sing."

"How?"

"Carefully. First of all, we move him off his own turf. And soon. The information's just starting to leak out. We don't want to give him too much time to think about it."

"I have no idea what you're talking about."

"Just pay attention." Murray sat back down on the bed, put his arm around Cindi's shoulder, and said to her, "Here's the plan. . . ."

It was 8:15 in the morning. Murray was sitting in the first-class section of a DC-10 on the way back to Chicago.

There had been no red-eye available last night, so he had spent the night alone in a room at the Marquette, pondering his strategy. What was he getting into? Obstruction of justice? Blackmail? Worse?

And why? Because he wanted to show those peabrains at CBS what network material was? Because he wanted to help his buddy Andy? Because he wanted to prove something to a woman who, despite his best instincts, he might actually be falling in love with?

Murray reasoned that he was acting within legal boundaries, up to a point. He wasn't suppressing any physical evidence. He could conveniently forget his conversation with Cindi, if anyone asked. As for his plan, he admitted that he was entering shady legal territory, not to mention questionable strategy. What would Beddicker do when Cindi Beamon called him and threatened to pour her heart out to the police? Would he agree to meet her, at her specifications? Or would he find someone to deal with her? Murray doubted whether Beddicker could find another killer on such short notice—hiring murders out could get messy; he'd already learned that. Murray was betting that Buddy Beddicker would take care of this problem himself.

But not in Chicago. Cindi would be in Los Angeles, and Beddicker would have to come after her. Could they get the truth out of him? Could they force him to compromise himself in a way that would protect both Steve and Cindi? Murray had tried his best to convince Cindi that they could, but he wondered if she really believed it.

He didn't believe it himself.

Ah, it should have all been so simple, Murray thought as the plane cruised in toward O'Hare. He'd been hired to solve a murder. He'd solved it. And the dramatic opportunities were rife, the commercial possibilities were limitless, he had every justification to haul Cindi Beamon up before the television cameras, stare directly into the red light, and say, like Bogart to Mary Astor, "You, Cindi, baby—you're taking the fall."

But Cindi Beamon was not going to take the fall; there was a much more deserving candidate.

And though Murray wished it weren't so, he was beginning to face the truth: the scenario he had plotted was a dangerous one. And there was more to his plan than he had revealed in the hotel room.

26

"Murray has gone berserk," said Andy Sussman.

"Well, he didn't have very far to go," replied Susie Ettenger. "Look, Andy, I've got about thirty pounds of legal briefs to go through, could you maybe call me after eight, I can cry about being all alone on a Saturday night while I watch *Love Story* on my VCR for the thirty-first time."

"I'm not kidding, Suse, he's gone off the deep end." Sussman was not very far from the deep end himself. He was standing fifty yards from the Pacific Ocean, at a phone booth a few feet from the bicycle path at the Santa Monica Beach. It was 2:30 in the afternoon. He'd driven the twenty-five miles north from Redondo on specific instructions from Murray: no telephone calls from the hotel or from anywhere near either Redondo Beach or the KCBS television studios on Sunset. "You want to know what I look like?" Sussman said. "I'm wearing torn blue jeans, an old trench coat, and sunglasses, I'm standing here on the beach raving like all the loonies who wander around on the boardwalk. All I need is a sleeping bag and a shopping cart."

"Sweetheart, believe me, I'm taking complete notes on all of this; we'll be discussing it in New York as soon as you finish the story. And I saw you on *Spectacular*. I just want you to know, Andy, you handled that with all the dignity that could possibly be expected."

"I'm touched," said Sussman. He knew there was a limit to how much dignity you could squeeze out of the bald head of a crazed wrestling manager, and that was just the beginning of his problems. Ben Garrison had come storming into the studio only minutes after they had gone on the air, live—the timing was obviously not accidental. Garrison had somehow talked his way past the security guards and was pounding on the glass window separating the studio from the control room as Sussman narrated to millions at home the true story of Dr. Double-X's championship match with Crash Kopeck.

"What kind of appreciation is this?" bellowed Garrison as *Sports Spectacular* broke for a commercial. "I give you two weeks of cooperation, I allow you to interview my wrestlers, I allow you to take a live segment from my memorial service for a fallen champion, and you go on live television and dispute the integrity of my sport!" Ninety seconds later, Garrison was still on the set. He was dressed in a lime-green sport jacket and gray slacks; Sussman noted that he had somehow gotten his TV makeup applied before crashing the show. "Ladies and gentlemen," Garrison said, speaking live and coast-to-coast, "I just want to assure every single wrasslin' fan in the United States that the Wrestling Federation of America is one-hundred-percent absolutely legit and on the level. There has *never* been a scandal involving our athletes, the greatest in the world—we have *never* had a drug problem, and do you know why? I'll tell you why—because professional wrestling is the most demanding sport in the world, with the greatest athletes, and not *one* of them could compete for *five seconds* if he were under the influence of the illegal substances that plague other so-called sports like baseball and basketball and football . . ." Garrison had continued his harangue until the next hurriedly applied commercial break. When the red light blinked off he flashed Sussman a crocodile grin, said, "Thanks for the time, Andy," and went back to the control room to watch the rest of the show from a monitor.

"Well, anyway, I thought you handled Wireless with

great restraint," Susie said. "He was obviously distraught about the whole police investigation and you showed genuine compassion, Andy, the audience could sense that."

"What was I supposed to do, Suse? I've got a two-hundred-fifty-pound bald Munchkin crying on my shoulder—he was chewing on my sport jacket, could you believe it? Chewing! It's a good thing it was one of Cliff's blazers. And he still thinks they were after him—after the show he literally *dived* on Captain Stevens, he was begging him for police protection—and he's still their number-one suspect! And Stevens wouldn't leave for an hour after the show, Susie, he was giving *me* the third degree."

Captain Stevens had given Sussman a short TV interview at the beginning of the program, explaining the proof of the poison and the direction the investigation was going in. He had remained in the studio until the end of the show, listening patiently as Andy broadcast his own "exclusive" report. Then he grilled Sussman in his polite but insistent way: How had Sussman known that Dr. Double-X was in reality Alvin Sassler? Who was the unnamed sports agent that Sassler/Double-X had been feuding with? Why hadn't he reported to the police that Wireless's apartment had been robbed from the beginning?

Andy had patiently explained his Fifth Amendment rights and his responsibility not to reveal sources. He certainly wasn't going to admit that the information on Dr. Double-X had come as a result of stolen documents. And Murray was adamant that neither Buddy Beddicker's name nor his own be mentioned for at least another week.

"So now I have the Redondo Beach police to worry about," Sussman told Susie. "I've got them tailing me, and Wireless calls my hotel room every hour, and Jill Weintraub wants me to get him out of their condo before their baby comes due, and now Murray's got me playing spook—"

"Andy, honey, I'm sure it's all very exasperating, but there's nothing I can do except bring the matter to the attention of Black Rock, and I can't do that until Monday morning at the soonest."

"Susie, I want you to come out here."

"*Now?* Andy, I'll be lucky if I don't spend all tomorrow in the office. I fell so far behind the last time I came out—"

"I know, I know. Susie, listen, I've got a feeling there's serious trouble brewing. Murray's been—"

"Murray can take care of himself."

"Murray's got a whole scheme cooked up, he won't tell me anything except the bare bones. He's got me renting cars and staking out restaurants up in Zuma and putting on these stupid disguises and driving up fire trails in the Santa Monica Mountains."

"Andy, you're ranting."

"*I am not ranting!*" Sussman stopped and looked around as two beautiful women in three-hundred-dollar jogging outfits roller-skated by with a pair of Alsatians on a leash. They turned away from him when he looked their way, he considered asking them for spare change, or maybe a date, but thought better of it. "Sweetheart, I am not ranting. This is serious business here. This is murder. One, so far."

Sussman thought he could hear the rustling of papers; he detected some classical music in the background. "Andy, if you're worried about doing anything illegal, just don't do it. Call me and check. Don't let Murray drag you around, he's probably doing this whole thing just so he can go on TV and sell his damned cruises."

"Suse, forget about Murray, okay? I need you here. Live and in person." Sussman hesitated. He was getting into territory that was not properly addressed in a trench coat from a telephone booth on the beach.

"Andy, what am I supposed to do, just drop everything so I can fly out there and let you cry on my shoulder?"

"No, not just that. Susie, listen . . ." Sussman could see the point of no return coming; he couldn't stall it off much longer. "Susan Ettenger, do you trust me?"

"Of course I trust you."

"Would I ask you to do something important without justification?"

"All the time."

"But would I ask you to make great personal sacrifices for no apparent reason, babe, if I didn't have some greater purpose in mind?"

"What greater purpose?"

Sussman took a deep breath of ocean air. "Come out here, Suse. On the next plane." There was silence for thirty seconds—it seemed about a lifetime. "Susie, babe. I love you. And I need you."

"In that order?"

"In that order."

"All right, then," Susie said in a whisper. "I'm on my way."

Sussman hung up the phone and walked out to the edge of the beach. It was a bright, clear winter's day, the smog had blown inland, he could see all the way to Catalina Island. He could look to his left and see the Palos Verdes peninsula, just south of Redondo Beach, where this whole thing had started. He could look north toward Malibu and the Santa Monica Mountains, where he suspected it would all finish. He had no idea what Murray was cooking up, but he suspected it would all happen soon.

And the sooner the better.

It was snowing again in Chicago, just a light dusting this time. It swirled around and blew into thin drifts, covering the dirty, melting remnants of the last storm with a clean white coat. Murray Glick was sitting at Diana's, a Greek restaurant on the Northwest Side, with Terry Tollison. He had tried to get her to come out to Northbrook, but she would have none of it. "I don't need to come out to the mall on a Saturday night, for God's sake," she told Murray. "You ought to get a jeep or something, if you're so worried about your car. I think all those cruises are turning you into a w-i-m-p."

Murray had caved in, although he still wasn't crazy about taking the Maz into the city in the snow. He was afraid it would disappear into a pothole on Halsted Street; he'd end up entombed in cheap asphalt, if they ever got around to filling it. And it wasn't that he felt compelled to prove his virility—he'd had plenty of time to contemplate that lately. The thing was, he wanted to have one last dinner with Terry before heading back to LA. He wanted to make sure he understood his own motivations. If he was going to take a risk, he wanted to make sure who and what he was doing it for.

Still, he had avoided any pressing issues. They had enjoyed an hour of flaming appetizers and Greek wine and roast lamb and a belly dancer who'd jiggled past them—Murray had done an admirable job of averting his eyes. He had concentrated on Terry, wearing a rust-colored cable-knit sweater and designer jeans, her overcoat wrapped around the back of her chair. Murray thought winter would never end.

It was Terry who broached the subject. "Murray," she said, finishing her baklava, "you know I'm not exactly ignorant about what's going on here. I read your cruise propaganda, three pages about the great Lester Beldon murder case."

"Glad to see you read the homework, Ter."

"Which involved one Andrew Sussman, your good buddy, I take it?"

"As fine a gentleman as you'll ever meet."

"Who, I just happened to notice, is showing up on CBS these days investigating the murder of a professional wrestler named Dr. Double-X, who died on that *Celebrity Superteams* show, in a boat that was being steered by Cindi Beamon, sister of Steve Beamon."

Murray leaned back in his chair; he reached for his wineglass but Terry poked it away.

"Now, coincidentally, Murray, who should show up

on my doorstep last week but Chicagoland's most famous detective, self-acclaimed."

"No brag, just fact, ma'am."

"Inquiring about the welfare of my patient—"

"Terry, that has nothing to do with us."

"Oh, please! It was all based on that wonderful relationship we carved out in the Caribbean?"

"All right, all right," Murray said. He wasn't used to this type of self-defense. "I'll admit, my initial reason for calling you was in the interest of seeing justice done to a vicious murderer."

"And getting another big score for yourself?"

"I don't suppose you could keep your voice down," Murray said. He didn't think anyone was listening, he assumed most of Diana's clientele was getting about as schnockered as he was, but it was too late in the game to take any risks.

"I suppose another case would look great on your brochure," Terry whispered sharply. "Especially one that's being covered coast-to-coast by CBS."

"Guilty, guilty, guilty," said Murray. "I'm a worthless, sleazy cad, I'm in this completely for my own selfish glory. I don't know why a kind, virtuous woman such as yourself even allows herself to be seen with such slime."

Terry pushed her chair back and stared quietly at Murray. She started to take a sip of wine, but she pulled her hand back. "I don't know why either. I thought maybe I'd have figured it out by now."

"Well, I'm afraid I can't help you out much tonight, Ter. Fact is, I think maybe we'd better head for home. I've got a flight to catch tomorrow."

"Where?"

"Can't say."

"Murray—"

"Shh," Murray said, putting his index to Terry's lips. "Enough table talk."

Terry sighed. Not a word passed between them until well after Murray had paid the bill. They were back in the Maserati, heading for Terry's apartment on Geneva

Terrace, just off Lincoln Avenue. "Murray," she said as they pulled up to the snowbank near her building, "there's two things I want to know."

"Ask me no questions, I'll tell you no lies."

"Talk, buster," she said, kicking him gently in the leg.

"Take your chances, then."

"Murray, what happens to Steve Beamon after all of this?"

"I made a promise," Murray said. "Sworn solemnly over a slice of Gino's deep-dish pizza, if you'll remember."

"And you're Mr. Virtue all of a sudden?"

Murray put his arm around Terry; it was the first time he'd held her closely. "I've got it in me somewhere, I'm reasonably sure. What was the second question?"

"The second question," said Terry, "was whether I should put a candle in my window while you march off to war, or just face reality and resume my search for a kind and generous and sensitive man who's also a helluva lot of fun."

"That seems like a difficult, if not hopeless task." Murray kissed Terry on the cheek. "If I were you, I'd give me at least till the end of the week."

"I suppose I can live with that." Terry turned to Murray and slid her arms around his chest. They hugged each other for a few more moments, then kissed again.

"Farewell, my lovely," said the Detective as Terry opened the car door and headed for her apartment. "I'm off for danger's lair. If I never return, treasure these few moments between us."

"Break a leg, Sherlock."

"Right." Murray blew Terry another kiss. He waved good-bye, slipped the Maserati into gear, and headed back into the winter's night.

27

It was nearly 9:30. The evening fog had rolled in off the ocean, pushing its way over the beach at Zuma and up against the Santa Monica Mountains. The Pacific Coast Highway was nearly empty. A few cars droned by in the night, most of them headed back to Los Angeles, an hour's drive south, or to Malibu.

There were less than a dozen customers at Marita's, a Mexican cantina half a mile north of the beach. A few winter surfers who had hung around all afternoon stood by the bar in their wet suits. There were the usual drifters; some of them had made their way down the coast from as far as Seattle. They sat at the bar or at small tables, munching on chips and salsa, drinking beer, devouring enchiladas.

When the black limousine pulled into the parking lot, it did not raise much of a stir. The limo was nearly invisible in the fog; the restaurant lights barely made an impact. And those who might have spotted it would not have been surprised. LA was awash in limousines; around Malibu they were more plentiful than Fords. It was probably just another punk movie actor, bored with his millions, going for a late-night spin.

In the far corner of the parking lot sat a beige Camaro with its hood up and a surfboard lashed to the top. A tall man in a wet suit leaned over the hood. He tinkered with the carburetor and jiggled the dipstick. He turned around when he saw the limousine and watched as a man got out, alone. He tried to look through the windshield, but he couldn't discern anything. He reached for a small pocket pager and pressed the button.

Inside Marita's, a man sat in the far corner. It was a small table. There was sawdust on the floor and some fake ceramic murals on the walls in back of him. The man wore a leather motorcycle jacket, he had black curly hair that fell to his shoulders. He sipped on a Corona beer. His ears were plugged into a radio; his eyes were glued to a television at the bar—the Lakers were playing up the coast in Oakland. He heard the beep in his earphones. He poured the Corona into an empty beer mug.

Across the room, a woman sat, alone. She had dark brown hair, it was long and straight, it flowed down to her waist. She was wearing jeans, a flannel shirt, and a pink down vest. She saw the man pour his beer, she turned her chair so that it faced the door. When Buddy Beddicker walked in, she tipped slightly backward. She might not have recognized him if she hadn't been expecting him; his collar was turned up, he wore dark glasses and a light blue golfing cap that was pulled over his forehead. They established eye contact, Beddicker walked over to her table. He placed a folded piece of notebook paper next to her beer and said, "Fan mail?"

Cindi Beamon took the letter and recognized her own handwriting. "Beddicker," it read, "the game's over. You screwed up, it's only a matter of time now. We want out." The letter had set the terms of the meeting: Beddicker to come alone, with money and passports. It carried a threat: if he didn't show, she would be appearing the following Saturday on network television to tell the whole story. "Sit down," she said. "Have a beer. A bon-voyage party."

"I like the hair," Beddicker said, running his hand along the back of Cindi's head. "Tough to play sports in, though. Somebody could trip on all that, take a very nasty fall. Have a very bad accident."

"I'll have to remember that when I make my comeback for the Swedes. Did you bring what I asked?"

"Oh, I haven't come empty-handed." Beddicker signaled the waitress and ordered a beer. When she left, he said, "I just thought we should have a short discussion first. You know, I really hate to see you quit the team, darling. All that work you've put in, it would be such a shame to drop out before the Olympic trials even begin."

Across the room, the man with the radio bent over his beer. Beddicker's voice was low, but Andy Sussman heard every word—Cindi had a wire on her. Another customer wandered in; the front door was open for a moment. Sussman scratched his head, his scalp itched underneath the wig; he could still see the vague outline of the limo in the fog.

"I think a few salient factors should be open to discussion," Buddy Beddicker was saying. He ground a large corn chip into the table. "You want to be a TV star? You want to sing to the gendarmes? Ask yourself what happens to poor little brother, sis."

"CBS'll cover everything. I give them the exclusive story, they'll take care of Steve. Maybe we'll be on *60 Minutes*, maybe we'll get our own TV mini-series. It'll work out."

"Now, that's very interesting," said Buddy Beddicker. "I'm fascinated by that. A class network like them, going for checkbook journalism. Maybe I think you're just pulling my leg, darling. Maybe I think you're a great kidder."

"Hey, take a chance. Sit down in front of the tube Saturday. Fix yourself a big bowl of popcorn."

Outside in the parking lot, the man in the wet suit got back in his Camaro and tried to start it; he revved the engine once, twice, but he couldn't get it to turn over. He looked around the parking lot, the fog was still rolling in, every once in a while it would ease up and he could see the big black limo clearly, sitting twenty yards from the front door. He wished he had gotten a better look. But in a few minutes the fog would be working for him.

He walked over to the limousine. The windows to the passenger side were dark; he couldn't see through them. He circled over to the driver's side and tapped on the window. The driver sat there, motionless. He tapped again. "Hey, buddy! Yo!"

The window opened a crack.

"Thanks, dude. Look, my Camaro's down—"

"Hey, 'at's terrible, kid. Go call the Motor Club," said the driver. The hair under his cap was black and slick; he had long sideburns.

"Hey, guy, just gimme a jump, okay? I got cables. C'mon, you can start a Saturn rocket with that buggy."

"Bug off, kid."

The driver closed the window but the surfer kept tapping on it. "Hey, dude, don't be ar asshole, okay?" He unzipped his wet suit to the navel. "It'll take an hour to get a tow truck out here. C'mon, buddy. Just two minutes, help me out—"

The driver opened his window all the way. "I said *bug off*, kid, or I'll plow that piece-of-shit sports car into the ocean."

"That's awfully inconsiderate, dude," said Murray Glick, pulling a snub-nosed revolver from his wet suit and pointing it at the driver's eyeballs. "Now, how about if you just open the door and move over a seat before I blow your fucking head off."

Inside Marita's, Andy Sussman heard two beeps on his headset. He guzzled down the rest of his beer and signaled the waitress for another.

"I asked for two passports," Cindi Beamon was saying. "And the money. That's for starters."

"Of course, of course," Beddicker was saying. "Just for starters. Anything else I can do for you? Maybe you want me to provide the jet. Maybe I should cater the meal?"

Cindi tapped her nails on the table; the expression on her face was no different from when she prepared for a serve or leapt for a spike. "Look, if you didn't bring what I asked for, we're both wasting our time here. And don't try anything cute, if that's what you had in mind. I wrote everything down in a sealed envelope. I've got it hidden away. Anything happens to me, it'll end up in the hands of the police."

"Is that right?" said Buddy Beddicker. "You're a bright little broad, you know that?"

"I do know it."

"And that really depresses me, sweetheart. I'm feeling lonely and depressed, so far away from my friends and family. I think I'd like to make a little phone call. Reach out and touch someone. Excuse me." Beddicker waved for a waitress. "Hey, miss. You got a phone in here?"

"Over there, in the corner," said the waitress.

"Hey, you're a doll," said Beddicker. "I'll be back in a minute," he told Cindi. "Keep my seat warm."

Murray drove the limo a mile past the beach, then turned onto a small dirt road, keeping his pistol trained on Beddicker's driver the whole time. He'd recognized the man right off; he'd seen him before with Beddicker in the Cape Cod Room. "Bring anybody else with you, dude?" he asked. He figured he'd stay in his surfer mode for a little while longer.

"You're dogmeat, buddy," the driver said. "You know that? They shoot people in this state for stealing a limousine."

Murray pulled the limo off the road about a half-mile up; he'd found a nice pocket of fog. But being seen wasn't the problem. Time was the problem. "Eddie, baby, I want you to talk to me."

"I think you got the wrong guy," the driver said, but he had flinched when he'd heard his name.

"Oh, I don't think so. Eddie Connors, I know your whole story. I know where you live. I know who you work for. I could write a book on you."

"Then I guess you don't need much in the way of conversation."

Murray shoved the pistol in Eddie's mouth. "Fact is, Eddie, I'd be most happy to drill you right now. Guys like you make me sick, picking on poor crippled kids and women. I can toss you in a canyon and no one'll ever know the difference." He jammed the pistol deeper into Eddie's throat. "Will they?"

"Aargh," sputtered the driver, choking on the gun barrel. "Awright. Whaddya want?"

"I'd like the cap," Murray said, bringing the pistol back a few inches and lifting the chauffeur's cap from his head. "Looks good with the wet suit. And I want a story, Eddie. I want to know what Dr. Double-X had on Buddy Beddicker, that Beddicker had to kill him. Can you tell me that, Eddie?"

Cindi Beamon sat alone at her table, sipping occasionally on her beer. She looked over at Sussman, who didn't even glance at her; he was engrossed in the Lakers basketball game. "Excuse me," said the waitress, tapping her on the shoulder. "The gentleman would like you to come over to the telephone."

Cindi reached back and swept her long hair from the back of the chair, got up, and walked over to the pay phone at the back of the restaurant. "It's for you," Beddicker said. "Small world."

"Hello?" Cindi said into the receiver.

"Sis, it's me, Steve-o."

"Steve! Steven—" She stopped and looked at Beddicker. "Where are you?"

"I'm, uh . . . I'm a guest at Buddy Beddicker's home."

"Steven, what happened? Are you okay?"

"Uh, yeah. I'm fine. Maybe you better do what he says."

Cindi looked at Sussman, who was still staring at the television. "Stevie, what happened to you? How did they—"

Buddy Beddicker tapped her on the shoulder. "Long-distance calls can get expensive, darling. Better wrap it up."

"Stevie," Cindi said, taking another glance at Sussman, "I want to talk to you about your medicine. Don't let them keep you without the medication . . ." She turned her back to Beddicker and spoke in a whisper. "Stretch it, Stevie," she said.

Beddicker tried to grab her by the shoulder, but Cindi walked as far as the cord would reach. Then, louder, she said, "Make sure they keep your legs warm, Stevie. And do your exercises. . . ."

"He was a fucking animal, you know that?" said Eddie Connors.

"And you didn't know how to deal with that?" Murray looked at the clock in the dashboard of the limo. Time was slipping away.

"He came in the broad daylight, for Chrissakes. 'Course, I'd never seen him before, I didn't know who he was. He didn't have the goddamn mask on. I wasn't workin' for Buddy back when he was just the Mad Assassin or whatever the hell he was. He just comes bargin' into the office an' he tells the girl he wants to see Buddy, he has some private business to attend to. So she says, 'He's busy, sir,' and he says, real gently, 'I see,' and then he just fuckin' walks in."

"You didn't stop him?"

"It was my fault, he took me by surprise. Broad daylight, for Chrissakes. He walks right into Buddy's office and I follow him in, and the first thing he does, he nails me one—he fuckin' coldcocks me."

"No shit, Eddie. Well, the Doctor never was known for his social conventions. What happened next?"

"Hell, I'm down on the carpet, I'm seein' stars. Alls I know is, he locks the door and he tells Buddy, 'No calls.' An' he takes the place apart, he takes the whole fuckin' place down. He empties the drawers an' tears out files an' he pulls pictures off the wall. Buddy's got a wall safe there, an' he grabs him—I'm a little woozy here, but I remember it. He grabs Buddy an' he shoves his face against the knob, an' he says, 'Open it!' "

"And what did the Doctor find in the safe, Eddie?"

"Ah, I don't know, exactly. 'At's not my territory. Whatever it was, he had Buddy by the short hairs."

"So I hear. And that's why Buddy dropped the lawsuit?"

" 'At's not my territory either. You ask me, it didn't make a difference. A man treats Buddy like that, he's askin' for it. Even if he didn't take nothin'."

Murray sat still for a moment, then opened the front door and instructed Eddie to follow him outside. He stood the driver up beside the car and frisked him. Eddie had a gun, a Smith & Wesson. Murray took it and checked the chambers—it was loaded. He took Eddie's chauffeur jacket and pulled it over his wet suit. It was a tight fit, but it would do for the thirty seconds or so he would be in danger of being recognized. He tied Eddie's hands behind his back. He put a gag in his mouth. He opened the trunk and tossed Eddie Connors inside it.

Then he got back into the car, placed Eddie's gun on the seat beside him, and drove back to Marita's.

In the back of Marita's, by the telephone, Cindi Beamon was warding off Buddy Beddicker for what seemed like an hour, but actually was only a few minutes. "He's got medication," she was saying into the phone. "And exercises. It's from the accident." She whispered into Beddicker's ear, "You wouldn't want a dead paraplegic on your hands. That could get awfully messy, Buddy."

Across the room, Andy Sussman jerked his head away from the basketball game. He heard three long beeps in his earphone. He banged an empty bottle of Corona on the table and asked the waitress for a refill.

From Cindi's perspective it all seemed a little too obvious, but then, she knew what was happening. She dragged the conversation with Steve on for another few minutes, then looked at Sussman, who had turned his attention back to the Lakers game. She hung up the phone. "So," she said to Beddicker, "now what?"

"Now we go for a ride, sweetheart."

"It's your ballgame."

They walked back to the table. Cindi picked up her purse and buttoned her pink down vest. Without saying another word, the two of them walked out the door.

When Murray saw Beddicker and Cindi leave Marita's, he started the motor running. The fog had gotten heavier, it had gotten colder. As they approached the car, Cindi grabbed Beddicker's arm and started whispering sharply in his ear. Murray didn't know what she was saying, but he knew that Beddicker was distracted; he would not glance through the windshield at him before getting in the car. Instead, he brusquely jerked the passenger door open, pushed Cindi inside, then slid in after her.

Murray immediately put the car into forward and pulled out of the parking lot. The panel between the driver and the passenger section was closed. Murray mumbled hello through the intercom and steered the limousine north along the PCH.

Andy Sussman waited inside Marita's for a few more minutes after Cindi and Beddicker left. He watched the end of the Lakers game—LA was way ahead—then walked over to the pay phone and called his hotel room. "So far so good," he told Susie Ettenger.

"As if I know what that means. So now what, desperate friend in need?"

"Nothing more on my end, just the ferry service. I'll be back by midnight. Stay awake, we'll have margaritas at P and W's, dancing at the Blue Moon."

"Sounds like a real treat. It's a good thing I flew out, so I could sit in a hotel room all night."

"Oh, I think the evening still has possibilities." Sussman rolled his fingers over the small object in his pocket. "See you once upon a midnight dreary." He hung up the phone and walked out of Marita's, over to the beige Camaro. The hood was still up. He leaned over the battery and reconnected the cables. He put the hood down, started the car, and roared off.

Murray drove the limo northward up the PCH, the fog so thick he could barely see in front of him; an accident or a traffic ticket would be disastrous. He tried to rehearse in his mind what would happen when they got to their destination. He'd explained it patiently to Cindi and Sussman, he'd made it all sound so logical. Buddy would see the truth. Buddy would cut a deal. He looked at Eddie Connors' pistol lying next to him on the seat. He hoped he wasn't giving Buddy Beddicker too much credit for pragmatism.

"So what now?" Cindi Beamon said to Beddicker in the back seat. "What are you going to do with Steve? What do you want from me?"

"Sweetheart, you made an unfortunate choice," Beddicker answered, staring out the window. "You should have trusted. I would have taken care of things."

"Sure. Just like you took care of my brother. So where are we going?"

"Cindi, darling, I bet you don't know what a beautiful city Los Angeles can be at night. Thousands of acres of desolate wilderness, just an hour's drive from the city." He rapped at the panel separating the driver from the passengers. "Almost there, Eddie?"

"Yo," Murray mumbled through the intercom.

Cindi moved a few inches away from Beddicker; she pushed herself toward the door.

"You want to jump out on the highway at fifty miles an hour? I don't think so, honey. Another bad decision. You should listen to your Uncle Buddy."

"You're going to kill me anyway."

"You jump out, you got no chance. I suggest you wait till we get there. Take a chance on my generosity. My kind, soft heart."

Murray steered the limousine past a huge crumbling sand dune, then slowed down. There were no traffic lights or highway signs; it would be easy to miss the cutoff.

He could end up all the way at the naval base at Point Mugu. He'd driven the route earlier in the day, but it was a different story in this fog. Crawling along, he was almost at a dead stop when he finally saw what he was looking for: Yorba Linda Road. He didn't signal. He turned off the PCH, eastward. In front of him loomed the Santa Monica Mountains. They could hardly be confused with the Himalayas, they never rose more than three-thousand feet, but they were full of desolate canyons. The coyotes outnumbered the people.

Murray moved slowly around the curves, climbing ever upward. The view of the ocean and the rocky coastline had been spectacular earlier in the day, but now he could barely see the road. He crawled along for another mile or so, and counted the bends: two, three, four. He stopped, then inched ahead. He found the turnoff and stopped the car.

"My, wasn't that a nice ride?" said Buddy Beddicker in the back seat. "Time to stretch our legs."

"This is the scenic vista?"

"Shoulda brought your camera, Cindi." Beddicker rapped on the driver's panel. "Eddie!"

"Yo," rasped Murray through the intercom.

"Time to escort Miss Beamon for a walk."

"Okay, boss."

Murray picked up Connors' Smith & Wesson and held it in the gloved right hand of his wet suit. He pushed a button and unlocked the door on Cindi's side. He opened his own door and got out, his chauffeur's cap pulled tightly over the wet suit's rubber hood. He opened up the rear passenger door, pointed the gun at Beddicker, and said, "Trick or treat, Buddy."

Beddicker froze for a moment, then made a grab for Cindi, but she had anticipated Murray's entrance and darted out the door on her side. She scampered around the side of the car and stood next to Murray.

"What the hell?" said Beddicker, looking faintly amused by all this. "Whattaya know, I been bushwhacked."

"Outta the car," said Murray, affecting a slight Indiana twang. "Move it."

"Aw, pal, I'm kinda comfortable in here. And we haven't even been formally introduced."

"Name's Ronnie Beamon," Murray said. "You know my cousin here."

"Well, Ronnie, it's a pleasure to meet you. I want you to know I think it's absolutely admirable that a family sticks up for its kin. Now, what can I do for you this beautiful winter's evening?"

"You can get your ass out of the car, that's what, before I blow you all the way to Point Mugu. Then you can start talking."

Beddicker arched an eyebrow and tapped his right index finger against the car seat. "And what would you like to know, Ronnie? Would you like to know where little Stevie is?"

"Get the information out of him first," Cindi said. "Get it straight, Ronnie. If I'm going to the police, I want the whole story."

"Sure, sure," Beddicker said. "You're going right to the police. A full confession. What can I tell you?"

"Out of the car," said Murray.

Beddicker yawned, stretched his arms over his head, and reclined in the car seat.

"On second thought," Cindi said, glaring straight at Beddicker, her voice quivering, "let's plug him now."

"Relax, honey—"

"Do it!"

Murray looked over at Cindi. She was delivering her lines much better than in rehearsal.

"Hey, hey, Ronnie boy! There ain't no cause for violence—"

"You made me kill someone!" Cindi said, her hands trembling. A tear streamed down her face; it was genuine. "There was never any reason—"

"There was every reason," snapped Beddicker. "Dr. Double-X was a filthy pig. Crash Kopeck knew it. Ben Garrison knew it. Half the wrestlers in America knew it. I just happened to be the one that did something about it."

"Wa-h-l-l now," drawled Murray, "that's mighty accommodating of you, Buddy." He looked over at Cindi. She was still shaking, but she'd gotten Beddicker started. "What did he have, Buddy? Did he know about Stevie?"

"Nah, Ronnie, he didn't have any of that." Beddicker sat straight up. "Nobody knew about Stevie but me. All the pig had was a few stock certificates. Just a few securities transactions that weren't filled out properly."

"I don't suppose," Murray drawled, "that them stock certificates was actually supposed to be goin' to your athlete clients, but instead they got to you personally— could that have been it, Buddy?"

"Hey, you're a bright boy, Ronnie."

"And Dr. Double-X, he jus' ripped all this information right outta your safe, is that right? And he said, 'Uncle Buddy, you better drop that breach-of-contract suit against me, and never tell a soul who the Doctor really is. Or else I'll turn all this over to the feds, and you'll be in jail for securities fraud and maybe mail fraud and forgery and a whole bunch of other things.' "

"Yeah, sure, that's exactly right," said Beddicker. "You figured it all out, genius. It's a simple business, that's why I represent hayseeds like you, not Albert fucking Einstein. Now, you want to put that gun down, Ronnie boy? I don't like doing negotiations by pistol point."

"Not unless you're holdin' it by the business end," Murray said smoothly. "Get your ass outta the car."

Beddicker edged toward the door. "That's enough, boys and girls. I got Stevie. I can keep him forever. You so much as scratch me, you'll never see him again."

"Well, now, Buddy, I got news for you." Murray gave his best impersonation of a country-hick grin and spun the gun in his hand. "You ain't got my cousin. Stevie's safe and sound."

"Bullshit."

"No brag, just fact. Your man Hennesey's an old pal

of mine, we go way back, Buddy. We been onto you from the start. We knew just what plane you took. We knew who your driver was. An' we know just where Stevie is—safe in his little bed back in Chicago."

Beddicker's face flushed for the first time, his mouth tightened. He positioned himself at the edge of the seat by the door.

"Buddy," said Murray Glick, "get out."

Beddicker licked his lips. "Sure, Ronnie, anything you say." His eyes shifted between Cindi and Murray. He eased his bulky torso out of the car slowly, his hands still by his side.

"Now, Buddy, we are going to cut a deal. I'll talk. You'll listen."

"I'm all ears, kid."

A sharp cry cut through the damp night air, followed by a long, deep wail. It was only two coyotes howling, but it startled Cindi. She stumbled backward on the gravel; she reached behind herself to break her fall. Murray made a reflexive move to grab her—he knew in an instant he'd made a mistake.

The next few seconds unfolded before Murray's eyes in an eerie slow motion. Buddy Beddicker actually smiled. He reached into his jacket and pulled out a small black handgun. In one fluid motion he pointed it at Murray and fired a shot.

Murray dived over Cindi. The bullet ricocheted off a rock behind him. She grabbed his arm and jerked him behind the limo. As he fell, he aimed the Smith & Wesson with his free hand. He squeezed off one round; it was all he needed. The bullet caught Buddy Beddicker square in the forehead. The force of the blast knocked him several feet away from the car. He staggered for a few yards, let out a small groan, then fell backward into the chaparral.

No one said a word. Murray pushed himself away from Cindi and got up to one knee. She bit her lip; the gravel had opened up a small cut on her hand. He reached for her, but she shrank back toward the limo. A volley of coyote howls echoed through the canyon.

Murray Glick unzipped his wet suit and stuck the gun back in his belt. He walked over to the body and kicked it over. He bent down and looked for the briefest moment at the remains of Buddy Beddicker's face. Then he walked back to Cindi and helped her up. Without a word, he dabbed the blood off her hand and escorted her out to the edge of Yorba Linda Road.

But the business was far from finished; there was still the driver to contend with. Murray walked back to the limo alone, pondering his alternatives. One man was already dead. In the back of his mind, he wondered if he could have played it any differently. Maybe he'd been kidding himself all along. Maybe it had had to end this way. But the truth was, it was Beddicker who had made the choice. Murray Glick's conscience was clean.

Eddie Connors, on the other hand, was bound and gagged in the trunk. Murray stared down the canyon, glanced back at the limo. There was a simple enough way to dispose of him, but he quickly dismissed the idea. Maybe his own code of ethics fell something short of Mosaic, Murray thought, but he still liked to think he acted with justification. And when he opened up the trunk of the limo, Connors was doing some serious groveling.

"Don't kill me, don't kill me!" he shouted through the gag. "Wait! Listen to me!"

"Keep your goddamn voice down," Murray said, "or I won't have any choice."

"Look," pleaded Connors, still lying prone in the trunk. "Ronnie, whoever the hell you are—I'm no threat to you, understand? What am I gonna do? Go to the police? I'm an accomplice to murder. And kidnapping. Beddicker's dead, I got no one to protect."

Murray pulled Connors out of the trunk and leaned him against the car.

"Listen, Ronnie, what're ya gonna do with the limo?

Back it down the canyon? The police'll find it tomorrow. They'll find out who rented it. I gotta better idea."

Murray glanced over at Cindi Beamon. She was standing at the edge of the road, lost in the fog a few yards away. "I can guess what your idea is. The limo was rented under a phony name?"

"Of course. I signed for it, I return it."

"And then you disappear, Eddie. You go away. Far away. You go become a shepherd somewhere."

"That's it exactly. Couldn'ta said it better—"

"Somewhere where you're not wanted for murder. And kidnapping. Not to mention robbery and extortion."

"Absolutely, pal. You bet."

Murray walked over to the body of Buddy Beddicker. He stared at it for a moment, grabbed it by the legs, then dropped it. "Take it," he told Connors. "By the legs. Take his clothes off, don't get any blood on you. Drag it out of sight."

"You're the boss." Connors did what he was told. When he returned from the hillside, Murray stood between him and the limo, holding the Smith & Wesson. "Eddie, this is your gun."

"I can see that."

"It's the gun that killed Buddy Beddicker. With your prints on it."

"So it is," Connors said. "I guess you maybe want to keep it as a souvenir?"

"Exactly. I'll keep it in a safe place, Eddie."

"I'm touched."

"Now, take the limo, Eddie. Drive west on Yorba Linda." Murray pointed to the right. Connors would have had no idea where to go, he'd been in the trunk for the whole ride. "You'll hit the PCH in a few miles. Return the limo. Buy yourself a shepherd's crook."

"Absolutely," said Eddie Connors.

"Bug off, now," said Murray Glick. He tossed Connors the key and stood with the gun in his hand as Connors got inside the limousine. "Have a nice life, Eddie."

Murray took Cindi Beamon by the arm and led her eastward on Yorba Linda, uphill for another half-hour, before the road leveled off and started to descend again. She walked steadily. She didn't cry or even shiver as they walked through the mist. Murray wondered if there was any tenderness left in her, if there had been any in the first place, before Steve's accident, before the Double-X murder. He wondered if she had a friend anywhere. He thought about taking her back to the hotel and sharing a bottle of wine with her. An arm around the waist, a soft caress.

But he knew it wouldn't happen, not tonight. It wasn't just the body he had left in the canyon. His mind was on Terry Tollison; he actually found himself eager to get the rest of the details tied down on this case so he could get back to cold, snowy, miserable old Chicago and give her a call.

It was not a healthy sign, Murray supposed.

He tried to clear his mind. He thought about a cold beer and a hot shower. As they approached the intersection with Deer Creek Road, he saw a pair of yellow parking lights shining through the fog. He saw the outlines of a beige Camaro slowing to a stop as it approached them. He took Cindi's hand and helped her inside the car.

28

"I have two questions," said Andy Sussman. He and Murray were alone in the Camaro; they had dropped Cindi Beamon off at her apartment in West Los Angeles. Sussman still had some lingering misgivings about her culpability, but he hadn't broached the subject. It was far too late in the operation for that.

"Personally, I'd lean toward being a little less inquisitive at this stage," Murray said. He opened the car window and rolled open the sun roof—it didn't give him much of a view except for the bottom of the surfboard that was still lashed to the roof. They were back on the Pacific Coast Highway, driving south toward Redondo Beach. It was 12:30 A.M.

"Just the journalistic training that I've only recently acquired, Mur. Question number one: have I done anything illegal?"

Murray reclined his bucket seat and rested his right foot against the glove compartment. "I wouldn't say you *did* anything illegal, Hoops. Quasi-legal, maybe. Buddy Beddicker attempted a kidnapping—two kidnappings, actually. I'd say we acted in the interests of what I'd characterize as the Greater Good."

"And what statute is that included in?"

"Statute?"

Sussman waited for some elaboration, but his friend slouched contentedly in his seat, working the zipper up and down on his wet suit.

"Uh, Murray?"

"What can I do for you, Andrew?"

"Murray, do I ever get to find out exactly what happened to Buddy Beddicker?"

"Sorry. Not the kind of thing a veteran sportscaster like yourself would be interested in. What was the last you saw of him, anyway—in case anyone ever asks."

"I saw him walk out the door of Marita's with some broad and get in a limo." Sussman took off his wig and gave it to Murray, who stuffed it in a paper sack and pushed it under his seat. "Hard to remember. I was watching the Lakers game."

"Good, Andrew. Very good. Who won?"

"Lakers by fifteen. I'm just guessing, Murray, but is it possible that I might have a hard time reaching Buddy Beddicker at his office tomorrow?"

Murray rolled down the window. He pulled a cigar from the inside of his wet suit and lit it; the smoke curled in with the fog and disappeared out the window.

"I see," Sussman said. "And of course, there's the Cindi Beamon question. She killed Dr. Double-X. I think we've established that."

"Strictly hearsay."

"I'm a great believer in your investigative genius, Murray. Am I supposed to hold back that information from the police?"

"Your choice, Hoops. Your conscience. You want to put her on trial? Send her to jail? Dig up Steve's past?"

"Of course I don't. I mean, in a fair world, it's not what I would do."

"The world's what we make it, Andrew. Not to mention that the only one who could corroborate any of that evidence is Buddy Beddicker."

"Who probably won't be at his office tomorrow."

"Highly unlikely." Murray exhaled a smoke ring.

"Which brings me to my second question, Mur. It so happens I've got this television story to wrap up."

Murray draped a rubber-coated arm around Sussman's shoulder. "Andy, did I mention what a great job you've been doing on that? My new girlfriend's been following it all, she's highly impressed."

Sussman was eager to hear about Murray's new girl-friend, but professional matters came first, barely. "Murray, the story's officially a murder now. It won't just go away."

"It will with proper management. And I have great confidence in your creative ability, Andrew. Just tell what you can prove."

"So what do I say about Buddy Beddicker? Is it all right to mention his name now as Alvin Sassler's agent?"

"No problem. The lawsuits between him and Winner's Circle are in the public record. That's your official link to Buddy."

"And what else am I supposed to say? Where do I go from there?"

Glick shrugged.

"That's all? Murray, you left me with a mess." Sussman stopped at a traffic light. They had arrived back at Redondo Beach; this was where they would part company. Murray would take the Camaro back down to San Diego, where he had rented it, and fly back to Chicago.

"Hoops," said Murray. "Old buddy, life is not always tidy. I believe I left you with a smaller mess than you started with."

"That's debatable."

"You wanted to know who Dr. Double-X was, I got you the answer. I found out who killed him, when no one even thought he was murdered. I even went so far as to ensure that certain innocent parties would not get their lives ruined, and at considerable risk to myself. And, Andrew, I did this for absolutely no personal gain."

Sussman swung off the beachside drive and parked the Camaro in the Sheraton parking lot. He looked Murray dead in the eye. He felt Murray's forehead. He took Murray's pulse. "Absolutely no personal gain, Murray?"

"As it turned out."

"Not by design, I take it."

"That's for powers higher than myself to decide."

Andy Sussman reached for the door. When cruise-directing shopping-mall detectives started talking about higher powers, he knew it was time to go.

"So I leave it to your powers of imagination," Murray said. "Tie up this story for CBS. You'll handle it with your characteristic grace under pressure, I'm sure. I'll see you in Chicago, Andrew, hopefully at a basketball game."

"If they don't put me on the first train back to Green Bay."

"Ah, quit worrying about your image so much, Hoops. You got another week here at least, enjoy yourself. Get a suntan. And give my highest regards to Susie. My offer to stand up for your wedding remains, by the way."

"So does her offer to put you in a Glad Bag and ship you off to Borneo." Sussman got out of the car. "Incidentally, one final question before you leave."

Murray moved into the driver's seat. He poked his head out the window and glanced at the surfboard. He'd bought it cheap down in San Diego when he rented the car. He thought it might make a nice keepsake from this adventure, but he supposed out of prudence he might have to loosen the cords and jettison it somewhere between Redondo Beach and San Diego. The only keepsake from this trip would be Eddie Connors' gun. "All right," he said, revving the engine. "Last chance, Andrew."

"Who's the girl?"

Murray smiled and puffed several more smoke rings into the fog.

"Hah! This is it, isn't it, Glick? You're smitten, I could tell by the look—"

"Easy, Hoops—"

"I know how it is with guys like you. Playboy of the Western World bites the dust—you'll go down like a rock. Am I right?"

"Too soon to tell. Could be she's just after me for good times, my great looks, and my reputation as a world-famous detective."

"Women can be so crass."

"A boy's always got to be on his guard. Sayonara, Hoopsie. Be good."

Murray Glick pushed the Camaro into drive and rolled out of the Sheraton parking lot back out onto the fog-shrouded Pacific Coast Highway. There were a few minor details to take care of before he bid California adieu. The odometer on the Camaro would have to be adjusted; he didn't think a few days in San Diego required three hundred miles' worth of driving. The bagful of wigs would have to be dispensed with, as would the surfboard and the wet suit. He would put in a call to Barney Hennesey to make sure Steve Beamon had gotten home safely. He would suggest that Barney make a last nostalgic tour of Beddicker's office and retrieve any evidence of Beddicker's relationship to Beamon, before Beddicker's body was found. Then he would return the car and catch the early-morning flight to Chicago.

Murray pulled his cigar from the ashtray and took a few puffs. He felt better. He was sorry that Andy would have to improvise on his television story. He assumed there would be some minor inconveniences in dealing with the police. It was true, he had left a minor mess, but Hoops could handle it. All in all, he was satisfied with what he had accomplished. He had left a small piece of the world in a better situation than he had found it. What more did people want?

Murray put the cigar back in the ashtray. He resisted the temptation to gun the Camaro to ninety as he pulled onto the San Diego freeway. It was no time for a speeding ticket. He glanced at a digital clock on a savings and loan off to the right; he could barely make it out in the haze.

It was a quarter to one.

He had killed a man less than an hour ago.

He guessed that it would be nice to have someone to talk to.

29

"So, as the strange, convoluted saga of Dr. Double-X comes to an end, what have we learned? Consider Alvin Sassler: blunt, headstrong, always ambitious, often ruthless. He donned a mask and clawed his way to the top of the wrestling profession, leaving a spate of enemies in his wake: Harvey "Crash" Kopeck, the great champion from Wisconsin—Dr. Double-X gracelessly stole his title, then jumped to Ben Garrison's cable TV empire; Leona Z, the rock mega-star, who approached Dr. Double-X for a wrestle-rock partnership, then had to flee his dingy hotel room for her life; Wireless, his manager, whose life has been haunted by treachery since Double-X died; finally, and perhaps fatally, Buddy Beddicker, his agent. Sassler broke his contract with Beddicker and went incognito as Dr. Double-X; when Beddicker discovered his secret identity, he sued him, but two months later mysteriously dropped the suit.

"Why did Buddy Beddicker drop that lawsuit? Was it because Alvin Sassler had turned up evidence linking Beddicker to forged and stolen securities, evidence that could have landed Beddicker in prison?

"Perhaps we'll never know. Alvin Sassler, aka Dr. Double-X, is dead—poisoned during the *Celebrity Superteams* boat race. And Buddy Beddicker's whereabouts are unknown—his office hasn't heard from him in several days, reports have it that he's disappeared.

"It's a twisted tale of betrayal and deception—it's a story whose final answers may be known only to the ghosts who roam the South Coast of California. One thing you can count on: if more evidence turns up, we'll be there. From Redondo Beach, I'm Andy Sussman, for CBS Sports."

"Bravo, bravo," said Susie Ettenger. Her applause echoed through the nearly empty parking lot at Redondo Beach. "Emmy award. Maybe a Peabody."

"How about a one-way ticket back to New York?" Sussman put down the margarita glass that had been serving as a microphone and leaned against the railing along the entrance to Pancho and Wong's.

"Give me a little time, Andy, I think I can manage it. I'll talk to Cliff Trager first thing in the morning—unless you want me to wait a few days. You're reasonably sure about this Buddy Beddicker thing?"

"Just a hunch. I'll put in calls to his office every day between now and Saturday. He'll have been gone five days—by that time, I think I can safely say that his whereabouts are unaccounted for."

"Sunday, then, I'll sit down with Trager. I'll point out that you've completely fulfilled your obligations as a sports journalist, and it's high time you were given more traditional assignments, in the spirit of your contractual agreement." Susie took Sussman by the arm and led him away from Pancho and Wong's, where they had stopped long enough to have a margarita apiece.

"Hope your radar's on tonight," Sussman said as they walked through the fog toward the Blue Moon Saloon. Like its namesake above, the Blue Moon was barely visible—if it wasn't for the band playing an old Buffalo Springfield song inside, they wouldn't have known it was there.

"Inner or outer?"

"How's that?"

"My radar. Andy, what went on tonight? Is there something happening that I should know about?"

"Yes and no. And yes again."

Susie stopped, they were at the entrance to the Blue Moon, the band had just finished playing "Mr. Soul." It was a quarter to two. The few patrons left inside were holding on for the last dance. "Yes, no, yes? Is that Morse code for something?"

"Sort of. Something went on tonight. It had to do with the perpetrators of a crime. The end result, I'm led to understand, is that certain people received their just rewards."

Susie finished her margarita and set the glass by the door to the Blue Moon. "In a legal manner? Or shouldn't I ask?"

"Allegedly. I think we've moved into the 'no' territory."

"So there's nothing going on that I should know about?"

"No. Well, yes." Sussman fumbled in his pocket. "Uh, Suse. I've been thinking. About this relationship of ours. I think, possibly, it could use some general improvement."

"Yes," said Susie. "We're into 'yes' now?"

"Definitely. By all means." Sussman put his arm around her. "It was just all this bi-coastal and semicoastal commuting, Suse, it's been driving me crazy. And I was thinking, uh . . ." Sussman held Susie and gazed out into the fog.

"Yes?"

"Well . . ." Sussman interpreted all these yeses as a positive sign and stumbled ahead. "I understand that you might have to make some sacrifices for a while, if you move to New York and everything and give up the law firm for a while. But it probably wouldn't be permanent—just till I get my career reestablished and everything . . ." Andy looked at Susie, but she didn't say anything; she had evidently given him all the help he was going to get on this one. Sussman took his hand out of his pocket and pulled out the engagement ring. "Susie, will you marry me?"

A slow smile spread across Susie's face. She touched the ring. She kissed Andy on the mouth. "Yes."

"Yes?"

"Yes, yes, yes." Susie gave Andy her hand and let him

slip the ring on her finger. She kissed him gently, then passionately. They melted into a soft embrace.

Just inside the door, the band was playing something by the Beatles—neither Andy nor Susie was of a mind to recall exactly what it was. They held on to each other for several minutes, then dropped their hands and stared into each other's eyes.

"Well," Sussman said. "It's history. Did I do that okay?"

"Best I've ever seen. I thought maybe you'd get on one knee or something, but it's all right."

"It's damp down there, Suse. And it's foggy, I might have tripped or something, hit a beer can. Ruined the moment completely."

"You were wonderful. Andy, do you think I could have the last dance? I think they're about ready to close the joint."

Andy took Susie by the hand; they opened the door to the Blue Moon Saloon and peeked in. There were five or six couples inside, a few single people hanging around at the bar. None of them looked as if they could truly appreciate the significance of the occasion. "Susan Ettenger," said Andy Sussman, "may I take this opportunity to waltz you back to the hotel?"

"Absolutely, Andrew. I'm lighter than air."

Andy tried to remember exactly what a waltz was. He placed one hand on Susie's back, the other around her waist—given his companions of the last several weeks, he was lucky he didn't put her in a half-nelson. "Am I close?" he asked.

"Perfect. Home, James."

And so they held each other and waltzed through the parking lot, humming the old Beatles tune, whatever it was. They dipped around an old Volkswagen van and sashayed between two BMW's and a Honda. By the time the song was over they had disappeared into the fog, welcomed by the omnipresent hospitality of the Sheraton Corporation, sheltered by their warm embrace.